Perfectly *Imperfect*

Angela Monteagle

Published by Angela Monteagle and Rando Works
New York, New York

ISBN: 979-8-9952593-0-5 (paperback)
ISBN: 979-8-9952593-1-2 (ebook)

Cover design: Mary Ann Smith
Editing: Kirstie Anders
Typesetting: Reedsy

First Edition

WWW.ANGELAWROTE.COM

For the strong women who have influenced my life, and the men who have shown their strength in solidarity.

Prologue: *Once Upon a Time*

I received an email today from a potential new client. She is a referral from a previous client that I remember warmly.

I automatically assume that I will get along with this new client if they are friends. I recall thinking that we moved similarly in the world and shared common thoughts and ideals. It very often makes my job easier. While I may like some clients more than others, it's human nature after all, my job is not to be my client's friend, but to support their journey to find themselves amongst their own. That is the greatest gift I could give any client. Likeable or not.

The referral is welcomed. It is always a nice feeling to know you have helped someone so much they tell their friends. It's a reassurance that you are doing something right. In this profession it is easy to question whether you are truly making a difference in someone's life or not. There are clients that I still think of today and wonder if they are happy.

My curious mind begins to wonder. What does this new client hope to resolve? My discovery call will reveal more, as her email didn't reveal too much.

Where is she on her journey?

Who is the person she thinks she is and how does she feel she is perceived by others?

How does she see herself when she looks in the mirror?

Is she ready to bare herself in complete abandonment, with the desire to piece herself back together?

That sounds dramatic, I know. Surprise! You just got a glimpse of my inner voice. I can be dramatic at times, just like a lot of other people. But when I'm with my clients, any such drama that lives in my head is delivered in the most objective way.

I think it would serve us well if we were to pull all our pieces apart and hold each of them in the palms of our hands. To feel the weight of each one and hold them up to the light for clarity. To protect the pieces we want to keep, to restore the pieces we forgot, to soften the edges of the pieces that painfully dig into our sides, and to leave some jagged as a reminder of where we have been. And finally, to throw away the pieces that no longer define who we are.

It's not always a perfect process, but I think it's a poetic experience.

I love what I do. I've been drawn to helping people for as long as I can remember. Certainly, as far back as a small child.

I think the seeds were planted as I watched my sister's journey in her self-discovery that often shook the foundations of our home. She was what some might call a rebellious teenager but underneath the mischief was a cacophony of feelings, crying out to be heard and longing for reconciliation. While I would spend my days with peace of mind, my sister often scurried under our roof in silent torment. Her experiences were her own but shared by many. It was then I had learnt not to judge one's actions without first understanding the path that led them there.

What came next solidified my resolve for helping others. One of my childhood friends had experienced the death of her father when we were in our teens. He had unexpectedly taken his own life and our high school counsellor, Ms. Walsh, was on standby for the students who had been affected by the news. For most, this was the first tragedy we had faced. We were a middle-class school filled with children who lived behind white picket fences and families that appeared happy, at least on the outside.

It was a shocking truth that I was subjected to when I learned of the despair my friend's father had lived with for so many years. I was saddened, and yet intrigued, by the fact many who walk among us have hearts as heavy as concrete boots.

I had made an appointment with Ms. Walsh to talk through how I felt. I was of an age that anyone over 20 seemed old, and while Ms. Walsh must have been in her 40s, she somehow seemed younger to me. She had bleached blonde hair cut into a bob, and blue eyes that you could see yourself in, and had a calmness about her that made you feel comfortable sitting in silence together.

I spoke at length with her over several meetings and discovered a hidden passion in understanding why people behaved the way they did. I wanted to know how I could help.

It was Ms. Walsh who asked me to consider studying psychology after I graduated high school. She found I was full of all the right questions, stemming from an innate and evident compassion. I was told by those who spent time with me that I was an old soul in a young woman's body. My teachers agreed it was likely thanks to being the last child in a family who actively participated in adult conversations while proactively encouraging time for play balanced with space for reflection.

I am lucky to have my own practice these days and most of my clients are females who confidently seek out support. However, I am thrilled to see my appointments are being progressively filled with patients, who in times gone by, would never have sought the guidance of a quack, let alone a woman. Something is working!

The way we view mental health has changed significantly over the years, and I'm grateful to see the advances that have been made. Did you know that it was only in 1952 that the first manual that focused on mental disorders was published in the US.? And it wasn't until the 1990s when there was a concerted effort across the nation to increase public awareness and reduce the stigma associated with mental health.

One thing as certain as death and taxes is that change takes time. It takes education, investment and the willingness of people to be open to something new. Fear derails change. To accept that whole health care includes mental health care also means accepting we are all vulnerable to more than just broken bones.

Through the work of professionals and organisations devoted to offering solutions to our unseen conditions, there is a global conversation that grows louder and louder. I'm proud to be part of that community.

It's without question younger generations are more willing and open to talk about their feelings while being far more adept at change. When you only have a few years rather than a few decades of life weighing on your mind, it's much easier to be swayed to try something new.

I know ultimately, as people, we are all desperate for connection. A shared collective longing to be seen and heard. Through therapy we can learn to accept this natural human instinct so often seen as a weakness. If only I could persuade everyone to seek out the tools for self-realisation and the opportunities for openly sharing all parts of ourselves.

I want to give that gift to as many people as possible. But I also understand the reality of that nirvana.

Nature versus nurture is a statement long heard by the masses and often discussed in my professional circle. But I also believe that more research and reflection should be applied when it comes to self-determination versus the amount of free will we each hold.

Through my many sessions with clients who seemingly make one bad decision after the other, the question of free will is one that is constant for me. I wish I knew the answer to better serve my clients.

Are we really self-determined if we keep repeating our mistakes or are we brimming with behaviour that is learned subconsciously? We are swayed by what we see and hear. We are conditioned to think and feel. We are born to fit into the society in which we find ourselves in.

Are we truly free to make our decisions? Or have our decisions been predetermined from the moment we entered the world and began consuming.

I have so many questions and it is a conversation that could go on and on and on inside my head, and one I am sure would never truly be resolved.

I am predisposed to question not just my behaviour but the behaviour of those around me. I grew up in a household where my father taught me to question everything.

He was a lawyer with his own small practice and when he first started out, he would daydream with my mother that they would bear a son who would one day take over his firm. This was not unusual for the times, nor is it even unusual today. A father believing his heir would of course be his son.

People are predisposed to believe in an ideology represented in their communities. Unless someone is brave enough to break the mould, everyone continues to live the status quo.

In those days, it was common practice and a firmly held belief that men were required to be successful, the breadwinners who provided for their families. Women were to take care of those around them and keep the peace at all costs.

My mother and father had somewhat bought into those gender-based ideals rooted in faith and tradition. While neither of my parents, as adults, considered attending a service to publicly embrace their faith, it was still this belief system guiding their unconscious daily lives.

Those biblical words interpreted and translated by the men who stood in front of a congregation lingered in my parents' minds and subtly determined the rules and religion they believed they would enforce in their household.

So, when my parents were not blessed with sons, but instead bestowed with three daughters, they were faced with a new choice on how to raise their children.

My parents gently rejected the tropes that their community considered necessary.

They had to fight against instinctively applying what they had learned from their parents, as we, their daughters, started to grow. Both came to realise they were not comfortable with the outdated notions applied to women in today's society.

My father grew to be forward thinking and progressive instead of listening to his friends at the golf club. Those men who would often make inconsiderate comments implying a lack of manhood at his inability to produce a son and therefore the loss of the family name. He had quietly decided his daughters would be given the same opportunities as any son may have and he would be damned if he'd let someone treat them differently.

My parents didn't rebel or march down the streets. Instead, quietly parented their girls behind closed doors their own way. They rejected the idea that their daughters would need to marry to be happy and that being a homemaker would be their lot in life. They dreamed their girls could grow up to be whatever they wanted to be and if the homemaker title was one they wanted by choice, they could still have that too. Most importantly, they didn't want their girls to grow up to be women upholding someone else's name and dreams ahead of their own.

My father was determined to change the status quo. As far as he was concerned, women had been fighting alone for long enough and it was time that men fought alongside them.

Or maybe it was just my fathers' ego and contempt at the thought that his daughters could be treated as less than equal, which drove him to squash the narrative and force success down our throats. Either way, my sisters and I were grateful for the opportunities that may not otherwise have been granted to us.

My father concluded that a lack of a son would not stop the family name from living on and hoped that it could possibly continue by way of his practice. He encouraged us to educate ourselves and asked that if not all three, would at least one of us learn his profession so that he could teach her everything he knew.

As children, we were told to ask 'why' about anything we didn't understand. To speak up when we had a question. And we did, relentlessly. My parents welcomed the discussions and as an adult it was not lost on me the patience my parents exuded with three girls close in age asking why at every opportunity.

As we grew older and began to view the world from our teenage resolve, my parents continued to encourage our curiosity and would engage in deep conversations at the dinner table. A ritual that was upheld five out of seven days a week, when on weekends we were excused from eating as a family in the formal room. Often though, we still ate together in front of the television.

My fathers' wish had come true when my oldest sister was accepted to law school and was genuinely excited about working with our father. They were similar in nature, and it made sense she would take over his business one day.

My other sister, who is the middle child, had a passion for the arts and had dropped out of college to pursue an acting career. It still makes me smile when I remember the disruptive times this caused in our household as I watched my parents do their best to support her as she abandoned a safe passageway and chose a riskier path. While my parents' friends questioned their judgement at allowing her to drop out of college, they had been proven right to give their daughter the space to explore her own future. She may not have forged the illustrious career some might wish for, nor was she afforded the opulent lifestyle we see of other actors, but she was making a living doing what she loved and didn't want for much else. Like it had made sense for my oldest sister to work with my father, it had made sense that this sister took her vivid imagination and tumultuous ups and downs, and turned her thoughts and feelings into art. She still struggles with her emotional wellbeing to this day, and I still find myself worrying about what may come of her future. Through our love and support and my sister's inherently beautiful nature, she has found her safe space in her craft. I am so proud of how far she has come.

You know my story of how I came to do this job. When I graduated as valedictorian, during my graduation speech I paid homage to my friend's father and how it set the career path I was about to embark upon. I spoke of my desire to help people. And while I was to build my career upon this, it should not be lost on anyone that we are all responsible for making meaningful differences in the lives of others. In essence, my vocation does not mean that after hours I get to stop concerning myself with those around me.

My closing statement was about taking care of each other, 'We do not get to the top without someone lifting us up or stepping on someone on the way. You choose how you get there.' A statement I continue to quote today.

I return to the email and draft a quick response.

My schedule is rather full for the next two weeks and I have limited availability, but I am confident we will find a time that works for both of us.

I am grateful I have so many clients who trust me. And I am grateful I get to be part of their story. My job is to help my clients look back and give them the tools they need to be able to move forward.

As I start to type, I once again allow myself to wonder ...

Who is Celeste?

– Nya, Therapist

Chapter 1: *Wake Up Sleeping Beauty*

It was 3:30 am, the sun would start to rise soon. As the bar closed its doors and bid its patrons goodnight, Celeste stood with her friends and swung her handbag over her shoulder. They stepped out onto the pavement filled with black bags of rubbish piling high, taking away the memories of the night before. It was mid-June, and summer was already in full swing in New York City. Gone were the coats and scarves for the briefest of springs before its inhabitants were showing a lot more forgotten skin in shirts and shorts and strapless dresses. Allowing the humid temperatures to warm their cold bones from a long winter.

"See you next time," Celeste hugged her friends goodbye and walked away with purpose. As the sun began its journey and the temperature politely dipped for the briefest of moments as it does at that time of day, it was the kind of New York morning you see in the movies. If you listened carefully enough, in between the sirens and the noise of the city that never sleeps, you could hear the birds singing. Their day was about to commence as she was about to put herself to bed.

She knew her recent fling was somewhere in the shadows, and she intentionally chose not to look for him. She had decided it was time to add his name in blue ink to her list of fuckups.

Celeste had a history of heartbreaks, or some might say her arteries were simply clogged by overindulgence. She was a purebred, a direct

"

descendant of a blood line of women who chose men that needed fixing. Men that would never truly be hers. Men that bled her of her generosity and either walked away healed or left because they couldn't kiss the lips of a woman drowning in disappointment, that he hadn't grown to be better. Servings of this nature should be kept to a minimum; however, she upsized with every inappropriate opportunity.

She crossed Amsterdam Avenue and strolled along the tree lined street that took her to her fifth floor walk-up. Celeste was proud of herself. She hadn't succumbed to the familiar pull of 'one last time', where she sometimes allowed herself to believe it could be different. This one she could help. This one could be the one. This one could be the proof it was possible. However, this one she knew was just like the last one, and the one before that. It was not lost on her, the pattern she followed, the steps she knew by memory. They weren't bad guys, but they were bad for her.

The gnawing feeling of wanting to be loved licked at her heels. She grappled with why she felt such love wasn't deserved. How she had insisted on creating love stories as doomed as the Titanic. It was a familiar feeling that she had grown accustomed to. It was almost comforting to find out she wasn't truly loved by the men that would never be good enough for her. She had a warped sense of self-righteousness in knowing this inevitable outcome.

She pushed open her door to her studio apartment, dropped her bag and keys on the bench, and walked over to close the curtains. She usually enjoyed waking to the light streaming into the small but comfortable space, but she needed more hours than the dawn was willing to give. The sky was about to start changing colour and the sun was already on its ascent to greet early risers out for morning jogs or weekend coffee.

She mused at her feelings of accomplishment mingled with a hint of anger; at whom she wasn't sure. At that moment she picked up a pen and noted the feeling – amongst a few others. She knew she needed to talk to Nya about it during her next session.

The fling had lasted a month. It was a month of familiar doubt and insecurities that signalled it would never be. It took her a month to come to her senses and walk away. It took her longer to understand any of it.

Chapter 2: *Dear Fairy Godmother*

Celeste looked around the comfortable office she found herself in for the third time. The walls were a shade of off white, with one holding certificates in frames and the others a mismatch of artwork that looked like they held fond memories of intrepid travel. There was a stylish and modern white desk that was littered with a few books, a stack of fresh notepads, some pink and yellow Post-it notes and an overflowing pen holder. There was a white Mac computer with its delicate keyboard and next to that, a mug clearly purchased at a tourist shop in Atlantic City that was emblazoned with the name 'Pamela'.

"Pamela?" Celeste asked as Nya picked up the mug, took a sip of black coffee and walked across the room to take a seat opposite her.

"Long story," Nya smiled with a look as if remembering a funny moment in time. "Are you sure you don't want a coffee?"

"No, thanks." Celeste was relaxed on an oversized grey armchair that was large enough for her to wrap her legs on, as she softly leaned on the opposing arm rest. Nya sat across from her in a chair that looked the same. Between them sat a white coffee table with gold trim and two drink coasters, one holding a glass of water Celeste had taken when she arrived. And of course, there was a box of tissues.

Nya was a therapist who was recommended to Celeste by her close friend Sarah. "How have you been?" Nya asked. She was in her mid-forties, or so Celeste guessed, with long brown hair in tight curls that hung to her waist. Nya was attractive and when she looked at you, you felt like she was really looking at you. Celeste had built an instant rapport with her the moment they had met, which was three weeks ago to the day.

Celeste felt very American having her own therapist. She knew her friends back in England would have a good but kind laugh over the fact she had Americanised to the point of therapy. It wasn't that any of them thought seeking help was bad, but the English weren't known for being candid about their mental health. They were known to have a proper disposition that somehow translated into resilience and, therefore, the ability to let issues slide off one's back like water off a duck. The Royals didn't air their dirty laundry, therefore neither should the rest of Britain.

She had moved to New York a year and a half ago, chasing her lifelong dream to live in the concrete jungle. After years working for nonprofits, and countless visits to build and foster professional relationships in New York City, she had decided the best path that would lead her to a life in Manhattan was not a struggling charity but a multinational company. She worried she was selling her soul to the devil as she started her search for the for-profit company that would scratch her itchy feet. She devised a plan to land a job in London, prove her professional prowess and slide into a transfer across the pond.

Finance, pharma and fashion were not part of her repertoire, nor her personality if she was honest with herself, but she had applied anyway. Luckily with no luck. As upon reflection of her rejections, Celeste was sure none of those industries would have given her the motivation to get up and go to work every day.

Where she had found a place to lay her laptop was at an advertising agency that was small but mighty. They had been steadily growing and had recently opened their NYC office right before she was offered her role in London. She had worked hard, dedicated herself to learning the ropes and the operations of their business and after a little over a year, she was signing forms declaring herself free of any criminal convictions to be welcomed into the United States of America with a shiny new visa to start her new job.

The city had not welcomed her with the open arms she expected. New York City was tough, with a capital T. If you didn't have your shit together upon arrival, you got it together quickly. Otherwise, the alternative was being chewed up and spat out.

Retreating to England was not an option for Celeste. She had worked too hard to get there. Although she was fortunate to have a job compared to other expats who landed at JFK with little more than a resume and optimism, learning to live the New York life was a culture shock most don't understand till they have made the pilgrimage themselves. Celeste likened living in New York City to being in an abusive relationship. One minute it's tearing you down, the next minute it's telling you how sorry it is and how much it loves you. New Yorkers themselves don't give off the impression they care too much for you. They'll shove you if you're in their way, but on the flipside, should you fall, they'll be the first to offer their hand to help you up.

Once the dust has settled, and you can see the bright lights of Broadway, you don't want to be anywhere else. The realisation that the dream has become a reality is one akin to having a child. Celeste knows when she makes that comment, if the mothers around the world scoffed simultaneously, it would cause a tsunami. She was childless and planned to keep it that way, and although she was sure it probably wasn't akin to the love of a child, the love she felt towards the city of New York and the life it offered made her heart swell like it never had before.

So now, eighteen months on, Celeste found herself in a therapist's office like thousands of New Yorkers before her. They say it takes ten years to call yourself a New Yorker, but Celeste was sure that getting your own therapist had to count as some time in lieu.

Celeste had decided it was time to talk to a professional about the decisions she made in relation to the men she chose. And truth be told, she had been questioning her mental health after choosing to get involved with yet another emotionally unavailable man in yet another failed attempt at so-called love. Her feelings of despair that she hadn't felt before, were the catalyst to making her first appointment with Nya.

"I'm good. I've stopped seeing Roman." Celeste waited for Nya to respond and she didn't. Roman had been her latest fling that had flung her mental health into a tumble dryer. Once again, she had been left wondering why she chose to throw her emotions into the heavy-duty spin setting. She knew she should opt for the wrinkle-free cycle but secretly didn't believe it worked.

Celeste had met Roman through a friend of a friend. He had recently broken up with his long-term girlfriend and wasn't looking for any-thing serious. Red flag one. He was quiet but charismatic and she found she had things in common with him. What they were she would struggle to tell you now. He was there, he was cute, he was somewhat available, and he was interested in her. He was kind and sensitive and seemed to have the weight of the world on his shoulders. Red flag two. They spent most of their time together with mutual friends and only really spoke over pints of beer and shots of vodka. However, during some moments alone, he admitted to personal struggles and desires to feed his addictions. He openly admitted he needed help. Red flag three.

Celeste found herself comfortable in this familiar territory and set about being available to help him. At least until the inevitable time came that she never could.

"I mean, I knew it was going to end anyway, and I should have known better to begin with. So, I haven't been in touch with him. And he hasn't been in touch with me. Which is fine, I guess."

"You guess?" Nya probed, "Is it fine?"

"Not really," Celeste admitted. "But it is what it is, and I can't make him do what I want him to do. I can't make him want me. So, it has to be fine. I felt angry last week but I feel better about it now."

"Why do you feel angry?"

"I'm angry at him for not calling. I'm angry at myself for thinking he will," she disclosed.

Nya noted, "This isn't the first time you've talked about being angry, and I think that is something we should explore."

"Oh God," Celeste gasped. "I'm a 38-year-old angry woman, no wonder I'm single," she joked. "Maliq would like that joke," she said. It wasn't the first time she had mentioned his name in these sessions. Maliq was an ex-boyfriend, though short lived, he still lived in her heart. Both Celeste and Nya were unsure as to why, but now wasn't the time for Nya to deviate and she wanted Celeste to continue.

"A 38-year-old woman who keeps making the same mistakes. Aren't I meant to know better by now?" Celeste asked Nya hoping she would get an answer that would help her understand herself better.

Nya answered her kindly, "I think we continue to learn till the day we die." She flipped the pages on her notepad that she had sat in her lap to a fresh page and continued, "You mentioned you can't make him want you, do you find yourself trying to make someone want you? And what do you mean by want?"

Celeste paused as she thought about what that meant. In all honesty she answered, "I want him to like me," she felt exposed.

"Do you think men don't?"

"I don't know," Celeste gazed past Nya to the window behind her, where she could see green trees gently swaying outside. She had always been somewhat of a people pleaser but at the same time considered herself independent. But now that she had said it aloud, she was reflecting on past behaviours. "Now that I think about it, I do find myself doing things that maybe I shouldn't. I mean, nothing really important but little things."

"Like what?" Nya pressed.

"Roman has a dog. Honestly, I'm not a huge pet person and I get allergies if I get their hair in my eyes. And yet whenever I was at his place, I would sit and pet that dog, and play with it, and talk to it. I'd catch myself doing it knowing full well it was so he would see me in a different light, maybe a better light, and it would make him like me more."

"Make him want you?" Nya asked.

"Yes," Celeste shamefully admitted.

"Have you done this in the past?"

Celeste hung her head as she considered the question, "Yes."

"I think we have two important factors to focus on right now. Your desire to be liked and the anger you feel."

Sounds about right, Celeste thought. In one short sentence Nya had ripped open Celeste's mind and exposed her. However, it felt good to air her grievances and she felt safe doing so in Nya's presence. Why she didn't feel comfortable telling anyone else this secret was a mystery. Celeste didn't have any issues revealing her emotions, thoughts and opinions to anyone who would listen. She was the kind of person that was so open and honest with those around her, they felt they could be open and honest back. Celeste had a knack of peeling back the layers of people she met and because of her sheer transparency they knew they could trust her in return. However, the deepest insecurity she felt, of not being liked or indeed wanted, was one she never revealed and because of her outgoing and happy disposition, no one ever questioned it.

"I want to talk a little more about you pretending to be someone you're not," Nya had her pen and notepad poised and ready. "How often do you do this?"

"Often enough now that I think about it." This wasn't news to Celeste but now that they had shone a spotlight on the issue, she was surprised to realise just how often she did indeed pander to a man's personality to make herself appear to be a better mate. She thought about the times she said she didn't mind where they ate even though she certainly did. When she would watch a movie she had no interest in because she thought he would find her more interesting, and how she would clean up after him because she thought she would seem domesticated. She wouldn't swear so she appeared lady-like and would dress in a manner that she felt spoke to his desires instead of her own. Was she mimicking her mother's behaviour during her parents' marriage? No wonder she was angry.

"Do you think I do this because of my upbringing?" Celeste pondered. "You said in our first session we go to what is familiar."

"What is familiar about these scenarios to you?"

"Mum used to wear these long flowing dresses and always set her hair a certain way because that's what Dad liked. Dad never asked her to do it, she just did. Because she knew he saw her in a certain way when she wore those dresses. We all knew it. I don't know how, but we did. And I never thought anything of it till after they broke up and Mum started wearing more tailored outfits and pants suits. She once mentioned it was nice to wear what made her feel good for a change. Do you think that's why I do this now?"

"Do you think you recreate your parent's relationship in your own?" Nya was good, it was like she could read her mind.

Celeste let her mind quickly scan her relationships over the years, "Yes."

She felt a wave of sadness wash over her. She wasn't that woman, was she? She recalled her parent's relationship and the example they had set. She had always viewed their marriage as one of hard knocks and tough times but that ultimately love would win, and their problems would be solved. Love didn't win and they separated after 30 years of marriage.

Thinking about it now, she isn't sure why she thought that. She was never sold the fairy tale dream any more than being read stories, like Cinderella and Sleeping Beauty, but it was unspoken that when you grow up you find someone to marry and have children and that you stay together forever.

There wasn't any anger or unkindness in her household, but what she does remember was a wife subservient to her husband to ensure a happy home. And as Celeste had grown into her teenage years, she can vividly recall her teenage angst spewing at her father that he shouldn't treat his wife like a child and that she had a mind of her own. Funny how she couldn't give you any specifics of what exactly he said or did that made Celeste see red, but she always attributed her stubbornness and innate need to be independent to those memories of watching her mother bend to the needs of a man. Her father was sweetly oblivious to the fact his wife did whatever he asked. Two individuals who had grown together from a young age recreating their own versions of what marriage meant to them, based on their naive accounts and memories.

And now to realise she wasn't as strong as she once believed, stunned her. She had continued that behaviour into her own relationships.

"It's okay," Nya pulled Celeste back from her memories. "I think you have a sense of needing control in your life. Changing your behaviour, the anger. I think these emotions and actions are symptoms of that need for control. How do you feel when I say that?" Nya asked.

Celeste looked over at Nya with gratitude as a wave of sadness washed over her. She felt unravelled as pieces of her life lay broken apart in her mind. Yet relieved and safe in Nya's care, she knew she would help put her back together again.

"It makes me feel like we have a lot to talk about," Celeste said with a smile.

"Anything else?" Nya asked.

Celeste was thoughtful and took time to flip through the memories in her mind, like a kaleidoscope shifting seamlessly from one scene to the next.

"Control is a funny word, isn't it," Celeste finally responded to Nya's question.

"How so?" Nya was curious to hear Celeste's take on it.

"When the word control is used in the same sentence as the word woman, it's always used negatively. Or assumed it's a bad thing. Why can't it be seen as powerful?"

"Do you want to be seen as powerful?" Nya pressed Celeste.

"Sure. Powerful sounds a hell of a lot better than controlling, doesn't it?"

Nya laughed and agreed. She pushed for more answers by asking, "Do you want to feel powerful then?"

Pondering the question, Celeste said, "It's all the same. Power, control. I guess I just want to feel ..." *What? What do I want to feel?* She asked herself.

In one word Celeste summed it up. "Heard," she finished her sentence.

Chapter 3: A Simple Twinkle in Her Eye

The hours after a therapy session usually saw Celeste swamped with memories of her past. Her therapist told her it was healthy to lean into them and truly reflect on the feelings that arose. 'Name them out loud,' Nya would say. 'Identify the feeling and seek the trigger.'

She had been sifting through the chambers of her mind, reminiscing about the dates she had been subjected to since her arrival in New York City. Not all bad of course, but she wanted to compile them to dissect the similarities that she had ignored until now. She laughed recalling the arrogance of the Brit she had met for a drink, who she quickly realised would not be a lover but could be an ally. They had connected over their experiences both in Britain and in coming to America and had split the check. She had given him a warm hug as she had said goodbye and was surprised to receive a text from him merely moments later, asking why she didn't give him a kiss. The audacity he had to expect a damsel in NY should indeed go weak at the knees for one of her own kind and offer herself as a prize for his candid time with her. It made her shake her head.

And this is why she found online dating exhausting. You never really know who you're going to get in real life. Although maybe that was just an excuse she liked to use; she hadn't seen that coming during the one and a half hours they sat drinking frozen margaritas outside the Mexican restaurant on the Lower East Side. With that thought in mind, she remembered another date that came after meeting the old-fashioned way. And had to admit, online or in real life, there are no guarantees. Your mind will make up its own version of a story it wants to project into reality.

She remembered it like it was yesterday.

***

The sun was high in the November sky and the water glistened under its presence. The leaves were turning, and she had not long celebrated her one-year anniversary of living in New York City. The weather was becoming brisk, and she was grateful for the unusually warm day. The sun's heat was making one of its final encores before farewelling its audience for the coming months.

Celeste and Trevor were perched on the bench seats inside the small rowboat they'd hired at the Loeb Boathouse in Central Park. Tourists flocked to this iconic destination, and she watched as families, friends and couples slowly made their way around the lake, snapping selfies and smiling broad smiles.

"I can't believe I've never done this before," Celeste gushed. She was genuinely as excited to be there as the tourists were. For all the times she had visited NYC, she had never taken her feet off land to ride the boats people flock to from around the world. She was happy to be finally experiencing this for herself, but also with a handsome beau.

She had met Trevor at a Rangers game at Madison Square Garden the weekend before. A friend had a spare ticket and had invited Celeste to join her and her boyfriend. Although far from a sports fan, Celeste quite enjoyed watching ice hockey. There was something about watching well-built men elegantly glide across the ice before using the full weight of their body to slam an opponent into the barrier. Celeste also didn't like violence but there was something primal in the way they played this game that turned her on. Plus, it was a great opportunity to be around other primal men and maybe she'd meet someone. She had yet to experience anything relatively close to what you see romanticised on sitcoms since her arrival in the city.

Celeste had been standing at the concession stand waiting to buy an overpriced under-whelming beer when Trevor and his friends joined the line up behind her. Trevor seemed to fit the bill of the stereotypical jock. He was at least 6 foot 4 inches, with blonde hair cut too short for Celeste's taste. It was almost military short. But he had bright blue eyes and a boyish smile that suggested you were about to have a good time whenever he flashed his perfectly set white teeth. He pushed his friends' locker-room style every time they made a joke to his liking, as he laughed a loud American laugh. A return push from one of his friends had sent him apologetically knocking into Celeste, and when she replied that it was fine in her British accent, he immediately asked her where she was from. It was a common line that she still didn't mind hearing. People always wanted to know more about her as soon as they heard her speak. It's funny how something as simple as an accent can open many doors or at least invite many conversations.

They approached the bar and the stand attendant asked both for their orders, hastily pushing plastic cups of beer with too much foam towards them. Trevor held out his credit card and paid for Celeste's drink along with his own.

They stepped aside to let his raucous friends place their order and it was then he had asked for her number.

She'd received a text from him later that night but knew better than to meet him. Instead, she sent him a reply telling him to have a fun night and to message her the next day. And to her pleasant surprise, he did. While she wasn't sure if he would, more to the point, she wasn't sure if she even wanted him to. He wasn't the kind of guy she would usually go out with. Jocks, or jocks-adjacent, were not her type. And he had to be at least seven years younger than her. What could really come of any rendezvous, except for the obvious? But he was devilishly handsome, and she couldn't resist.

When he had met her at the boathouse, he was wearing a Ranger's shirt and a Yankees cap. He was a walking billboard for New York sports teams.

She had laughed to herself that she was on a date with the type of guy you see on an American sitcom. Red, white and blue with stars in his eyes; wholesome to boot but not a lot under the hood. Maybe she was finally getting the sitcom romance she had long-been exposed to and expecting.

His outfit quickly reminded her that he was not her type, and she couldn't see how this could possibly go anywhere, but then he gave her one of his winning smiles and she swooned. She couldn't wait to tell her friends about it back in England. This would be ammunition they would long use against her in their playful way. She was aware it was another mistake in the making but let herself be fooled in the moment that maybe this time it was different. Maybe she could find space in her wardrobe? It varied from casual capris to little black dresses to hippy skirts to pressed pin striped suits. Was there room for a jersey of her own? She already knew the answer but entertained the idea for a moment in time. Deep down she knew she had no interest in wearing any sort of jersey. But she also recognised the character she could play.

They made small talk as they made their way to the boat rental kiosk. He talked about sports results and some outrage at a player being poached. She wasn't overly interested but he seemed excited when he spoke, and she decided it was easier just to smile and nod along.

Probably not the kind of guy to talk about the current political climate with, she reminded herself.

He had helped her into the boat like a gentleman and climbed in after her. With their oars at the ready, a boat rental crew member gave them a push off and away they floated towards the middle of the lake.

"You mean to say you've lived here a year and you're only just doing this now?" Trevor asked.

She turned her attention away from his chiselled face that had day-old stubble. "Look at the color of the water. It's more green than blue. Why?" she smiled sweetly at him.

"It's actually a reflection of the trees and vegetation around us. Usually when it looks blue, it's a reflection of the sky."

"Really?"

"Well, that and other factors like molecules and particles." He'd read it somewhere once and wasn't sure.

Celeste sensed he wasn't entirely confident in his reply but decided to indulge him. It was a tried and tested method. Make him feel smart. "How scientific. I don't know anything about that stuff. Oh look, a frog! Okay, smarty pants, why are frogs green?"

What is the tone of your voice? she asked herself.

"They've got three types of pigment cells that work together." The only reason he knew that was because of the science class he attended at the expensive private school his parents had sent him to.

"Oh my gosh, you really are a smarty pants. I can't believe you know this stuff." Celeste found herself praising him in a voice an octave higher than it should be.

What are you doing?

"It's not a big deal," Trevor replied.

And yet she continued. "I think it is. I think you're very smart. I bet you know all sorts of things I have no idea about."

The voice in her head continued. *You are ridiculous! You sound like a fool. But I guess that's the game you are playing.*

Trevor looked pleased with himself. "I'm sure that's not true."

"I could tell you everything about nail polish. But you, well, you know about all sorts of important stuff." She paused and the voice in her head said she may as well go for it now. "I bet you know how to do lots of important stuff too. I bet you are handy."

"Now that you mention it, I actually do like to build things."

"Shut up!" Another couple in a boat were drifting past them and they looked in her direction as she delivered that line. She could feel them looking at her. She knew what they were thinking. She sounded like an idiot. She sounded like a teenager.

In for a penny, in for a pound, she thought. She was sure she heard the other woman say, 'someone save her from herself'.

Trevor was smiling smugly. "No really, I do."

"Wow! You are so clever."

"Oh, stop," he said even though he didn't mean it.

Celeste continued, "You are so clever. What have you built?"

Celeste watched his arms as he moved the oars through the water, considering her question. He was tanned from a recent holiday to Cancun and his shirt was tight against his firm chest and triceps. "Pretty much all the furniture in my place," he finally answered.

She didn't know if it was true but something about the way he said it made her believe him. "How did you learn how to do that?"

Celeste was genuinely curious to know him better. She had let go of her silly girl act for a moment and considered whether there might be more to Trevor than his tight top.

"A woodwork class I took in school. I guess I found I was good at it and just kept it up. It's not that hard."

Forget it, she thought. *He isn't going to give you what you want. And the real you is not his type. Play the game girl.*

"Stop that. You make it sound easy when I bet you have to be super talented to do what you do."

Trevor was looking at her the way a child looks at his first-grade teacher who just told him his finger painting was a work of art. "I don't know ..."

She was wrapping him around her little finger. *This is too easy*, she thought.

"Well, I do." She took hold of one of his hands as he let the oar rest on his thigh. Then reached for the other. "I mean just look at these hands. They are like magic hands. Clever, magic hands." She giggled. She heard herself and wanted to throw up with embarrassment.

But Trevor was looking at his hands and she could tell he was feeling very good about himself. "Do you think so?"

"Yes! I bet everything you do with these hands is perfection."

She was feeling giddy now. A girlish curse had come over her and she was all in. She knew this wasn't who she really was, but Trevor was responding in a way that made him look at her the way a starving man looked at food. Eager for her to speak again and tell him how wonderful he was.

Are men really this easy to please, she wondered?

"And your arms. Gosh, they are so muscly." She said as she gently ran her right hand over his buff arm.

"I haven't been to the gym in a week." Was he really feeling vulnerable or was he just looking for more attention?

She gave his arm a little squeeze. "Could have fooled me," she smiled.

Trevor picked up the oars again and started rowing.

Celeste was in awe of how easy it had been to inflate his ego. Although, if she was honest, just ten minutes of that pathetic show felt like three hours. She felt exhausted from her performance already and wondered how she would keep it up. She was an intelligent, thirty-seven-year-old woman acting like a teenage girl trying to impress the popular boy at school.

It made her reflect on her first crush who was tall, blonde and athletic, with the same mischievous smile. She had fallen in love with him at the ripe age of twelve. But he had fallen in love with her best friend, Virginia. Virginia was a year older and had a bust that made the rest of the girls jealous and all the boy's notice. Was it at this time that Celeste started to learn that men didn't notice intellect and were merely drawn to simpler pleasures?

She recalled the foolish girl act she started to play hoping to get his attention... and it had worked. He liked it when she was acting silly. Somehow, she became more desirable. But still not as desirable as the girls who had blossomed already. Celeste had to wait another couple of years to combine both efforts.

As she sat in the boat, she recognised she had opened the silly-girl toolbox and was using all the tools she had collected over the years.

Trevor interrupted her thoughts, "What do you think of this place?"

Celeste looked around again. They had ventured away from the boat house and had passed under the famous Bow Bridge. When she took in the view she saw the midtown city skyline. Mirrored towers reaching high for the white fluffy clouds that hung in the clear blue sky above. She counted at least three cranes perched on top of skyscrapers being built that would sell at rates that could feed a small nation for a year.

The scene took your breath away. The water lapped at the edge of the grey rocks that acted as daybeds for turtles warming in the sun, and ducks drying off lakeside. The leaves were playful in hues of green, red and brown as autumn was taking over. They were still full and lush and hadn't started to shed, but the occasional star shaped leaf would float by to remind you winter was approaching.

To the west, stood the famous San Remo towers as if straight from a child's fairy tale story. The same ones you see dawning in every tourist photo.

"Oh, I just love it. You really know the best places to take a girl on a date." Celeste looked around and took in the landscape and felt a rush of happiness. Then, for a moment, she dropped the act, "I mean it. This is just perfect. I couldn't be happier right now." The real Celeste meant it.

"I'm glad you like it. I really enjoy coming out here. A bit of down time when you need it, you know."

"Absolutely. But surely you don't really need down time. I mean, you just seem like the kind of guy who's always so relaxed."

It was a simple question that she knew would be answered candidly. It was a knack she had, as if by magic, she could retrieve the sincerest emotions and deepest memories from the men she dated. Most of the time they couldn't explain, even to themselves, why they had the courage to confide in her.

She wasn't sure if it was her apparent foolishness that led him to believe she'd be too silly to judge him when he exposed his true self, or if he saw past the act itself and inherently knew she was a woman who genuinely cared, a little too much sometimes.

"Most of the time, but I have my moments. To be honest, I have some dark days, but I try to stay positive and keep my chin up. I don't know why I'm telling you this stuff, sorry."

Bingo! That didn't take long, she thought. *That must be a record, even for me.*

"That's okay."

Trevor continued, "I guess it's not uncommon these days. Everyone has their battles."

Normally Celeste would have jumped on this information and taken a deep dive into what he meant. She would have turned him inside out to get to the root of the problem and try to find a way to help him. After all, she was practically a professional with all the years of experience she had racked up. Yet, she chose not to indulge this opportunity for him. Something about him made her think he didn't really need fixing. He was just being his honest self with her and that scared her more.

She had already predetermined this would end sooner rather than later. And even if those reasons were valid, she would rather orchestrate the ending than leave it up to fate. She didn't want to risk being hurt on someone else's terms. She had her own version of the story to tell.

To protect herself, Celeste shifted the tone in her voice again to continue playing the game. But she was already fading trying to uphold the ridiculous act she was performing, and she didn't think she had it in her to last much longer. Something about when you know there is no future and the relationship is short term, that makes the process more exhausting. "Mmmm, the pressures of the world can be tough."

She knew how unenthusiastic she sounded and quickly changed the subject, "Oh look, turtles!"

Trevor turned to look at the turtles and at the same time he took out his mobile phone. He looked down at the device in his hand and Celeste stared at him with irritation.

She found it rude when anyone turned their attention to their mobile phone when they were meant to be having some meaningful time together. Her insecurities were high at this moment due the impressive show she was performing in and she started to worry she wasn't good enough.

Is he expecting a message or call? Who from? Another girl? Someone prettier than me? Younger than me? What am I doing here?

For a moment she considered turning off the act, telling him to turn the boat around and take her back, so she could go home.

How would you explain that? she asked herself.

It's fine, it's fine, it's fine, she repeated in her mind.

"Looks like there is a family of them," Trevor broke her reverie.

"What?"

"The turtles, it looks like there is a baby one with its parents."

"Oh, how cute." *Quick, say something more interesting than whoever he was waiting for a message from.*

"I recently started doing yoga. It's awesome and it makes you so bendy," she blurted.

Trevor laughed, she wasn't sure if he was laughing at her because he didn't believe her or if he just laughed at everything before he spoke. "I actually do yoga," he offered.

"Shut up! You do not." *God lord,* Celeste thought, *of course you do.* She knew it wasn't uncommon for men to do yoga and honestly didn't have a problem with it, but for some reason she didn't want to date a man who did it. She always associated it with men who were more in touch with their feminine side. Another thought process probably passed down as she remembered her dad hurting his back once and saying he didn't want to do Pilates to help himself heal. It just wasn't for him, he had said. Celeste's father was a man's man, so it made sense to her. Was she now projecting this into her taste in men?

"I do. It's great for the soul. There is actually a lot of research proving it has modern medicine benefits."

"Is there anything you don't know?" Celeste said playfully but was losing interest.

"Shut up!" he teased, mimicking her.

This she found funny. She wasn't sure if she was laughing at his perfect impersonation or if she was just laughing at herself, but she laughed a hearty laugh.

"You're hilarious, gosh. Funny, smart, handsome. Aren't I lucky?"

"You really know how to make a guy feel good about himself," Trevor replied.

Celeste had simply smiled at him in response.

They returned to the boat house not long after, just as the sun was setting.

As they pulled up and waited their turn to row the boat back into the dock, Trevor kissed her.

It was a good kiss. Not as selfish as Celeste had anticipated it could be. She had assumed that his looks had served him well and he had never had to work at it. Not all men who are lucky in lust are bothered to learn how to do it right. But he had reached out one arm and had cupped his hand around the side of her neck. He had pulled her towards him as he leaned in. He kissed her firmly but with a warmth that suggested it was likely a long-term girlfriend taught him how to make a woman feel special.

She took him home that night. Her apartment wasn't far from the park, and it made sense to her at the time. She'd put on a good show. Didn't she deserve her own sitcom romance?

***

They had woken with the sun beaming into her apartment. Celeste woke first and had risen to use the bathroom. When she came back into the room Trevor was getting dressed. He slid his mobile in his pocket and said he had plans that day and had to get going. He said that he had a great time and that he would call her. He left her apartment with a quick kiss on the lips and Celeste never heard from him again.

While she had secretly fantasised theirs would be a love story that would give hope to all single women; that it too could happen to them, but deep down she had known he wasn't the one. While he was a lovely guy, he wasn't the guy for her. He'd be great to flash around your friends because he is the type of guy that fits in everywhere. He'll make you smile and laugh and forget about the world for a while. But there was no more depth to his personality than the water they had sailed upon the day prior. He was sweet and hospitable and that was in part what she yearned for in a man, but she also longed for someone that would stay up till all hours, debating the rights and wrongs in the world.

Sure, she hadn't given him the chance to show that side of his personality. If it did in fact exist at all. But she had promptly put him in the box that suited her ending. It was easier to put him in said box rather than wish for anything more. So, she didn't particularly want to see him again. *What's the point, it'll never work. Let it go now.* And it seemed he had her in his own box. For whatever reason, he didn't want to see her again either.

Even though Celeste genuinely felt she was satisfied with the outcome, she couldn't understand why the rejection still hurt so much.

Chapter 4: *Whispers in the Chamber*

Celeste was meeting with Nya for the fourth time and was telling her about the date she'd had with Trevor on the lake. She told her how she had recalled it after their last session, and how reflecting on her interaction with him, helped her learn a lot about herself thanks to these sessions.

Celeste had always had strong convictions that therapy was an essential part of selfcare and healthcare, and would recommend it to anyone who would take her advice. She wondered if it was a profession she should have gone into herself, given how often she found herself lending an ear and giving life advice that she wasn't sure she was qualified to offer.

She had never sought it for herself though, at least not from a professional. Given her open and talkative nature, Celeste was always comfortable sharing her feelings and discussing issues with those around her. She had mistakenly believed that her openness was an outlet on its own. However, she was finding herself opening up to Nya in ways she didn't to her friends and family. And it was because of this she wondered how it had taken her so long to take her own advice.

"I played the part," Celeste said. "Look good, play dumb, make him feel wise and superior. It's a simple girl fact and most girls were taught this in school."

"You were taught to play stupid, is that what I'm hearing?" Nya asked.

"Yes. Play the fool. Don't put up any fight. Agree."

"Agree?"

"Sure. That's the way to win a man, right?"

"Why do you use the word 'win'?"

Celeste answered with hesitation. "Maybe because then I'll feel worthy." She almost stopped herself from speaking the words. This was a depth of conversation she wasn't comfortable swimming in. She felt it was a weakness and that she should feel ashamed to share her vulnerability.

But she also knew she could trust Nya. And had to if she was going to get her money's worth.

"Do you think you aren't worthy of a man's love?"

"I think I am. But then it seems my actions speak another language. And after my last session with you, I think we worked out why. It's a learned behaviour, and I keep repeating it. In some form or another."

"And how does it make you feel to recognise this behaviour now?" Nya pressed.

"Pathetic. Sad." Celeste admitted.

"Why those two words?"

Celeste pondered this. "Pathetic because I should be stronger than that. Sad because I'm not," she said.

"And it's important to you to be strong?"

"Of course. I don't want my parent's relationship. I don't want my boyfriend or husband telling me what to do. I want to feel supported."

"Did you feel supported growing up?" Nya enquired.

She's good, Celeste thought. "I think so. Definitely by mum. Honestly, I think I tried to get my dad's approval. He wasn't disapproving, but emotionally absent is probably the best way to describe it."

Nya continued, "And talk to me about what the outcome usually is when you find yourself becoming someone else to impress a man?"

Celeste knew the answer without even thinking about it. "I get angry when he doesn't do the same in return."

"You want him to be someone else?" Nya questioned.

Celeste paused and answered. "No, I want to be able to be myself. But I usually can't, so then why should he get to be?"

She wasn't sure if she was making sense and sat with her thoughts for a moment. "I just find myself changing and giving way too much. I think that somehow, if I am a better version of me for him, then he'll be a better version in return. But he never is. All of me is taken and it's never reciprocated."

"He never gives himself to you?" Nya asks.

"Not how I want him to. He is taken care of and I'm not. Then I get angry."

"Why's that," Nya was working her magic.

"Because it makes me realise I am the one giving up myself for little to nothing in return. I spend all my time taking care of him. When is it my turn?"

Nya didn't say anything. She waited for Celeste to turn the conversation over in her head for a few more seconds.

Celeste was reflecting on all the times this had happened throughout her relationships. "And now that I think about it, it's a common theme." Pausing for a moment, her eyes flickering with memories. She spat out a laugh that was telling of someone who had come to a realisation.

"Actually, almost all of my relationships." It was a statement.

Nya made a quick note, "All? Or just romantic?"

Celeste had never really thought about her behaviour in relationships beyond her love life and considered it for a moment.

She recognised that certain feelings surfaced in her family relationships and echoed in her friendships. She was sure if she pondered more, it likely extended to her work relationships too.

"Maybe all," Celeste answered honestly. "I haven't really thought about it."

"Have you read the book yet?" Nya was referencing the book she had asked her to read when they first started their sessions, *Codependent No More*.

With guilt, Celeste replied, "I've flicked over some pages ... I think I read the first chapter."

Celeste looked at Nya and waited to see if she was in trouble. *Am I doing it now?* She thought. *Trying to be the person Nya wants me to be?*

Nya met Celeste's eyes and smiled, "In your own time," was all she said.

Celeste felt relieved and made a mental note to find the book that she was sure was either amongst the stack of novels on her dresser or sitting neatly on her bookshelf.

"Let's talk about your last relationship," Nya continued.

"Sure," Celeste quipped.

"You've mentioned Maliq a few times throughout our sessions. You throw his name around every now and then, but we haven't delved into it."

"What do you want to know?"

"He seems important to you, and I'd like to better understand that relationship."

It was true. Maliq was very important to Celeste. They had met in a pub in London where he had taken her hand and danced with her in front of the band that played. It was a romantic story that she wanted to be able to tell people about for the rest of their lives. He was a kind man who had given as much of his heart to her that he could afford. Unfortunately, it was barely a sliver, as he himself acknowledged he had been broken in the past and wasn't sure he could give many more pieces away.

This was new to Celeste. A man who admitted his faults. Could it be possible he would stay the course and help himself, rather than seek to lean on her?

The answer was no. Celeste had done what she always did. She had thrown herself into the relationship, forged a path of restoration for Maliq that included giving up many parts of herself—and it was one that he didn't follow. She had once again expected more in return than he was willing or able to give.

When Maliq didn't put in the work, she got angry and ran for the hills. Actually, she ran for America.

"It must be a good sign that for once I found a man who at least admitted he needed help, rather than just leaping in and providing it without being asked, right?"

Nya nodded her head.

"And I left! I left him before it became too toxic," Celeste was proud of herself.

"That is true," Nya agreed.

"And Roman. He also admitted he needed help. Two in a row." Celeste added, looking for a pat on the back.

"Sure. But you're still going from men who need help but won't admit it, to men who need help and are willing to admit it—all the while, neither are willing to do anything about it. You may have left Maliq in a moment of clarity, but you picked up where you left off when you chose Roman. The pattern of behaviour seems to have followed you across the Atlantic," Nya said with a kind smile.

Celeste knew she was right. While one could argue she had made progress in dating men who at least understood their own demons, she was still chasing someone else's problem as she believed she was the solution.

Nya continued, "How long did you and Maliq date?"

"Not long enough. Or maybe just long enough. It was just over six months by the time I left."

"And he is in London, right?"

"He is."

"And you talk a lot?"

"Sometimes. And then he'll do something to make me angry," Celeste paused and smiled at Nya. "There is that word again. Something will happen and I am usually the one who will slam on the brakes until I have calmed down."

Celeste crosses one arm over her waist and raises the other to rest her chin in the palm of her hand; her eyes reveal she is considering what this means.

"What is your relationship with him now?" Celeste was aware that Nya needed to know so that she could help.

"A friendship. He is the one I want to call when I feel scared or sad. Or if I need a rational point of view. I do wonder if maybe one day, we will be together again ... but then I think about it and I get frustrated at the reality."

"What does the reality look like?"

"He has his stuff. Like we all do. I feel like he doesn't let me in when he is going through a hard time, and I just need him to let me help. He doesn't like to be told what to do, even though he's told me he knows I'm right. And it's just frustrating. If he knows I'm right, why won't he just do it then? And I feel like I don't have any control over anything."

Nya writes something in her notepad and Celeste wonders what she has just said that is so important. *Was it the word 'control'*, she wondered?

"You've talked about helping Maliq. I want to hear how he makes you feel. Why do you like him?"

Celeste pondered for longer than normal. It wasn't that she didn't have the words, but sitting in front of Nya, she was now considering what they meant. "He's a good man, you know." She emphasised the word good when she repeated herself, "you know, like a *good* man."

"What does that mean?"

"He cares about people. About me. Maybe too much about other people."

"What makes you say that?"

"I feel like he prioritises other people's feelings above mine. Which is fine sometimes, but when you're in a relationship, shouldn't you feel like your partner has your back one hundred per cent of the time?"

Nya answered with a statement rather than a question, "It's important to you to feel like you're supported."

"Yes."

"And we know this because of your relationship with your dad. This makes sense." Celeste felt validated in her perceived neurosis and Nya asked, "So how did you feel when this would happen, what would you do?"

The feeling washing over Celeste was becoming familiar. A realisation, a moment of clarity, a spotlight on an emotion she was given permission to recognise as tangible and not fictional. "It made me feel the same way Dad would make me feel. Not seen. Important but not important enough to be taken care of. And then silly that I should expect anything different. And then I would get angry. Because anger is less humiliating than sadness."

"Do you think Maliq is like your dad?"

Celeste was quick to reply, "No." She paused. "Well, in some ways but not fundamentally. Fundamentally he was more like my mum. He was kind and considerate and cared so much about others."

"And we know your mom pandered to your dad's needs. Have you considered that your anger at Maliq was not just about your feelings towards your dad, but also that he represented your mom in a lot of ways? He didn't make you feel seen, much like your dad. But he also pandered to the needs of others above your own. Somewhat like your mom did when she catered to the needs of your dad and you felt it was unfair to the rest of the family. And unfair to you."

Celeste sat silently in her thoughts. Her mum pandered to the needs of her entire family but in hierarchical terms, her dad's needs were usually put first. Nya was right, her response was two-fold. One part her father, one part her mother. She had a much easier time blaming her dad for the impact his behaviour had on her, rather than to place any blame at her mum's feet.

Nya knew her client well by now, "Remember, this is not a blame game. This doesn't mean we are now blaming your mom."

Celeste smiled as Nya read her mind.

Nya continued, "Your mom did the best she could, with the tools she was given as a child and into adulthood. But through our conversations we understand that the impact of how pandering to your dad's needs wasn't the best approach. Even your mom admits that."

It was true. Celeste had many previous conversations with her mother over the years about her parent's relationship. Her mum did what she thought was best. She was raised to keep a marriage together at all costs and was taught in an era that prioritised men's needs over women's. Then the family needs over everyone else. Although truth be told, her mum pandered to everyone around her and never put herself first. As Celeste contemplated this, she knew that the trait had been passed down to her too.

"Maliq on the other hand didn't believe in marriage. He barely believed in relationships. His childhood had taught him love wasn't to be trusted, that appearances were important, your private life should be kept private and to keep your chin up at all costs." Celeste had a moment of clarity, Okay, so maybe he was a little more like my dad than I realised."

Celeste was quickly realising the consequential nature of her relationship with Maliq and that he had fed into her pattern of relationship behaviour seamlessly. And why she was still so enamoured with him today.

"He's a safe bet."

"Safe bet?" Nya questioned.

"You asked why I like him. I could say all the usual things about what a good guy he is, how kind and funny he is, blah blah. But at the end of the day, it's because he is a safe bet. I know exactly what I am getting with him. What comes next. How this will end. Just like every other guy I've dated."

Celeste thought this was what Nya would call a breakthrough.

"I agree. What you need to unpack now is what you think you will do with this information."

"Can I stay friends with him?" Celeste asked.

People always say therapists won't give you a straight answer, but Nya did, "Of course. I don't see him harming you or being a threat to your wellbeing. Besides, he is thousands of miles away," she smiled. "However, I think what you need to establish about your relationship with Maliq, is what it really brings to your life now."

Celeste would sometimes romanticise her relationship with Maliq. Play it out like a scene from a movie. He would visit her in New York, he would change into a man who could put the woman he loved ahead of his own needs and those around him, declare it in grand fashion even. She would find freedom in allowing herself to believe that he will not take her for granted or ask her to change. They would marry, even if she didn't truly care if marriage was on the cards as long as there was commitment, and she would live happily ever after.

She laughed out loud at this notion and offered to Nya, "I know that I trust him. And I think that deep down, I know he and I are not meant to be more than friends. I think what this friendship means to me is that it brings me peace."

"Peace?" Nya needed to understand this statement.

"I didn't get it totally wrong with him. Although he was still not the right one for me, he was the closest I've gotten to a relationship with someone who respected me and still respects me. I know he loves me in the way he knows how and wants only the best for me. To know there is a man like that out there who feels that way about me, brings me peace. Maybe that is the wrong word?" Celeste asked.

"I think if it's a word you identify with, then you should use it. Peace can bring silence and stillness. So, it makes sense that he brings peace to your thoughts and possibly helps you to pause in your decision process."

It made complete sense to Celeste now that Nya was analysing the nature of her relationship with Maliq. What she was still disturbed about was her decision making of late that led her to fall into the pit of desperation that was her last love affair. A stark reminder of all the other men who she felt broke her heart. She had barely dated when she first arrived in New York City as she was busy dating the city itself. Trevor had been one of the first who had taken her heart on a ride that left it whiplashed, or whatever it was it felt after their one night together. She was still perplexed at how hurt she had been and contemplated why she had willingly taken the quick hit after such a stint of sobriety. She had quickly slid back into her old habits that she had so longed to kick.

"So why did I fall into that last love affair with yet another man I knew was not right for me?" She wanted answers from Nya.

"Why do you think?" Nya countered.

I think I'm paying you $150 an hour, and you should just tell me, is what Celeste thought, but instead replied with a smile, "I honestly don't know. Any insight?"

"Well, you've been living this way for 38 years and I think that you shouldn't be so hard on yourself."

Celeste felt a wave of emotion wash over her and thought for a second she might cry. This was another outcome of therapy that she was becoming accustomed to—out of the blue emotions. Triggers that make you want to weep without any rationale other than a release is needed.

"I made another mistake. The same one I keep making, or so it seems," Celeste said.

"You made another mistake, you leaned into what you know," Nya concurred. "Changing your pattern of behaviour isn't going to happen overnight. This is a long process that you have committed to. And you need to be kind to yourself when you slip. And you won't always get it right, even when you think you've mastered it. We've spoken about the fact he fit the mould, a man that you unconsciously recognised. You had other stresses in your life at the time."

"I definitely felt like things were out of my control." Celeste had been having a hard time at work with a female colleague. Weren't women meant to stick together? She was older than Celeste, with grown children and had been in her job a long time.

Celeste had thought they could be friends at first, until she had been told by other colleagues of the unkind words being said behind her back. It had brought her to tears in her office that day. This woman was ruthless. She was out for blood and had a target on Celeste's back. She had a higher opinion of herself than management had and firmly believed she should have been in line for a promotion that would have taken her into Celeste's role.

Celeste, like her mother, didn't know how to handle the emotions of being unliked by someone. Especially by one who had no reason not to befriend her. Instead, this colleague's jealousy had gotten in the way, and she made it her priority to defame Celeste at any opportunity she got.

Celeste had also been due for her first visit home to London since leaving but had to postpone due to some work commitments. This had also left her feeling vulnerable as she was homesick and wanted some quality time with friends and family.

"I guess I wasn't overly happy with life when I met him."

"And it's common practice to go back to what we know," Nya offered. "The good news is, you came to me and now we are giving you the tools you need to help you the next time you are faced with the same situation."

"This is going to happen again?" Celeste laughed as if she didn't mind, but Nya saw the desire in her eyes to mend the broken path she walked.

"More than likely, but the thing to keep in mind is, it will happen less and less."

"Well, I've got you on speed dial as I have just signed up for Hinge," Celeste did not look happy as she announced this.

"Want to expand on that?"

"Everyone keeps telling me Hinge is better than the rest. Better quality men with better outcomes. But I'm sure it's just the same. And besides, I really don't want to meet someone on an online dating app." It was true, she didn't. With all her being, Celeste was certain she would never meet her mate through technology and algorithms.

"Maybe you shouldn't be so adverse," Nya compelled her. "You have told me about friends who have met online that have gone on to marry, have children, be happy."

"Yes, but I don't want that."

"To be happy?" Nya countered.

Celeste let the words float through her mind and imagined the word *happy* breaking apart and coming back together, before breaking apart and repeating the cycle. Much like her pattern of behaviour in choosing inappropriate men. Was she really avoiding the opportunity to be happy? Why did she have this fairy tale idea that she would meet someone the traditional way? And in fact, the era of meeting online would one day become the traditional way of meeting your mate. Why was she hellbent on standing out from the crowd of modern technology in an idealised fantasy of finding some Prince Charming who would fall at her feet.

Nya broke her chain of thought, "Our time is almost up so what I would like you to do for our next session is think about why you are so averse to online dating. What do you think will happen if you do meet someone you are genuinely interested in and what do you think that outcome might be?"

"Homework, I love it," Celeste stood, picked up the short round glass Nya had offered to her when she had arrived and drank the last of the water. She usually had to force herself to drink water, as she favoured soft drinks far too frequently. She had been making a conscious effort to drink less sugar and more water, no matter how boring she found that to be. This of course did not apply to wine or any alcoholic beverage.

"Same time next week?" Nya asked as she perched in front of her Mac to schedule the appointment.

"Sounds good," Celeste pulled out her iPhone to add the session to her calendar. It was several versions behind the current one and was always a talking point. It was technically new as she purchased it at AT&T when she first arrived in New York. She had asked for the oldest iPhone version the shop had to offer. She wasn't interested in paying $1,000 for the newest version of anything.

She considered if that was why her dating life was so disastrous. Was she several models behind in her men? It would make sense as most of the time they were in desperate need of an upgrade.

"See you next week," Celeste waved to Nya as she threw her mobile into her handbag and pulled open the door to leave.

She was getting used to her sessions with Nya and was finding she was already putting some of her tools into practice. Nya was a rare find and she was grateful to have been privy to her service. *If she wasn't my therapist, I reckon we could be friends,* Celeste thought.

Chapter 5: *Fairy Tales and French Toast*

It was the pap smear time of year again. Celeste was at a new practice on the Upper East Side that she had found using a popular medical app. She wondered if any celebrities came here given the location. Maybe she would run into Drew Barrymore or Mariah Carey, she was sure she read somewhere they lived in the neighbourhood. The receptionist had been Russian with a prompt, yet personable, demeanour.

The doctor's assistant, who was also Russian, laughed sympathetically when she noticed Celeste had paused when asked what her height was. She still hadn't gotten used to speaking in feet and inches and the co-metric-system-user in the room caught on to her dilemma and responded with a smile. "Centimetres are fine too."

As Celeste stood clad only in a paper gown in the sterile exam room, complete with crisp white walls, a privacy curtain, and two laundry hampers; one with new gowns and the other used, she spotted the scales and stepped on. She was pleasantly surprised to see she had lost weight. Automatically judging herself for being happy to be thinner. She had a small frame and was fortunate enough to be blessed with good genes, however her size was also in part thanks to her portion control. She was not averse to eating what she wanted and had her blow out days, but she also wasn't particularly fond of exercise that required special clothing, shoes or equipment. So, she compromised and ensured she ate appropriately. She also figured living in a fifth-floor walk-up was exercise enough.

There were two boxes of blue latex gloves positioned on the wall and the chair with the paper sheet was prepared and waiting for her. The stirrups thoughtfully hidden away, would only be exposed at the same time she would.

On the bench next to a sink, there was a brochure for radiant and beautiful contours with a smiling woman on the cover. She wasn't sure exactly what the material was about but assumed anti-aging, unless of course there was some new craze where women could now contour their vaginas. It wouldn't have surprised her. *The beauty industry hasn't made billions of dollars by telling women the truth so why start now*, she thought as she waited for the OB-GYN to grace her with her presence.

Luckily the doctor didn't keep Celeste waiting too long. She introduced herself and asked Celeste to pop up on the chair, and to *spread 'em*. She didn't say spread 'em but that's what ran through Celeste's mind as she tried to gracefully slide her feet in the stirrups that had magically appeared. As she shuffled her bottom closer to the end of the chair so the doctor could see her in all her glory, she could understand why some women felt uncomfortable. Celeste didn't, well not really. She had long since understood it was a part of being a woman and that the doctor was simply there to do their job. This was a positive trait that had been passed on from her mother. She grew up in a household that might have been bordering on conservative due to her father's beliefs, but where her mother wasn't ashamed to show her naked body to her daughters and taught them that a woman's healthcare was paramount, and they shouldn't feel ashamed when visiting the doctor's.

The doctor performed the necessary steps, inserted the speculum and explained she would insert the swab to take a sample. Celeste laid back and recalled the time another doctor had told her she had a good cervix that made getting a pap smear easy. She'd taken pride in the comment, which she always wondered if it was an odd thing to take pride in. Can you be proud of the way your cervix looks? She wouldn't know what a good or a bad cervix looked like. This memory made her wonder if this was yet another symptom of wanting to be liked. Could she really be associating the praise of her cervix as some sort of validation she was a good woman?

The doctor had finished in the time she had taken to think that through.

Celeste watched her walk over to the urine sample she had given to the doctor's assistant when she first arrived. She was worried she would not be able to give a sample as she had already gone to the bathroom just before leaving her apartment and had not had a drop of water all morning. Luckily, she filled the cup, but it was bright yellow, and Celeste was sure they would judge her for it.

"Not pregnant?" Celeste enquired jokingly.

"Not pregnant." The doctor confirmed. *Did she think I was asking?*

"Oh, I didn't think I actually was ..." Celeste trailed off.

"Of course," The doctor replied, without asking any questions.

Celeste wondered if she should explain it was a joke. *What is she thinking? Is she judging me? Does she assume I'm just reckless and careless and that was why I asked about being pregnant?* Why did it matter to Celeste if the doctor was thinking any of those things? Realistically, Celeste was sure that at the end of the day, the doctor didn't care either way.

The doctor finished whatever she was doing with the samples and looked at Celeste. "All done! Your results will be on the online portal in about a week."

"Great, thanks," Celeste smiled.

The doctor left the room for Celeste to dress. She slipped on a pink skirt that hung to her ankles and swayed when she walked, teamed with a loose white top she casually tucked in that also accentuated her waist. She took her brown leather bag that was small enough to sling across her body but deceptively large enough to carry her essentials and then some. She had taken to using smaller handbags again, a trend she went through whenever she recognised that the larger the bag she carried, the more unneeded crap went into it and everywhere with her.

Since she was a teenager, her wardrobe always leaned slightly hippy, or boho as it was now more fashionably referenced. Celeste would never have called herself a fashionista, and while she admired some trends, she was comfortable buying clothes she knew fit her personality rather than what the magazines were telling her to be.

Celeste was meeting Sarah for brunch. Not just brunch, but bottom-less brunch. It was one of her favourite things to do in New York. And it was relatively unique to the city. On Saturday's and Sunday's, the weekly menus were set aside and brunch menus adorned the tables. For an extra $20 or so you could also partake in bottomless mimosas, sangrias or margaritas in most establishments. Some restaurants allowed reservations while others observed a first come first served rule. This quite often led to long lines of brunch-goers eagerly waiting for their name to be called after placing it on the waitlist upon arrival. Or depending on how long the wait was, and the street you were on, you might breeze into a bar for a drink or two to pass the time.

They were meeting in the neighbourhood of Kips Bay; their favourite brunch spot. The Bluebell Café was on 2nd and 23rd, an easy ride on the number 6 subway that was just a couple of blocks from the doctor's practice.

She walked out of the consultation room into reception to make sure she didn't owe anything. Another system she was still growing accustomed to, health insurance and what it does or doesn't cover. Turns out an annual pap smear was on offer as part of her plan. Interestingly, she had mused that in the UK it is the same test and research had proved you only have to be tested every five years. However, in the USA and with insurance involved, it had become an annual excursion that your doctor could charge for.

Celeste thanked the Russian who politely reminded her to check her results in a week and to call if she had any further questions about her visit.

Pushing open the door into the hot July sun, she had one of those moments where sheer joy washed over her unexpectedly as she took in her surroundings and was reminded she was living in Manhattan. She wondered how long those feelings would last. And if the time came that they didn't occur anymore, was that the indication it was time to leave the concrete jungle?

Tapping her phone, the turnstile buzzed her in to enter the sticky and humid subway, Celeste saw the next train was only two minutes away. A Godsend at this time of year when it takes mere seconds for the humidity in the underground system to eat you alive and ruin any attempt of make-up or fashioned hair style. As the train pulled up, she was grateful she was in a subway car that had air-conditioning. If you get in an empty car at this time of year, you can put all your money on a bet it's because the AC was not working. A short fifteen minutes later, Celeste was exiting the station on Park Avenue and walking the two blocks east.

As she rounded the corner, she saw Sarah standing by the restaurant. Sarah was basically the same height as Celeste, maybe slightly taller with straight, healthy, brown hair that hung to her waist, and Celeste was always envious of how luxurious it looked. It was a topic of conversation every time Sarah wore it out, which was rare, and she attributed it to her doing absolutely nothing to it. She wore light cotton green cargo pants that sat comfortably on her slight hips and an oversized button up denim shirt that was spotted with tiny colourful flowers and hid her larger than average bust underneath. For as long as Celeste had known Sarah, she was always comfortable in her own skin and was never one to flaunt her body.

Sarah had arrived five minutes early and Celeste was right on time. It was a personality trait they both admired in each other, being on time. Something they both took great pride in and great despair in if they were ever late. Celeste attributes her timeliness to the fact her family was late for everything as a child, a habit she swore she would never acquire. Sarah's was due to anxiety, a condition she had taken 29 years to realise she had.

Sarah was born in New York to an American mother and a Belgian father. They had left when she was still a baby in nappies to her father's homeland. Her anxiety was an inheritance from her dad and fear of being late was in part due to growing up with a mum that didn't speak the language, so everything took a little longer.

Celeste and Sarah had met in New York ten years earlier. Sarah had moved from Belgium to study in New York and to make a home in the city that had long called her name. She had been living on the Upper West Side for almost six months when Celeste had rented a room in the same apartment. Celeste was volunteering for a month at a local nonprofit, helping run an event to raise money for a hospital. Celeste, although not from New York, had also had a burning desire to make it her home. It was harder for her without a US passport, so she had to find alternate means and start making inroads and contacts.

The apartment was owned by a kind couple originally from the Dominican Republic, who had become empty nesters after their three children had grown and moved out. They had rooms to spare and so rented them out for a little company and a quick dollar on the side didn't hurt.

Sarah was only nineteen years old when Celeste, nine years her senior, met her. They had become fast friends, and thanks to Sarah's older sister's ID, they were able to frequent the local bars in the neighbourhood. Many nights were spent at Brother Jimmy's and Jake's Dilemma. $1 shots and $1 well drinks were too hard to pass up, especially when both were living on a tight budget at the time.

Celeste had already had her fair share of heartbreak by the time she met Sarah, and although Sarah was considerably younger, she had an old soul that meant she was able to empathise and advise Celeste in ways older more experienced women may not have.

Sarah had been in a long-distance relationship with a long-term boyfriend she had left behind in Belgium, up until a month before Celeste landed on her doorstep.

Maybe it was this long-term relationship, and Sarah's decision to start a sexual relationship with someone who Celeste considered not worthy that aided Sarah in delivering words of wisdom.

As it turned out, Sarah's bad decision making when it came to men didn't last for very long as a year later, she came out and started dating a woman.

Celeste had pointed out that picking inappropriate men seemed not to be a practice relegated to only straight women. Even some of the most sensible of lesbians still tested the waters with men waving red flags. Goes to show that when women know there is some soul searching to be done it's not uncommon for them to engage in behaviour that distracts from the core issue and creates another to focus on instead.

Celeste and Sarah spent almost all their free time together over the next month. Their friendship grew stronger every day. Celeste and Sarah shared their dreams of making it in New York, they walked the streets and discovered cafes only locals knew of and restaurants that were on the brink of exploding in popularity thanks to location scouts for hit TV shows. They visited the museums, went to comedy nights and musicals and familiarised themselves as best anyone could with Central Park.

Sarah had found a part time job at an art gallery dedicated to Belgian artists and Celeste would attend the many events they hosted, taking advantage of their free wine while watching Sarah mingle with the guests. Afterwards they would play a game guessing the net wealth of the attendees and conjure up stories of their mildly satisfactory lives that money couldn't make up for.

Celeste would share with Sarah the details of her volunteer work, the people she had met and hoped would one day lead to finding a job that meant she could stay in New York forever. They would dream up business plans together that would only ever come to fruition with the support of a wealthy backer. Maybe one of the Belgian gallery clients would see the potential, they often joked.

The closer the month's end drew near, the less they talked about Celeste's impending departure.

The time passed too quickly and before they knew it, it was time for Celeste to go home to London. She hadn't managed to find a way to wrangle a job out of the charity she had thrown her experience into. Although they were impressed with her skillset, there was no budget. Such is the way of the nonprofit world. When Celeste had left to return to London, they had hugged a sad and tearful goodbye and promised to stay in touch.

This was not the first time Sarah had bonded with a roommate. Prior to Celeste's arrival another woman closer to her age had rented what would become Celeste's room for three months. Missy was her name, and she was doing an internship at a hedge fund downtown. As her internship was drawing to an end, she was offered a job in Texas, and she promised to stay in touch when she left. She hadn't. This had led Sarah to think that if an interstate friendship couldn't survive, an international friendship was all but dead on the runway before the plane even took off.

To Sarah's surprise, Celeste had indeed kept her promise and had continued to visit every year, sometimes even twice a year. Their friendship had blossomed, and they spoke frequently about when the time would come that Celeste would finally move to New York.

When that day came eight years later, they both felt that it was just a natural moment in history they had predicted would happen. They fell into step of wandering the streets of New York together again, and the only thing that had changed was that the drinks were no longer only $1.

Sarah looked up from her phone and smiled when she spotted Celeste crossing the street on the red sign. It was New York and no one paid attention to the walk signs, especially Celeste who had quickly picked up the New York habit of stepping off the pavement and inching closer to passing cars waiting for a break in the traffic.

As she crossed the road to greet Sarah with a warm hug, Celeste felt blessed to have such a good friend in a city that sometimes feels full of enemies.

"Shall we?" Celeste motioned for the door.

They were welcomed by the hostess who wore dark eyeliner, a white tank that hung to her hips, rolled up three-quarter light blue jeans and white sneakers in the casual way you see in fashion blogs. Celeste thought to herself that although her fashion style was good, she was never going to be one of those women that looked like she literally stepped out of the pages of a magazine.

The hostess smiled as Sarah gave their details for the envious reservation they had been able to secure. Surprisingly, they were shown to their table right away.

The hostess was quickly replaced with a server that introduced himself as Evan and said he would be looking after them today. They immediately ordered a round of mimosas as part of the bottomless brunch and had no need to look at the menus that had been placed in front of them.

The Bluebell Café had a delicious brunch offering but the two friends always ordered the same thing. Celeste took the Bluebell Big Breakfast consisting of poached eggs, bacon, sausage, breakfast potatoes and a buttermilk biscuit with strawberry jam on the side. Sarah chose the omelette with cheese, mushrooms and peppers with breakfast potatoes and of course a buttermilk biscuit that came standard with most meals. Although not a vegetarian, Sarah preferred vegetables. Celeste was the opposite.

"Why were you coming from the Upper East?" Sarah asked, referring to a text message Celeste had sent when she was on her way.

"Gyney appointment. Imagine looking at vaginas all day long," Celeste pondered.

Sarah laughed and Celeste realised the inadvertent joke she'd made.

"I was once told I had a lovely cervix," Celeste shared. "To be clear, it was a physician, not a man."

"What constitutes a lovely cervix?" Sarah asked a valid question.

"I still don't really know what she meant, but a compliment is a compliment," replied Celeste.

"Add that to your dating profile," Sarah joked.

"Imagine," Celeste laughed.

A couple in their sixties, seated next to them, had clearly overheard their conversation as they stood to gather their belongings to leave. The husband shot them a dirty look while the wife stood behind him. She looked sideways in their direction suggesting she had had this type of conversation with her own friends when her husband wasn't within earshot.

Celeste and Sarah felt obliged enough to hold their laughs till they had stepped out of range.

Sarah correctly noted, "He is definitely not from New York."

"If he is, you know it's one of the Islands," Celeste countered, and they laughed.

Society had somehow managed to give off the impression that when ladies lunch, they didn't speak of such intimate details.

"The men who created that version of women must have run the best propaganda program in history. Ask any woman what she talks about with her friends, and it's not the latest mop." Sarah commented.

Celeste interjected, "Having said that, years ago I listened to colleagues talk at length about a new steam mop and I was embarrassed on their behalf–did they not have better things to talk about? But then I bought a steam mop and oh my God ... it changed my life."

"Do you think men sitting around talking about mops when they catch up?" Sarah asked.

Celeste considered the question, "Not the ones I know. Maybe that's where I'm going wrong."

"How is Roman?" Sarah enquired. She had warned Celeste not to get involved with him. Only because she knew she gave her heart too quickly, usually to inappropriate men and would likely need repair at some point.

"Wouldn't know," Celeste replied with a proud look on her face.

"Good."

"Ask me again in a week." Celeste replied and continued, "And Nya said it seems to be bringing out some of my issues for us to discuss, so maybe it's not so bad if I go back to seeing him again." Celeste joked with a hint of truth.

"Did Nya tell you to keep seeing him?"

"Not exactly."

"Doesn't sound like something she would say," Sarah smiled. After all it was she who referred Celeste to Nya, so she knew the therapist's style.

Sarah had sought therapy a couple of years ago to help her combat her anxiety and to dig into some qualms she had about her own behaviour in relationships.

Celeste remembered when Sarah had first told her that she had a therapist. It sounded very New York of her, and they had laughed about it at the time. But she had watched Sarah become a slightly calmer version of herself and noticed she looked more content than she had been pre-therapy.

"Thanks again for the referral. She really is amazing."

"I know, right!"

"It's like she can read your mind," Celeste said. "And she knows the perfect questions to ask that have you spilling all your thoughts."

"It's great when you find a counsellor you can connect with. I knew you'd like her."

It made sense Celeste would connect with Nya, if Sarah had. Celeste and Sarah's strong bond grew out of their similarities, and if Sarah liked someone or something, there was a high likelihood Celeste would too.

"I'm surprised how much I'm learning about myself," Celeste shared. "I mean, I'm not suggesting I didn't have anything more to find out but I kind of figured I had my shit together and knew myself well enough."

"And even though I analyse the shit out of myself, this goes deeper, and it feels like things are clicking into place that I didn't know were even unhinged."

Sarah took the segue, "Speaking of unhinged, did you get on Hinge?"

Sarah was a firm believer in online dating. She had been trying to coerce Celeste into creating a profile for a long time. But Celeste had resisted. She was holding onto the dream of meeting a man in real life, maybe in a bar on a dance floor, like she did with Maliq. But it was a fantasy proving difficult to materialise. She had dabbled on other platforms in the past, but she always lost interest within days of commencing the search. It was tiresome. Swiping left and right, reviewing their virtues and vices, judging someone based on their photo selection.

Gym selfie, out.

Tiger photo, out.

Shirtless, out.

Bathroom selfie, out.

Lives in Jersey, out. Even though Hoboken was technically closer to her apartment than someone who lived in Brooklyn.

No wonder I'm single, Celeste would often think as she swiped through the images with as much enthusiasm as one might have for visiting the dentist.

At one point in time, Celeste had narrowed her search down so much and had swiped left so often that the platform told her she had exhausted her search and that she should consider changing her settings to find more men. Celeste looked at the notification and thought, I think what you meant to say was, please lower your standards and start again.

But she had heard from several friends that Hinge was the app to be on these days. With trepidation she had finally succumbed and created a profile.

"You'll be very happy to hear I did."

"Finally!" Sarah exclaimed. "And?"

Celeste was worried she was putting way too much pressure on herself, and the men she matched with, to be much better virtual versions of the inappropriate real-life versions she found on the street. She wasn't convinced she could filter out the treasure from the rubbish online. She was barely able to find the patience to scour through charity stores for second hand clothes, what made her think she had the endurance to repeatedly swipe left or right?

"It actually isn't as bad as I thought. Although my expectations were pretty low," she joked. After her last experience with Roman, she wasn't sure she was ready to date again. But her time with Nya gave her some hope, even if it was at the very pit of her stomach.

"Any luck? Have you met anyone yet?" Sarah wanted all the details.

"I went on a date last week with a fellow subject of the Queen. He was lovely but after we both headed home, he sent me a text asking why I didn't kiss him."

Sarah screwed up her face and said, "Such a dick."

"Right?" Celeste countered. "This is why I'm not so sure about online dating ..."

"Nope, you're not giving up yet." Sarah said, adding, "Out of curiosity, why didn't you?"

Celeste paused and pictured his face. "I just wasn't into him like that. I mean we had a great chat, but ..." she trailed off. "To send a text asking why I didn't kiss him? Come on friend, if you have to ask then maybe you shouldn't be asking at all."

Sarah screwed up her face again in agreement. "Are you matching with many guys?"

"A few. I've got to admit there does seem to be better quality there. It's still not without its dickheads mind you. Obviously," Celeste said, referencing her last story. "But I am going to persevere. With all this self-discovery I'm doing with Nya, I'm realising that I need to expand my horizons a bit more. Not lower my standards but try not to judge as much as I do. My point is, I shouldn't say no because they don't appear to fit the criteria. Maybe I'm letting some of the good ones slip through the conditional cracks."

"I agree, meeting in real life definitely makes things easier. You're more likely to spot an asshole a lot sooner," Sarah said cynically, but added, "but who knows, maybe a guy from New Jersey won't be so bad. Stay away from those shirtless, gym selfie guys though!"

Celeste laughed. "Totally agree. And I really need to let them tell me their story before I create my own in my head. So, that being said, I have another date tomorrow."

"This is great! Its progress. I'm proud of you".

Celeste laughed, "Don't get your hopes up just yet. You'll never guess what his name is."

"Tell," Sarah couldn't wait.

"Prince," Celeste said as she rolled her eyes. She couldn't roll them harder if she tried.

Sarah laughed so hard it turned into a coughing fit. She collected herself using a napkin Celeste had handed her.

Celeste continued, "At least that's what this profile says."

Sarah continued to laugh, "You didn't ask?"

"I figured I'd wait till I met him in person. Ironic, right?" The name of her forthcoming date was not lost on Celeste. She felt like she actively rebelled against finding any sort of Prince Charming and now her independent nature was bursting at the seams–she told herself she had even more reason to split the check. She was not going to be swindled into some make believe love story based on the man's name. A wicked witch already lived in her head; she needn't have any more fictitious characters intruding on her life. But she was curious to know whether this bachelor was at least a gentleman.

"It would be hilarious if this worked out." Sarah gleefully said, her eyes wide with romantic hope.

Celeste was cynical but had to admit she was looking forward to meeting him. "I am a little excited about the date. We've been texting, and he seems lovely, as lovely as you can be over text. And he even called me for a quick chat to confirm our date and the time he'd pick me up. His profile said he likes to talk about politics and philosophy, and he was telling me about some philosophical book that he is currently reading. So, we might be a good match?"

"Sounds perfect for you! Someone to talk politics with is right up your alley."

"I know, right! I don't have to dumb myself down. Maybe I can let loose and be the real me."

"Do it," Sarah urged. "And if he doesn't like it, fuck him."

Chapter 6: *A Sandcastle Serenade*

He was tall, easily six foot two, and wore a big smile that made his brown eyes twinkle in a way that made you feel that everything was right in the world. His shoulders were broad, and he carried himself with confidence. Celeste automatically started berating herself for getting butterflies so soon, before moving onto justifying her feelings. She stopped, took a deep breath, and thought, *just be yourself*. She immediately wondered, *is that good enough?*

Prince turned to Celeste and his smile widened at the sight of her. In his right hand he carried a wicker basket with a towel draped over it. With his free arm he reached out and placed his hand gently on her arm and kissed her cheek. Celeste blushed and pushed aside the butterflies that were still harassing her.

Prince took her hand, "Shall we?" He gestured towards the beach that beckoned them. She didn't feel like she had the petite hands many women have, but inside his they felt small, and seemed to fit perfectly together.

Jones Beach was a popular beach on the shores of Long Island, New York. Prince had been the perfect gentleman in picking Celeste up from her front door in Manhattan and driving the one and a half hours, thanks to traffic, that it took to get to the national park that surrounded the white sands New Yorkers fled to in summer. It was August, it was hot and humid, and every man and his dog had the same idea. They shuffled along the sand and darted around children playing until they came across a spot that appeared to have been recently departed, likely early risers who got the hell off the beach when the throngs of sweaty bodies showed up.

"Sorry I was a little late. Traffic was crazy. I hope you weren't waiting long," Prince said apologetically.

"Oh, that's okay, not at all." Celeste had been ready early but had taken the time to pop out and grab an iced coffee from her local café. She turned to look at the waves crashing before her and felt the warmth of the sun on her face. "I love summer! I can't believe I've never been here. And this view, the beach, the water, the sun!" Celeste added as she turned her gaze from the rolling waves to the bright blue sky.

"You like it?" he asked with a hint of anticipation of seeking reassurance he had pleased her.

"I love it!" she answered.

Prince placed the basket on the ground, slung off the backpack he had also brought, and unzipped it to pull out a red and black tartan picnic blanket. He unfolded it to gently lay it on the soft sand and swept his hand indicating she should take a seat. Celeste smiled at him as she sat down, legs crossed. She had worn a summer dress in hues of blue that matched her eyes and had let her hair fall in waves that day as she thought it gave the impression of a carefree beach dweller that was best suited to sea-salt spray in her tendrils rather than hair spray to tame them. She wanted him to think she belonged at the beach as much as he did. Although looking at him now, she wasn't so sure he was the beach bum she assumed when he suggested a day by the water.

Celeste watched as Prince squatted down next to the basket and peered inside. "What have you got in there," she asked as he started to rummage.

Prince began to pull out items, "I've got cheese and crackers," he paused as he continued to scan its contents. "More cheese!" he announced as he pulled out another type of cheese.

"I can't believe you've gone to all this trouble." Celeste said with a tone in her voice that he didn't recognise as hopefulness.

"It was no trouble, really. Now," he returned his attention back to the basket, "do you want juice, water, Coke?"

With a look of surprise and delight, Celeste laughed, "Seriously, what have you got in there?"

Prince smiled and delivered another surprise, "Or how about this?" he asked as he held up a bottle of Bulmers cider. "This is the cider you like, right?" he asked with an air of confidence that almost masked his eagerness to please her.

Celeste beamed, "It is. How did you know?"

"You mentioned it when we were chatting."

"Did I?" she smiled in delight at his attention.

Prince took a bottle opener, popped the lid and handed Celeste the open bottle. He opened one for himself and held out his bottle to meet hers. "Cheers," they said in unison and their eyes met and they both took a sip.

Prince sat smiling proudly, "What's that cheeky grin for?" she probed.

"I've really been looking forward to this," he smiled, then added as if the words slipped out of his mouth before thinking, "I even bought new shoes." He glanced towards his discarded Veja shoes that he had kicked off when they had settled upon their location. Was he nervous? She wasn't sure. "I just mean I realised when I thought about bringing you here, I didn't really have any beach stuff. So I went shopping for beach shoes, whatever they are. And ended up with those instead," he laughed. "Truth be told, I'm not a massive beach guy."

She smiled at him and felt pleased that she had pondered on the thought of whether the beach was really his first choice of places to be.

"It is a very important item. You can tell a lot about a man by his shoes," Celeste imparted, hoping the light heartedness would make him feel more comfortable.

"What do mine say about me?" he questioned.

Celeste played along, "They are very playful. I'd say you're a bit of a fashionista." Prince laughed and Celeste changed subjects, "What did you get up to this week?"

"Work and more work. Although I took a half day yesterday and went to visit my grandma in Jersey. I had to break the news that I wouldn't be taking her to church tomorrow."

"Church?" Celeste enquired.

"She's a devout Catholic. I go with her sometimes," Prince divulged.

Celeste's first instincts were to run, she had once believed in religion, but she had done a complete about face on anything faith based, much to her own Grandmother's dismay. Instead, she replied, "You're Catholic? I'm Catholic." She found herself slipping into her alter ego; the words slipping out before she could think about it. She was portraying a version of herself she thought he wanted and she didn't like it. She was raised Catholic but certainly didn't want anyone to consider her religious.

"I used to be an altar boy," Prince said with a wry smile.

RUN! her mind screamed and yet she smiled sweetly and jested, "You were not!"

"I was!" he replied as he offered more insight into his beliefs. "That was a long time ago now. I've got to admit, I don't buy into any of it anymore and I only go with my grandma because it makes her happy."

Celeste quietly thanked a God she didn't believe in as she relaxed into her conversation again, "Wow, a real-life altar boy. I don't think I've ever met one before. Are you from a big family then?"

"Just three kids."

"There are six in mine."

"Sounds more Catholic than my family," he laughed.

"I'm a middle child," Celeste offered.

"First boy," he returned.

Not to be outdone, Celeste said, "Apparently middle children are the most well-rounded. The first born however is either one of two things."

Prince stared at her with mock anticipation, and she laughed.

"You're either spoiled as the golden child or you're the black sheep they made all the mistakes on."

Prince joked in return, "It's not my fault I was the favourite."

Celeste found herself softening inside when she looked at him, "With that cheeky grin, I can see why."

"Six kids, that's a lot," Prince said without judgement. "Are you close?"

Celeste pondered his question and wondered how much she should share. She had been accused of talking too much in the past and offering too much information beyond the necessary amount of disclosure. Not that she had any skeletons in her closet, at least none that she found held any value, but when you have a lot of people in your family, you have a lot of stories. *Did he really want to hear them all at this time? Probably not*, she thought.

"More or less," she offered. "I think like most families," she continued, "we've had our ups and downs. I always joke that with so many of us, if one pisses you off, at least you have a spare lying around." She laughed in a way that made it obvious her family was comfortable in uncomfortableness.

Enough about her, she decided, "How about you?"

"Yeah, very. We talk all the time. Family group chats, family holidays, that kind of thing." Celeste wasn't sure if the jarring feeling she had was jealousy or a warning. While she was indeed close to her family, she had long since learnt that blood was not thicker than water and often found herself judging those who relied so heavily on their family to provide fulfillment. Relying on family as your key to happiness was like exposing an open wound to a salt mine. A risk she was not willing to take. As the thought flickered through her mind, she realised it was money being well spent with Nya.

Celeste pulled her gaze away from his brown eyes, and took in the view once more, "It really is gorgeous here."

Prince followed her stare and they both looked towards the horizon, "I guess I was lucky to grow up with this so close. While I'm not a massive beach guy, I do like coming out here with a good book. When it's a bit cooler," he added.

Celeste turned to him, "Oh that's right, you're a reader." She had always found it arousing when a man was well read. She wasn't sure where that attraction had developed, possibly due to her own upbringing and the emphasis that was placed upon the importance of reading. Maybe because it mirrored her own interest in reading, and not on a kindle or device, but the old-fashioned way of pages formed in the shape of a book.

"It was in your profile," she reminded him when she wondered if his look of surprise was one of questioning how she knew.

"Oh, so it is." He smiled. "I read a lot. And you?" he asked.

"I can't get enough," she replied, insinuating reading but alluding to his company. *Here we go*, she thought, as the familiar feeling of butterflies and dreams were enveloping her.

"I love biographies," Prince interrupted her daydream.

Celeste agreed, "I love to read about musicians. Some of their stories are just so outrageous and so fascinating."

They spoke in unison, "Have you read Scar Tissue?" and laughed an easy and familiar laugh as if they had just shared an inside joke.

"You've got good taste then," Prince complimented her and she blushed.

"So do you. I may have to check out your collection sometime. Book club." A pit in her stomach formed as she started to succumb to the familiar feeling of foolishness. *Seriously? Book club? That's so lame*, she told herself.

Her insecurity in saying the wrong thing took hold and she asked, "Oh gosh, is that lame?"

To which he kindly replied, "Not at all. Now, how about something to eat?" Prince turned to once again rummage through the basket full of treats he had handpicked that morning.

Celeste watched him as she chastised herself. *Book club IS lame*, she told herself. And began a conversation with her insecurities in her head. *I didn't mean book club … It was a stupid thing to say. But I do love to read, and he does too. Stop it,* she concluded as she spoke again, "You've really thought of everything."

Prince was in the process of taking the packaging off the cheeses and opening up the cracker packets and bags of chips. "I aim to please. Closet romantic right here," he smiled.

Celeste once again looked into his eyes and replied, "And here I thought this only happened in fairy tales."

There was no better time than now to ask, it was the perfect segue. Celeste said, "So, speaking of fairy tales …"

Prince turned and had a smile that suggested he already knew what she was going to ask before she said it out loud, "I think I know what you're going to ask."

"Do you have hopeless romantics for parents, or …" Celeste trailed off.

"Not that my parents aren't hopeless romantics. Wait till you meet my dad." Prince laughed and rolled his eyes.

Is he going to introduce me to his dad? Oh my God! Has he told his dad about me? This is a good sign, right? Stop it. Stop it. Stop it.

Prince didn't appear to notice Celeste had drifted off into her own head for a moment and he continued. "Mom loved Prince. You know, The Artist Formerly Known As," he shrugged his shoulders in a way that suggested he had told this story time and time again.

"Simple as that," he continued. "It was either going to be Prince or some philosopher's name if Dad got his way."

"I assume you know every lyric to every song," Celeste joked.

"You joke, but if we ever go to karaoke, I don't need to look at the screen for the words!"

"So, what I'm hearing is that we need to go to karaoke sometime then," Celeste said casually.

"We should do that sometime. Do you sing?" he asked.

"Oh God no, no one needs to hear that," she replied.

He gently poked her leg with his finger and said, "We'll see about that." Celeste felt electricity jolt through her. *There is no way I'm singing in front of him, how embarrassing*, she thought.

As if reading her mind, Prince said, "No one cares if you can't sing, as long as you are having a good time."

They spent three hours lazing on the beach, taking intermittent breaks from the sun's rays in the energetic waves of the North Atlantic Ocean to cool down. They people-watched, and talked, and talked some more. They covered almost every topic Celeste thought imaginable. She forgot about her concerns earlier that she should be mindful of how much she shares and there was an ease between them she had never felt before, to the point that strangers assumed they must have been long-time lovers.

Prince had asked what felt like a hundred questions when they spoke about her homeland, and her journey to relocate to the United States of America. Celeste herself didn't find her story newsworthy, as she found it to not be much different to any other western immigrant story. But for people who had never been offered the opportunity, or had never pursued the dream of the unknown, they were always fascinated to hear what they considered to be a brave story.

"Have you thought about living overseas?" Celeste asked. She knew he had travelled a lot and wondered if they might have this in common too.

"Of course, if you want to go somewhere else tomorrow, I'll meet you at the airport," she felt her stomach flip and wondered if he was speaking generically or if he specifically meant it with her.

Prince continued, "My brother lives in Ireland, has been there for the last three years." This was news to Celeste, and she was surprised he had kept that to himself for this long.

"Why didn't you tell me?" She was curious to know.

"I just did," he joked. "Besides, I wanted to know about you." She was taken aback at his words and wondered if she was reading too much into them. She felt like he meant it, but her guardrails were still intact, and she wondered if she could trust him.

"Would you ever move to Ireland?" she asked as she had always hoped that if she were to meet someone in New York City, they would be open to the concept of moving home to England with her one day, or at least in the near vicinity, should she ever decide the time had come to leave. She thought that by asking if he would move to be near his brother was a softer question than suggesting he might want to move with her one day.

"Sure, Ireland, England, Spain. You name it, I'll be there." He had reached out and rubbed her hand at the same time he had said the word you. It was an overreach for her, but she leaned into it anyway, and she took him to mean he would go anywhere with her. She allowed herself this moment.

"Okay," Prince appeared to be making an announcement, and she shook her thoughts loose from her head. "As much as I love hanging out with you, I have to admit my time at the beach and this heat may be coming to an end."

Celeste was flattered by the fact he seemed to have made the effort of spending so much time somewhere he would prefer to not be. It wasn't that he didn't recognise the beauty of the beach, and appreciate its cooling waters, but he had long ago determined that the sun was not his friend, and he preferred to be under the shade of a tree rather than go to battle with nature.

"How would you feel about packing up here and grabbing an ice cream?" he asked.

"I'd love that," Celeste answered honestly. While she loved spending time at the beach, she too had her limits. She often found the thought of spending time soaking up the sun way more appealing than the actual act itself. While she thoroughly enjoyed the first hour of feeling her body warm up by several degrees and the act of being able to wash away the sweat with salt water, she would often find herself getting bored. She mostly enjoyed the time it allowed her to read one of the many books that sat on her bookshelf, or on her nightstand, on her dresser, or on her coffee table. She had so many books to read yet couldn't stop buying more.

Together they packed up what was left, or more so gathered the rubbish that was left over as they had managed to devour most of what Prince had brought.

"Thank you again," Celeste said to Prince as they folded the blanket together.

He winked at her as he stepped toward her to take the half-folded blanket. She took a deep breath as he stood so close to her at that moment. She looked up at him and he leaned in to kiss her. He dropped the blanket, and it interrupted their kiss.

Smiling shyly, he blushed as he picked up the blanket and finished folding it.

"Shall we?" he asked as he reached out for her hand. She took it and they made their way back past the group of friends who had gathered after their arrival, with music blaring and drinks being shared, past the solo sunbathers who should have put on more sunscreen, past other couples who sat quietly next to each other with books in hands, or earbuds in ears, and past the families who looked beaten by the heat and the rambunctiousness of their children. She assumed those kids would sleep well tonight and the parents would hope to have a quiet wine together, only to fall asleep on the couch in front of the TV before they could see the bottom of their glasses.

They walked onto the wooden boardwalk and towards the ice cream stand, taking their place in the queue. The girls ahead of them were in their early teens. Celeste watched them as they giggled with each other and placed their orders. Some enjoyed three scoops a piece. Celeste recalled when she was their age, when crushes on boys seemed so complicated but life was still so easy.

It was their turn to order from one of the young attendants who was excited to be working at the beach for the summer. Prince gestured for Celeste to order first. *Should I just get one scoop? Because I really want two. Fuck it.*

"I'll have a cone with salted caramel and mint choc chip, please" Celeste ordered and considered whether she had made the right call as she watched the ice cream pile up on her cone.

Prince didn't flinch or make any sort of face, so Celeste assumed he wasn't judging her for her two-scoop order.

"A cone with salted caramel," he turned and winked at Celeste to acknowledge their common taste. "And black raspberry, and cookie dough, thanks."

"That's quite the combo." Celeste was impressed, and thankful to a degree that he had ordered not two but three scoops.

They walked over to a bench and sat next to each other, facing the ocean. They quickly ate their ice creams before they melted down their hands and arms. The heat was not accommodating and instead of being able to slowly enjoy their treat, they fussed and devoured their cones the only way one can in the summertime.

"That was delicious, thanks," Celeste said. She had offered to pay but Prince already had his phone out and was tapping the device before she could finish her sentence.

"Great way to end the day," Prince proclaimed as he collected their belongings from the ground next to them.

He once again reached for her hand and she apologised if it was sticky. "You did make a bit of a mess," he teased her. Then he lifted her hand and lightly licked the tip of her finger. It was a sweet gesture that sent shock waves through Celeste. *I think my knees just went weak!* She had to stop herself from jumping up and down and clapping like a child. She felt giddy and she was letting herself enjoy it.

They walked back towards the car park and slipped on their flip flops before stepping on the black tar that would surely burn their feet. They walked across the vast parking lot that occupied a sea of vehicles. One could have argued for the need for a shuttle bus to get from one side to the other, but she enjoyed the time it afforded them to walk along in comfortable silence until they reached his car.

They threw their belongings in the boot and settled themselves into the front seats for their drive home. It would take at least another one and a half hours to get back to the city, if they were lucky and didn't hit any additional traffic. They had avoided extended delays in the morning as they had left relatively early, the heat already licking at their heels. But at this time of day, given the sun was still so high in the sky, it was unlikely many others were leaving at the same time as they were.

As they drove home, Prince had handed her his phone that was connected to the stereo. She was appointed Chief DJ for their drive home, and she wasn't sure she was ready to be judged for her musical selection but being of the same generation she thought she'd go back to her roots and hoped for the best. She leaned into a time when she was carefree and playful in a brand-new world that was opening to her as an adult. When pop music and grunge were seemingly the only real great divides that existed, especially compared to the fractured world they lived in today. Whether you preferred one over the other, at least in music you could always find some sort of common ground. So, she started tapping in his Spotify account and scrolling through albums till she came across a band that she hoped would resonate for them both.

With the windows down, they blasted Incubus the whole way home, and Celeste had never felt so free. She could hear Prince's voice permeate through the soundwaves that cascaded over them both. She too knew every word and on occasion let go of any embarrassment of not being able to hold a note and sung the lyrics loudly along with him. She sang, she smiled, she laughed, and she let herself feel good. She didn't want this time to end. As they crossed over the waters of the East River and the end of their day drew near, she almost invited him to dinner with her friends. But she decided against it as she wanted uninterrupted time with her girlfriends where she could inappropriately gush about Prince and take up too much of their conversation with thoughts of this man.

They weaved their way through Manhattan, dodging impatient pedestrians who crossed against the light. Celeste was a good driver but she in no way felt comfortable driving in the city. The fast-paced nature on the pavement translated over to the streets and if you were not aggressive in nature, you would find yourself sitting at green lights while accommodating droves of people taking over the roads, hearing horns honking and drivers yelling at you to *move your fucking ass*.

Prince pulled up to her apartment block and got out to retrieve her belongings for her. "Want a hand taking anything up?" he asked.

"Thanks, but I've got it," she lied. While she didn't need help, she did want him to spend more of his time with her. But she also wanted to play the game as she was taught she should and instead declined his kind offer.

He put her beach bag on the first step of the building, as she used her hands to feel the mess she was sure her hair was. "What are your plans for the rest of the night then?" he asked.

"Dinner with Sarah and Holland." She had already told him about her friends earlier in the day, that the girls had been together for two years now, how she had watched Sarah become a stronger version of herself through the strength of Holland's love. And in return, how Holland had calmed in nature, from a woman who had so much energy to expel, to a woman who became fierce with quiet confidence. Celeste had been lucky to have witnessed some of her friends' relationships that had evolved in all the right ways. While her direct experience differed and she had been exposed to turmoil, she felt blessed to see the kind of love story that goes beyond the fairy tales we are taught. Sarah and Holland were one of those examples. Through them she had learnt the importance of communication, and forgiveness. Through them she had learnt you should grow larger not smaller in a relationship. Through them she had seen the results of being truly seen. And deep down, she wanted what they had.

"I had a great day," Celeste told Prince.

"It was perfect. Truly, just perfect," Prince replied, and Celeste felt a wave of relief. *Phew, perfect,* she thought.

Prince leaned in and kissed her softly. Celeste felt herself blush as she waved him goodbye. *Perfect.*

***

After a fun evening and several cocktails with Sarah and Holland, Celeste had farewelled her friends, thanked them for listening to her ramblings and had taken the subway home.

She now sat on her bed eating a Turkish Delight chocolate bar because it reminded her of home. She had found quite an assortment of sweets and chocolates, that she suddenly craved for more often these days than she did when she lived in London, in one of those British stores that sell overpriced items to homesick expats willing to pay the price of their first born if it meant reliving a memory of home.

She fell back onto the many pillows she had bought during a fourth of July sale when she decided she should spend the money on making her bed feel just like the ones in hotels do. *He's amazing!* she thought as she re-lived her day with Prince.

And it started. *Amazing you say*, came the mocking response derived from her insecurities.

She pushed back; *I can't wait to see him again.*

Well, that's good, she told herself.

I hope I see him again; she started to panic.

I'm sure I'll see him again.

What if he doesn't want to see me again? What if he didn't think the date was as good as I did?

Should I text him? No, it's too soon. Or is it?

And around and around in her own head she went.

Rationale kicked in, *do whatever you are comfortable with.*

Insecurities pushed back, *but is that the right thing to do?*

Is there such a thing as the right thing? I was reading a magazine article the other day about what men want. I should find that ...

What if I get in touch and he doesn't reply?

Insecurities are a cruel monster. *It means maybe you weren't as funny as you thought you were!*

Maybe I should call him?

And if he doesn't answer?

Fuck it, then that's his loss.

Why does it have to be so hard?

Don't complicate things.

Keep it simple, stupid.

Chapter 7: *A Determined Damsel*

Celeste reached for her mobile after she felt it vibrate. It was a text from Prince. 'See you in a sec,' it read.

She quickly replied, 'I'm just three blocks away. Sorry I'm late! P.S. By the time I get to you I may just be a puddle of water and a green dress on top. I'm melting in this heat'. She didn't like being late, but she was also aware the faster she moved, the more she perspired. And she wasn't sure which was worse at this point.

Four days and about a hundred text messages had passed since their date at the beach. Prince had asked Celeste to dinner at Bacaro, a candlelit Italian restaurant on the Lower East Side.

Celeste was scared to admit that she already really liked this guy. She considered the butterflies in her stomach and summed them up as indigestion or possibly the onset of a stomach flu. She knew full well it was the thought of Prince that made her feel funny inside but wasn't ready to firmly acknowledge that. Funny good and funny bad. She had had these feelings before of course, but for all the wrong men. *Am I jumping into another mistake? He seemed so different to the others, but what would I know?* She was now doubting herself in ways she never had before. Reminding herself Nya would be proud that she was thinking things through, she had pushed through her sense of dread and tried to focus on the good. She told herself she deserved to be happy. She told herself that she should allow herself to trust in this man and what he seemed to represent. Even though that terrified her. Prince was different. Period. However, she wasn't sure if that was good because he offered a sense of hope or it was bad because he was putting on a good act and eventually, he would be just the same as the others and would hurt her.

Now, as she rushed to meet him, she worried her makeup had run off her face and onto the pavement. *Wow, for someone who tells the world you've got it together, you're pretty messed up,* she thought to herself. She chastised herself with the same ease as taking a breath. Nya's words were slipping away from her mind and without realising, Celeste's defence mechanism was slowly taking Nya's place. She didn't even know it in her haste to be on time and make the right impression.

I can't believe I'm late. I hate being late! I've had a bad day. I don't want to start this date in this mood.

Gah, get out of my head.

Take a breath. Slow down. He'll understand.

She caught a glimpse of herself in a shop window. *Oh my god, my hair is a mess! It looks bad. And I should have changed. I just didn't have time.*

As a woman in red stilettos and hair that looked like it had been done in a salon and untouched by the weather, sauntered by. Celeste's mind screamed, *you should be more like that! That will get his attention.*

I look good, she countered.

I've seen you look better.

If he doesn't like me because of what I'm wearing, well then, he can just ...

Oh. My. God. Woman. Stop it.

Celeste rounded the corner and walked quickly towards Prince. "You beat me!" she exclaimed. Prince didn't let on he had barely beaten her and had been running behind as well. He didn't mean to be deceitful, he just wanted to take it as a win that in her eyes, he was waiting for her arrival. He leaned in to kiss her cheek.

Celeste wanted him to kiss her on the lips but was also grateful he didn't as she considered the amount of sweat she was sure was on more than her brow. Summer in the city was a killer. But she wouldn't have it any other way as it was the compromise to the killer winters she endured. She noticed Prince was also feeling the effects of the concrete jungle. "Shall we escape into some air-conditioning?" she asked.

Prince, being the gentleman he was, reached around Celeste and opened the door for her. He placed his hand on her lower back as she walked past him into the welcoming cool air. She worried that he could feel the dampness on her clothes as the sweat had seeped through.

Gross, she thought, but noted he didn't pull away. She wondered after feeling first-hand the sweaty mess she was, he was not as inclined to kiss her as she hoped.

Exposed brick walls and slate floors transported you to Italy. After confirming their reservation and waiting for another twenty minutes, after all, this is New York City and a reservation at a popular restaurant doesn't guarantee you'll be seated on time, they were led down wooden stairs that seemed to be from a century ago. The basement was warmly lit with lighting that made the worst of us look good, and seated small groups of friends that laughed in ways that made you want to join their conversation and find out what the inside joke was.

The server showed them to their small wooden table, and although in New York it's not uncommon to be sat next to a perfect stranger so close you'd think they were part of your party, they were lucky enough to be bestowed a corner table with some privacy.

"I'm so sorry I was late," she offered.

"That's okay. You were five minutes late. Late in this city could technically mean an hour and even then, some would say it's acceptable."

"Not in my books," Celeste replied.

"Noted," Prince vowed.

"It's just been one hell of a day at work. Seriously, what is wrong with people? You're employed to do a job, just do it. Last time I checked I'm your boss, not your mother. You know? And now I'm late. Which I hate."

"For this date. That was at eight," he wasn't sure if Celeste didn't find his sense of humour amusing or if she didn't hear him over the buzzing exchanges between fellow diners. *She mustn't have heard me,* he assured himself and continued. "Anyway ... Wine? Shall we get a bottle?"

"You read my mind."

"How about cabernet sav?"

"Yes!" Celeste replied a little too eagerly. "Thank you. This makes for a nice change."

"Nice change?" he enquired.

"My day is full of decision making. It's nice to not have to. It might sound silly, but a simple gesture of picking the wine is a grand gesture in my books." *Too much?* she wondered?

"I'm glad I could help."

Prince smiled at the server and ordered the bottle of wine, which was promptly delivered to the table, along with a basket of warm bread and sides of butter. The server poured the wine and Prince asked Celeste to try, rather than himself. Another gesture she did not take for granted.

"Delicious," she approved, and the server filled Prince's glass and then her own.

Celeste took several full mouthfuls before realising she was chugging her wine like a man downing a beer after labouring on the docks for twelve hours. "Sorry; it's been one of those days. How are you?"

"I'm good. I had the day off today. Spoiled it by getting some work done around the apartment."

"Don't you hate it when being a grown up interrupts your fun time. That's why I like to pay people to do those things for me," she joked as Celeste knew full well she rarely forked out money for someone to do any chore she was simply being too lazy to do herself.

"I don't mind so much."

"Well, that's good to know."

"Apart from the mothering, how was your day?" Prince took a drink of his wine as he relaxed in his chair. His eyes were fully on her.

"Mothering aside, apparently, I'm a ball breaker. Or so my colleague says. He doesn't like that I've been given the lead on a project, and he has to work under me for the next eight weeks. He isn't achieving his KPIs, and I called him on it today. I simply told him his performance was unacceptable, and he needed to show me some results."

Celeste could feel her temperature start to rise when remembering the disparaging way she was treated that day and forgot for a moment that she should probably be more bashful on a date.

She continued, "And then he said I was being irrational, that I was just trying to throw my weight around because I'm one of 'those' women; nothing but a ball breaker."

Prince seemed genuinely astonished that someone would dare speak to her that way, "Wow, he actually said that?"

"So, I told him I'm pretty sure my balls are bigger than his. Which wouldn't be hard considering I didn't believe he had any to break in the first place. God, men! They can be so pathetic when challenged."

Prince smiled, said nothing and took a sip of his wine.

Celeste's brain went into overdrive. *Oh my God. Shut up. No man wants to hear that you can break his balls, or that you have your own set to play with.*

She tried to wipe the spew that had just come out of her mouth with all the sweetness she could muster. "Sorry, I didn't mean to imply all men. Hell, I'm sure your balls are huge!"

WHAT! she wanted to climb under the table, as Prince laughed out loud.

Instead, she took another big gulp of wine and said, "Oh my God! I can't believe I just said that."

As she placed her glass back on the table, Prince picked up the bottle and refilled her glass, "More wine? Mothering, ball breaking, you've had a busy day!"

"It wasn't all bad. I found out I was accepted to do my MBA today. I'm pretty excited." Celeste was incredibly proud of herself, and it showed. She wasn't sure if that was a good thing or bad thing. *Will he deem me arrogant or view me as courageous? Does he think I'm gloating or gleeful?*

He broke into her thoughts, "Congratulations! So, you'll be a student again. With student discounts."

"Exactly! Stick with me and you'll never pay full price again."

Prince threw out the gauntlet, "Cheap public transport."

"Discounts at fast food outlets." Celeste rivalled.

"Cheap museum tickets."

"Cheap theatre tickets." Celeste was quick on her feet, and Prince was matching her pace.

"Late nights and late sleep-ins."

"Those were the days. Dorm parties."

"Dollar drinks at the college campus bar!"

"Beer pong!"

"And dress up parties!" Celeste paused as if to remember.

"I expect to see you in your best golf costume and at least one toga outfit!" Prince teased.

Celeste continued, "Oh and foam parties! Don't forget the foam parties!"

"No responsibility and care-free."

"Until your parents found out what you were really getting up to. The number of times I tried playing dumb to get out of being busted. Oh, if only I didn't have to work for a living this time around."

Prince reached across the table and took Celeste's hand. "Seriously though. I'm impressed."

The butterflies were playing field hockey in her stomach as she looked at him. *Is he feeling the same way?* If she was reading his eyes right, he was. *But that's ridiculous, isn't it. To be able to read his eyes?* "Thanks," was all she was able to mutter as she looked away.

Pulling herself together and concentrating on wiggling her toes instead of the college party in her stomach, she continued, "So I'm going to be busy. Work and study. But it'll be worth it."

"Good on you," Prince was impressed and felt proud of her. Which felt somewhat strange as he barely knew her, yet somewhat familiar as if he'd know her a lifetime. One could mistake that he knew Celeste well enough with his genuine feelings of pride and joy for her. This was a new feeling for Prince, and he was enjoying the crash of emotions arresting him.

"So, what are your plans for the weekend?" he continued.

"Jam packed as usual. Never enough hours in the day, but I like to keep busy. How about you?"

"I'm a bit the same. I do enjoy some lazy days at home though."

Celeste cast her mind back and gave that comment some consideration, "I can't remember the last time I had a lazy day."

"You should give it a go sometime." Prince suggested with a jovial smile.

"I know. I always seem to fill my calendar with plans. I barely have a spare minute let alone a day to spare. According to my mother, that's why I'm single."

Intrigued to learn more, he asked, "How does that work?"

"I'm sure she means well, but life is not all about having a boyfriend. She says I don't make enough time for men in my life. Which is ridiculous. I mean, I'm here now, right?"

She had done it again. Said the wrong thing. That little voice inside her head was back, as if it was constantly on watch for when she would make yet another mistake. *Come on! You're giving off the impression you don't even like men. Although maybe that's what you're going for.*

Celeste tried to ignore it. "How about your mum, is she anything like mine?"

"Mom is always on at me to make more time for men too," Prince felt a wave of relief as Celeste gave a hearty laugh. He added points to his mental scorecard and assured himself that she hadn't heard his joke earlier, and continued, "No, she stays out of it."

"It's not just my mum either, it's everyone. It seems when people find out you're single, you must be on the hunt. I mean, men don't have to deal with this."

And then she was on a roll again. "Lucky for some. I'm fine being single. I don't know what the big deal is. Besides, I think having a boyfriend should be about wanting one, not needing one."

"I get that. Do you want one then?" Prince asked. Celeste had begun to notice that Prince didn't seem to mind her tangents and that he was almost eager to participate. Or was she imagining it?

"That depends on who's asking. And how they are asking. The stupid things people say to single independent women. Let's see, I've had ... how are you still single? Why are you single? Don't you want to get married? Aren't you lonely living alone?"

Prince enjoyed this banter and threw himself into the theatre of the conversation. "Oh, why don't you get yourself a pet."

Celeste couldn't hide her delight at his participation, "Yes!" she exclaimed. "Don't worry, it'll happen for you."

"He's out there looking for you too." Prince facetiously patronised.

"I work with a guy who's single, want me to set you up?" Celeste countered.

His next reply made Celeste roar with laughter that brought a grin to his face, "Do you think your standards are too high?"

"What do you do on Valentine's Day?"

"Are you doing the online dating thing?" Prince replied as they shared a smile acknowledging their digital chance encounter.

"Do you think men are intimidated by you?" And he gave her a look as if to say 'good one' to her quip.

Not to be outdone, he retorted, "You're so brave doing it all on your own."

She knew she made a decent income by some people's standards, so she jived, "Money doesn't buy you happiness."

"You wouldn't have to give up your career if you had kids."

"You could be a stay-at-home dad." *Oops*, should she have referenced Prince specifically. *Does he now think I want to have kids with him? Stop it.*

She was relieved when he took the joke and ran with it. "You don't know love until you've had a child."

"Maybe you could be one of those women who have it all."

"What if you already are?" he said in a way that sounded almost like a statement rather than a question.

It was one of the kindest sentences ever delivered to Celeste. "Exactly. Thank you."

On a high, she took full advantage of his compliment and spoke her truth.

"I'm an independent woman, and might I add, an unapologetically independent woman. You know, they always say 'don't speak up, don't say too much'. Which really pisses me off. Why can't I refuse to take shit from anyone, just like a man, without the name calling associated with it?"

It was a fair question, but Celeste automatically regretted it when she heard his response.

"You're certainly not shy and retiring." He said but his tone didn't give away exactly how he meant it.

Celeste took it the only way she knew how. Her stomach dropped, and not in a good way. *Am I being 'too much?'* She had been accused of this in the past. At that exact moment one of the women from a nearby table had excused herself from her party and walked by theirs. She was tall, thin and oozed sex. *Was that sex she could smell on her as she drifted by. Don't be ridiculous, Celeste. She can't smell of sex. Although this is New York, she very well could.*

She watched as Prince's eyes briefly turned away from hers and took in the sex goddess that had entered into their realm. She couldn't blame him; she had just done the same thing. Yet her insecurities seized on this moment like gas to a flame.

You've blown it now haven't you. Too chatty Cathy and not enough sexy Susan. Celeste was sure she was frowning as she tried to rationalise not only the paranoia of Aphrodite stealing her man, but the inane sentence that fell about her head just now.

Before she knew it, she blurted out, "Is that what you want?"

Prince immediately turned his gaze back to Celeste and took her in for a moment. She seemed perturbed and almost sad. "Are you okay?" he asked.

Celeste stood, "Excuse me for a moment." And walked to the bathrooms.

Should I have been shyer and retiring? Was I bantering too much? Could I have kept his attention if I'd been more ... whatever he wanted?

Meanwhile, Celeste was in the bathroom staving off a panic attack about the sheer stupidity she felt because a pretty woman had made her feel shit about herself. Okay, it wasn't just the pretty woman, it was all her nonsensical talking too. And her bravado. Was she being too showy? She leaned her head against the mirror and let out a deep sigh.

Celeste could feel someone standing next to her.

"You okay?" Aphrodite asked.

Of course you're fucking nice too, she thought.

Celeste smiled and got her head together, "A few too many wines after a long day, but thanks."

"I hear that, have a good one," she winked at Celeste as she left the bathroom.

Celeste used the bathroom and mustered some confidence to return to her date.

Prince watched her walk towards him and gave her that smile that seemed to say he only had eyes for her. *Am I imagining it?*

Prince was a thoughtful man and sensitive to other people's emotions. It hadn't gone unnoticed that Celeste had felt something, threatened perhaps, by the woman that had walked by their table. He had watched her look at the woman and back at him, and the look in her eyes when he had turned his attention back to her after briefly taking in what took Celeste's attention away from him in the first place.

She sat and he handed Celeste her glass of wine and said "I think a strong woman is great. I respect that."

Surprised, Celeste asked, "You do?"

"Sure! The world needs women like you."

Holy crap! Maybe I haven't blown it after all, she thought. But instead said, "I wish my mother was here."

Prince's humour didn't let him down, "Do you take her on dates very often?"

Celeste felt comfortable enough to tell him what she secretly thought to herself, "I swear she thinks men won't tolerate an independent woman."

"Well, just so you know, I'm definitely not that kind of guy."

Could it be? Could she really have found a man who likes her independence? Even praise it? Here, lurking in the wild of New York City, has she found one of the remaining species of men courageous enough to take on the modern woman in her natural form? "Wow. How are you still single?" she bantered.

With wit as quick as a fox, he answered, "Your mom would probably say it's because I'm a feminist."

Celeste was giddy. She was letting herself believe this could be something. She knew it was dangerous. This man had serious potential to take her down. It was a huge risk but after some brief risk analysis, she gathered she had enough intel at this stage to allow herself to feel good about him. To allow herself to imagine he could be different to all the others. What if she wasn't wrong this time? Something about him was different from the others, in a way she couldn't quite describe yet could write a novel about. It was a new sensation, and a five-letter word she never believed in was bubbling in her throat. *Trust.*

"Yes, she would. So, Mr. Feminist, would you like to do this again sometime?"

"That would be great." And with that, she leaned over and kissed him on the mouth.

***

Two days had passed, and Celeste sat staring at Nya's face that was on her screen for their virtual appointment. Celeste had a smile on her face that looked like a Cheshire cat.

"Maybe I was wrong about online dating," Celeste conceded.

"Tell me more," Nya enquired.

"So, I met this guy. His name, you ask?" Celeste said without Nya asking and continued before she could say anything in return, "Prince." Celeste paused and waited for Nya to appropriately respond.

Celeste wasn't disappointed as Nya laughed out loud. Not disrespecting his name, but at the obvious irony Celeste had already dissected in her mind and with Sarah.

"I mean, you have said that you are looking for a guy who doesn't need rescuing," Nya laughed again.

"Yes, but I don't need to be rescued." Celeste said, and the words swam around her mind as she wondered if deep down she did.

"Not rescued, no." Nya agreed.

"I mean, can you believe it?" Celeste said to Nya without waiting for her reply. "What is the universe trying to tell me? It is so ironic, and I don't know whether to love it or hate it."

"If nothing else, it gives you even more reason to unpack your feelings about your independence and your expectations in relationships." Nya offered. "But is he the namesake of Prince Charming or Prince of Purple Rain?"

"The latter," confirmed Celeste.

Nya smiled and replied, "I'm not going to lie. I love Prince too."

"I mean, who doesn't?" Celeste wasn't sure if she meant the musician or if she secretly also loved the thought of a real-life Prince Charming. *Don't be ridiculous*, she thought. *Fairy tales are for fools.*

"So, tell me more," Nya sat back with a genuine smile of anticipation.

"We matched and had a few chats before arranging to meet up. He took me on the most romantic picnic I think I've ever been on. We went to Jones Beach. He packed this amazing lunch; he even remembered the cider I like to drink and surprised me with it. He had everything planned. Which amazed me. I wore this dress because I thought it made me look beachy, whatever that is. He seemed to like it. Not that it matters. Well, I guess it does matter. Anyway, we have so much in common and even though I had a few moments of wanting to run for the hills it turns out, he is incredible. And we had a second date a few days later. Which, well, you might want to dissect. But anyway, this guy ..." Celeste trailed off as she realised she was gushing and rambling at the same time.

Nya laughed and was genuinely happy to see Celeste happy. "Okay, let's start with why you were amazed that he planned everything?"

"Because apparently he is some sort of bloody Prince Charming!" Celeste circled back on what she was somewhat considering ironically serendipitous.

She then took a moment to seriously consider Nya's question. "Because I'm the planner. It's always me. I don't date men who take charge or really take care of me. I guess I was surprised to realise he really listened and paid attention to the things I like. The cider was a small gesture, but it was a big deal to me."

"So, what made you want to run for the hills?" Nya asked.

"He told me he was an altar boy as a child and I freaked out and thought he was still some devout Catholic."

"And that worried you?"

"Yes." That was an easy answer for Celeste. She was raised by a Catholic father and Baptist mother, and although religion didn't play a significant role in their upbringing, it certainly influenced the style in which her homelife was conducted. It took many years for Celeste to denounce her relationship with God, not that she was sure she had one to start with. However, she was comfortable letting go of a religious-based belief to hold steadfastly to one of science. Although her time in America had heavily influenced her decision to let go of any religious practice thanks to the actions of some so-called-Christians in the United States, she didn't oppose people's belief in a God and their faith in something greater than themselves. But religious organisations had come to scare her as she had bear witness to some horrific displays of humanity by members of such groups. Therefore, she knew she couldn't date someone who spent their time praying to an institution that she wanted no part of. Faith was one thing; organised religion was off the table.

Celeste continued, "But it turns out he isn't. He says he believes in science but won't call himself an atheist and is far more comfortable with agnosticism. For now, anyway. I'm okay with that."

"So that was all that made you want to run?"

"Yeah, and I got that wrong, so I didn't have to worry about it at all. It's funny because since seeing you, I now see myself and my reactions differently," Celeste offered.

"How so?"

"I think that ..." Celeste paused, "no, I know that I can make a snap decision and then it can be very hard to change my mind. I think in the past I would have taken that simple statement and made it into something bigger than it was. I would have played with those words and forced him into a corner to say what I wanted to hear. And then still would have walked away with my own interpretation of what he was trying to say."

Nya thought she knew where Celeste was going with this, but asked, "Can you elaborate?"

"I think it's a defence mechanism. I think the fear of being happy and trusting in a man to give me that happiness sometimes leads me to form irrational judgements about their personality and opinions. It's easier to be let down early, than to trust and be let down later."

"So, you conjure up an idea of who they are and force it upon them?" asked Nya.

"I guess I do."

"It's great that you are recognising it," Nya praised.

"Well, you haven't heard about our second date," Celeste retorted. "I walked away from our first date on cloud nine, I even want to use the word swooning. Ugh, that makes me feel sick to even say that out loud."

"It's okay to feel that way," Nya interjected and reassured her.

"So, you tell me," Celeste smiled. "We messaged constantly after that date, and I was so excited to see him again. We went to this great Italian place downtown and as soon as I neared the restaurant, I could feel myself getting all worked up. I started to stress that I was running late, that it was a bad impression. Then I was hot and sweaty and thought it was an even worse impression. And then I started to panic in my head, what if he didn't like me, what if I wasn't good enough. What if?" Celeste almost looked embarrassed to be saying such things out loud.

"And what happened?" Nya questioned.

"I decided he could go fuck himself before I even gave him the chance to decide if I was good enough," Celeste declared with a look of a layperson trying to understand the theory of relativity.

"Okay, so how did the date go after that?"

Celeste looked like she was trying to work through why she did this herself, and her expressions continued to change as she detailed the night to Nya. "It was great! He was great, as great as he was on our first date. He saw I was a bit ruffled around the feathers, and I was certain he wasn't going to stand for it, but instead he ordered us a bottle of wine, let me taste it when the server returned – me! How often does that happen, that a man will defer to the woman at the table to decide. And then he listened to my crap day at work and sided with me the whole time."

"Sided with you?" Nya repeated her words to her.

"Yeah, took my side and made me feel like I had a right to be upset. It felt like he was on my team."

"You felt supported," Nya stated.

Celeste could see where this was going. Nya was laying out the puzzle pieces that Celeste was slowly putting together. The feeling of being supported was an unfamiliar one and she didn't know how to accept it. When she reflected on the rest of that night, she remembered the moments of feeling not worthy and mystified at his calm demeanour, his interest in her and the banter that so easily flowed. She now understood her reaction was instinctual, her mistrust buried deep in her bones and the new sensation of feeling, feeling ...

Nya interrupted her train of thought as if she were speaking out loud, "How does all of this make you feel?" Celeste knew this question held a lot of weight.

She dug deep to understand what those butterflies in her stomach really meant. And three little words popped into her head, "He sees me."

Their time was up, and Celeste scheduled her next appointment. She closed her laptop and said goodbye.

Celeste wasn't sure how she felt about her revelation. She wriggled on her couch as she sat in silence while her heart skipped a beat or two. She decided a pint was in order. She promptly got to her feet and took a quick pee in her small bathroom where her knees didn't quite touch the wall when you sat down on the toilet. She washed her hands and splashed cold water on her face, assessing whether she should apply foundation. She decided to put on a touch of tinted moisturiser and ran a ChapStick over her lips. She was out the door within minutes and would be at her local in about the same amount of time.

Is it really possible? she pondered as she walked along her pavement to Amsterdam Avenue. Prince seemed perfect, but is that really possible? *No one is perfect, but maybe he is perfect for me. But am I perfect enough for him?*

Could this man be the one? She still wasn't even sure there was such a thing as 'the one'. He seemed almost too good to be true. She hated that she was possibly putting him on a pedestal. But something in her gut, and thanks to the debits in her bank account to Nya, made her think that maybe there could be a happy ending in her life. *Maybe he could love me like no one has loved me before?* She was getting ahead of herself but allowed her mind to continue to wander a little more before reining herself in.

"No one is perfect," she said out loud. And no one on the street looked twice at the lone woman talking to herself. "Man, I love this city," she said to no one.

Chapter 8: *Bachelor Charming*

Prince looked up from his menu as he felt the familiar weight of a hand on his shoulder. He hadn't noticed his father walking into the small Thai restaurant they had agreed to meet at for lunch. Prince stood and his dad hugged him with the warmth of a parent who loved unconditionally.

"You never arrive before me!" his dad declared with a smile as he took a seat opposite at the small wooden table. It was true, Prince was lackadaisical when it came to conforming to time constraints. The road to arriving on time was paved with good intentions, but Prince was easily distracted, and time became an illusion. While his family and friends were accustomed to his tardiness, there had been several occasions throughout his love life that a new love interest was not as forgiving. Prince wasn't inconsiderate of others' time, but he was aware that he may come across as thoughtless and it was something he was trying to work on. Some may have argued he should have mastered the artistry of time management by his age already.

Prince smiled and replied, "I even managed to stop by a new gallery that opened up around the corner."

Prince had woken early that morning and found himself feeling vibrant. He usually roused relaxed but opposed the morning sun. He was a night owl who would find himself fully realised the closer the hands on the clock reached towards midnight. While he functioned at his best on around six hours sleep, an extended sleep in was customary when the opportunity arose.

That morning, he found himself wide awake at the same time he imagined people with children might arise. He swung his long legs out from under his bed sheet and stood to throw open the heavy black out curtains in his bedroom. He pulled upwards on the window and invited the sounds of the neighbourhood into his home. He lived on a quiet street on the Upper East Side closer to the river than the park. It was a stabilised apartment in a building that was surrounded by old money. The Upper East side wasn't for everyone; it was steeped in history of outrageous wealth and had not always welcomed people who had come from humble beginnings like he did. But when you left Madison Avenue and the stores filled with clothing that cost pennies to make but were sold at a premium, you found the Avenues filled with Irish American bars and local restaurateurs offering delicacies from cultures abroad.

Prince had lived at home in New Jersey longer than his siblings had. While he had moved out of home in his early twenties to live with friends not too far away, he was often still home having dinner with his folks. He had odd jobs here and there. He had taken on some labouring work with a friend for a while, a much-longer-than-anticipated stint working at a restaurant in Princeton, and then he had landed a job at a small charity that supported previously incarcerated men integrate back into their communities. It was the perfect role for Prince, supporting a service that gives people a second chance and seeks solutions rather than prescribing punishment.

Here he found his passion, but certainly not his pay day. Like most charitable work that warmed your heart and made you feel like you were truly making a difference in the world, what you were not making a scrap of difference to, was any sort of retirement security. His bi-weekly pay-check was a constant reminder of how much of society relied on people like him, but how little they valued their contribution.

However, Prince had found a nine to five that he believed in, and as far as he was concerned, money was not the motivating factor in his career choices.

He had decided to leave New Jersey eight years ago when an opportunity arose to be transferred to the Boston office. The stars aligned as his sister lived in Somerville, a creative, progressive, community-oriented neighbourhood and she had a departing roommate. So, Prince packed up what few possessions he owned, bar some that every child leaves behind in their parents unused cupboards and drove the five or so hours to his new abode. He was close to his sister, as he was to his brother. He came from a tight knit family, and he knew how lucky he was. When he looks back on the time he got to spend with his sister, he is fondly reminded of how it solidified their relationship as adults. He had spent a year in Boston and during that time, watched her blossom in a new relationship with a man that reminded him of himself. They say you seek in a partner what you know and what is familiar to you, so Prince was quietly thrilled that his sister was with someone that respected her as much as he did. As their relationship grew stronger and more than just his toothbrush was left in his sister's space, Prince decided it was time for the next chapter in his life.

He started applying for jobs and it hadn't taken him long to find another in his field. New York City was not short of wayward men who had found themselves oppressed under the spotlight of the law, willing to accept rehabilitation but often only receiving retribution.

He needed to find an apartment and was aware it was a challenging city to land the right one in. While in the midst of applying for work, he decided to make the short drive down one Saturday to walk through some of her neighbourhoods and get a feel for what he wanted. He had spent so much time in the city throughout his life, it was just a hop, skip and jump away from his home. There is a reason New Jersey properties with easy access to the Hudson River are so high, and as an adult he understood that proximity and convenience could be a tax line item all on its own. It seemed to him that New York City was always part of his unknown plan, because as he strolled along the pavements, at a slower pace than those who lived there, bustling with people from all walks of life and littered with black rubbish bags waiting to be collected by loud trucks at 3:00 am, he realised it already felt like home.

He had toyed with the idea of living in the East Village and had viewed apartments further down on the Lower East Side, as well as China Town. He looked at least four apartments in Hell's Kitchen and two more in Chelsea before he had found a form of respite on the Upper East Side, offering him what he considered the best of all worlds. Close enough to the bright lights of all the city had to offer, but far enough away from the chaos of 24-hour nightlife that was sometimes too tempting. He was also an art enthusiast, and living so close to The Met made his heart swell. And anyone would be a fool to turn down a rent stabilised apartment.

In good traffic, he lived only a little over an hour's drive away from his parents' home and he still saw them regularly. He wasn't sure at what point this routine came about with his father, but they had been coming to this same restaurant in his neighbourhood for at least five years now and it had become a custom that no one else intruded on. It was just their time together to talk shit about the world over a spicy curry that made your eyes water.

"Buy anything?" his father joked, referring to his trip to the new gallery. They both knew that neither of them could afford the masterpieces that adorned many of the gallery's walls. But he had acquired his love of art from his dad and they appreciated the viewing pleasure, nonetheless.

Prince shared with him that the gallery was part of a conglomerate, which aligned with the notion that an independent gallerist was far less likely to pay the extortionate rent required to open its doors, and its exhibit was featuring an up-and-coming Japanese artist. It was the kind of gallery that didn't list price tags, the blank space next to the pieces screamed at Prince that he shouldn't even bother to ask.

He shared a strong bond with his father. While his outgoing nature came from his mother and together they would be in fits of laughter, his quiet reflection was passed down from his dad. He looked up to his parents with gratitude and respect and idealised their relationship. He was intent on mirroring what he saw as perfection in how two people combine their lives together.

"So, I think I've met someone," Prince told his dad, who noticed his eyes smiled as he said the words.

"You think?" he asked. "Is she real or imagined?" he laughed at his own joke.

Smiling, Prince answered, "Real. Very real. She's great. Really great. Smart, independent, pretty. Smart."

He was aware he was not articulating her as well as he could, but the words tumbled out of his mouth without any control.

"Where did you meet?" his dad asked with sincere anticipation. His son had not dated in some time, and he was curious to learn more about this woman who appeared to have made an impact on his son losing his vocabulary.

"Online, of course."

"Of course," his dad replied. Not that he really knew at all. The last time he was in the dating game you had to ask the bartender for a pen to write a phone number down on the back of a coaster.

"We clicked right away when we first connected. Like, in the easiest of ways. Even when we spoke on the phone for the first time, it was like we had done it a thousand times before."

Prince's dad watched as his son told his story, waving his hands this way and that as he fought to still himself and to sit calmly as he normally would.

"So, I was actually really nervous to go on our first date," Prince admitted.

"That's not like you," his dad observed. Prince may have been somewhat shy when it came to women, but he had an uncanny ease about him when it came to meeting new people. It was how he had been friend-zoned time and time again. Too timid to take the next step, but too comfortable in forming friendships that opportunities were quite often missed. He was confident in his own skin, and it had been quite some time since Prince had met someone who made him aware of his tongue getting tied when he spoke.

"I'm pretty sure I made some stupid comment about my shoes. She's really funny and just has this ..." he paused as he wanted to use the right words to introduce her into their conversation, "way about her." It wasn't as eloquent as he had wanted, and given he was a man of many words, he was once again surprised at the way his brain seemed full of clouds, which was exactly where his head was at.

His father knew his son well and watched as he fidgeted with his napkin while he spoke. "Wow, you really do seem flustered by this girl." It made him happy to see the impact she was having on him.

"Pull yourself together man," Prince jokingly chided himself out loud.

"Now what fun is that?"

"I don't know why I get nervous thinking about her. Keep this up and she might change her mind about seeing me again."

"So, there is going to be a next time?" his dad asked in anticipation.

"We've already been on a couple of dates," Prince had waited till now to tell his dad about her. He didn't hide his love life from his parents, but he often felt it only necessary to share when there was something worth sharing.

He was acutely aware that it made him nervous there was something worth sharing.

"I mean, she really is great. But it wouldn't be the first time I got it wrong," Prince shared a comfortable honesty with his father that had been encouraged his whole life.

It was true that Prince had had his heart bruised in the past, but he had quickly brushed it off as an error of judgement and that the next one would be better than the last.

"Well, you know what I say, take a little from this mistake and a little from that, and what do you get?" his dad paused for Prince to answer.

"One massive shit show and all out huge mistake," Prince replied.

His dad laughed with a wide smile. "Your perfect woman," he stated.

"So, you think perfection exists, Dad?"

"You know what I mean," he replied as he leant back in his chair to give his son the space he seemed to need to work through his feelings.

"Maybe I shouldn't rush into anything? I mean, I kind of want to delete the apps because I'm not too bothered to keep talking to anyone else, but maybe it's too soon?"

"Is it wrong to put all your eggs in one basket?" His dad was a romantic at heart, so it wasn't a surprise to hear him make such a statement. Prince thought his dad was going to offer more solid advice, instead he followed up by saying, "I've never really understood that—what's wrong with putting all your eggs in one basket? How else do you carry them?"

Prince rolled his eyes and shook his head at his head, "Bad dad joke."

"It's been a while since you really dated someone."

"Exactly. Would it hurt to see what else is out there? I mean, this is New York." Prince wasn't wrong in wondering who else might be out there. It was a fact there were more single women than men in New York City so his odds were dramatically better than that of the average New York City independent woman who can take care of herself, seeking the time and attention of a man who possibly can't handle the fact she might earn more money than him.

"Or should I say fuck it, and just jump in headfirst?" He was genuinely eager for his father's advice. It was rare for Prince to feel the fragility of his heart in the hands of a woman, and he was seeking answers to protect it.

"Go with your gut, because when you know, you know."

"You think?" Prince asked with all curiosity. "I'm not convinced your gut instinctively has the right answers. After all, we are but animals and I'm not sure our brains have truly caught up to our bodies."

Prince knew he wasn't wrong. He had seen too many friends make decisions with their hearts instead of their minds and watched as relationships had crumbled before his eyes. He also knew it wasn't realistic to ignore that instinct his father was referring to. Prince may prefer an evidence-based approach to most things in life, but he was still his father's son and he was open to feeling the sting of cupid's arrow.

"Headfirst it is then, assuming you've given it a lot of thought," his dad offered.

"I think you guys would love her. Mom would have a lot to talk to her about."

"Why don't you bring her over to the house?" he suggested.

"Okay, let's not rush. You'll have me married off before you even know her last name." Prince knew that was a blatant mistruth. He was grateful his parents had never pushed for marriage and grand babies and quite frankly, he wasn't sure if either appealed to him.

"Take it easy and take it slow. Have fun." His dad countered. "And I'll take a first name to start."

"Celeste," as her name fell from his lips he felt a tingle across his forearms. Rubbing them, he looked around the restaurant.

***

His dad watched as his son pressed the hairs on his arms back into place, and his eyes darted around the room as if in search of an answer to a question his body was asking.

Prince was a good man, and any woman would be lucky to have him. Of course, any father would think the same of his children. While he knew Prince's life was fulfilling, he had hoped that he would find someone to share it with, if for no other reason than he believed everyone deserved to be loved.

He wondered if he had prepared his son for the rollercoaster ride that came with matters of the heart. While Prince didn't spend his nights writing poetry about soul mates, his dad was aware Prince had an unconscious expectation that should he come across locks of hair falling from a high tower, they would surely be accompanied with a happy fairy tale ending. If only relationships were always that easy and graceful, he thought to himself.

Prince's father had always been very open with his own heart and his pursuit of finding happiness in his wife's love was evident. He thrived under her gaze. But now his dad wondered if he should have taken more opportunities to teach Prince the important lessons about the work that truly went into successful relationships.

They had raised him in a home full of love and respect and under the blanket of a marriage still strong after thirty-seven years. Prince was aware of cross words and stony silences that all relationships endure at some point or another, but as parents they had promised each they would raise their children in a home where communication thrived, and the truth was spoken. There was an honesty and respect in their home that was always evident and expected.

While Prince's eyes were not shut to the pain that love can bring, he himself had never directly experienced it. His dad was surprised that he hadn't considered this before now. Prince had never truly known what it was like to lose love and had shed very few tears on the loss of a life with someone that had not quite bloomed into existence.

While he was thankful his son had escaped the cold hard realities most of us face at some point in our lives, he now wondered if he was missing out on an experience that would support his growth as a person. Although, upon reflection, he was not sure we could definitively say people learn their lessons and go on to be better versions of themselves.

Maybe his son was all the better for having read about Romeo and Juliet rather than having to live through his own reality of it.

He just hoped that Prince didn't have an unrealistic expectation of what to expect when someone did capture his heart and mind. He hoped that Prince would see through the facade of widely romanticised versions of how love should fall at one's feet. He was aware he had contributed to this theory as he had showered his son with his own grandiose stories about courting his mother. But storytelling aside, he hoped he had prepared him for the beautiful experiences that vulnerability can bring if we see past imperfections and acknowledge our own.

***

Prince had caught the attention of the server, and she was headed their way.

They both picked up their menus as if they hadn't been to this same restaurant a hundred times before and didn't know that they were going to order the same dishes they always ordered when they met there.

Prince felt his dad's eyes upon him as he blindly looked at the letters on the laminated piece of paper in his hand.

He looked up and straight into his dad's eyes.

He was excited to tell Celeste about him.

Chapter 9: *Let Your Hair Down... Or Not*

Celeste skipped down the stairs at 79th and Broadway to take the subway to dinner. She had picked a restaurant in Gramercy, which meant she had to swap trains at Times Square to get there. The air was thick as she waited on the platform for the next train to arrive. Two minutes felt like two hours as she felt sweat run down the back of her leg. She wore a cotton dress that would have swayed in the wind if there was any such reprieve, it was white and covered in black love hearts and she had picked it up on sale at Anthropologie during winter. She was grateful it didn't show the sweat marks she was sure were forming in all the usual places. Her hair was pulled up in a ponytail to avoid the inevitable frizz on a night as humid as this one was.

It was 7:25 pm and she should arrive right on time for their 8 pm reservation. They were dining at Isabelle's Osteria on Park Avenue. She had been walking home from a brunch in the East Village one weekend when it had caught her eye as she passed by. It looked inviting and when she stopped to look at the menu, she found it was reasonably priced given the location. She had made a note of it in her list of places to try, a list that was as long as her arm and then some.

When her friend, Abigail, had reached out to catch up, she suggested Isabelle's as it was convenient for both. With Abigail living in Tribeca, it was almost halfway to each other's apartments. Plus, it was an easy walk to some great bars nearby should they choose to stay for drinks after. Which they always did.

She was meeting Abigail and her new boyfriend, Alexander. She had met Abigail when she first moved to New York City. Celeste had been at a networking event that her company had sent her on, when she met Abigail in the long line for the free cocktails. After the cursory introductions, they started talking about where they were both from and how they had found themselves in New York City.

Abigail had grown up in Connecticut and had moved to the city to go to school. She was an NYU graduate with a trust fund that provided a large one-bedroom apartment in her posh neighbourhood. She still worked, which Celeste found honourable but as the months wore on she realised Abigail's lacklustre for a career and instead a want to continue living like she was still in college, didn't quite align with Celeste's desires.

That first year was a blast though. Celeste and Abigail had partied their way through every neighbourhood in Manhattan and Celeste had made it their mission to taste test an espresso martini at every bar they walked into. She maintained the cocktail was invented in England and she was here to taste the American versions as often as possible.

As Celeste became more comfortable in her New York skin and made new friends, she realised her friendship with Abigail was one forged out of a desperate need for female companionship that was hard to find, more so than compatibility. Nothing tests your tenacity more than moving to a new country and trying to make friends as an adult. Celeste didn't have any troubles taking a seat at a bar by herself and ordering a pint, but being at a destination where cliques were clicking and you were the outsider looking for an avenue into their conversations was difficult.

And while she found it somewhat easier to strike up a conversation with another solo patron, even if one finds herself immersed in a conversation with a would-be friend, she often found herself awkwardly attempting to ask for a phone number without sounding like she was looking for a date. More often than not, Celeste would avoid what she perceived as a possible uncomfortable conversation and would simply say it was lovely to meet and wished her farewell.

So, when Abigail had struck up a conversation and invited her to leave the networking event for a new restaurant opening she had been invited to, Celeste jumped at the chance.

While Celeste loved Abigail and would be forever grateful that she had taken her under her wing while she navigated the many lessons the city dished out, she found that she was seeking a stability that she both craved and feared.

Celeste took pride in her ability to do everything all at once; to try the new bar, to go to a show, to hit up the comedy club, to go back to a trusted restaurant, to attend a festival, to stay out late, to get up on time for work. Celeste almost always said yes. However, the one thing she detested and often refused to do, was line-up. Unless she could add her name to a waitlist where they would call her phone and not her name while languishing outside the venue, she would rather eat dollar slice pizza than spend her time deteriorating while waiting to dine. Dramatic words but that was how desperate Celeste felt about not waiting in lines.

So, when Celeste realised she was craving some solace in the apart-ment she had proudly made a home, she questioned how others would perceive her since they had always known her as the girl who jumped at an invitation. Would they still be her friend? It was around this time that she met Roman and after unpacking her baggage with Nya, she was piecing together that her desire to be liked reached far and wide.

She was excited about piecing the puzzle together to see the full picture that guided her beliefs and her decision making. She knew she had a long way to go and that this journey had only just begun. But she was fascinated that when she focused, she could indeed see how one inconsequential decision led to the next.

It had been many weeks since she had last seen Abigail, and in that time, Abigail had taken possession of a new boyfriend. She used that word as Abigail was not without a man on her arm for long. She churned through boyfriends like a kid tearing through FAO Schwarz. They were toys to her and thanks to her looks and her money, she usually had her pick. They were harmless men who often had their hearts broken over her. Usually younger and always handsome, their bank accounts didn't matter to Abigail, only their stamina. Because of the nature of her dating life, Celeste often found herself double dating with a current fling's friend. Their nights out were often fuelled by expensive champagne and cocktails and often left one reaching for Tylenol and water the day after. Abigail would frequently depart with her beau, leaving Celeste to her own devices with her new acquaintance. Rarely would she succumb to their charms and most often she found herself alone in her bed, sometimes with a slice of pizza from the all-night pizzeria on the corner of her street.

Celeste walked up the subway stairs at 14th street station and headed a few blocks north to the restaurant. The pink shade sails adorned the venue and pink and white lattice chairs were filled with laughing groups of friends and lovers on dates. She entered the restaurant and spotted Abigail already seated with her boyfriend. Celeste pointed her friends out to the hostess and as she squeezed past diners enjoying their meals, Abigail stood to hug Celeste when she arrived at their table.

"So great to see you," Abigail squealed and didn't give Celeste a chance to reply when she added, "This is Alexander."

Alexander had to be at least seven years younger, easily in his later twenties, with a devilish smile that would soon be wiped from his pretty face if her previous relationships were any example of what was to come for him. "I've heard so much about you," he said in a voice as deep as his tan as he leaned in and gave her a kiss on each cheek.

Celeste was always astonished by the diverse range of men Abigail chose to date. One thing was for sure, there was never a dull moment in the life of Abigail.

"So nice to meet you too," Celeste obliged. "And you," she turned to Abigail, "look amazing!"

Abigail gave an obligatory smile that Celeste had seen hundreds of times before. Abigail knew she was attractive, but she was never conceited and that was a quality that Celeste admired most about her. She may be a lot of things, spoiled, impatient, and careless, but never egotistical.

As they sat down, a server placed large menus in front of them. While Celeste would have preferred time to catch up with Abigail alone, she understood the rules of engagement in this friendship. Meaningful one on one catch ups usually occurred during daytime hours, preferably after a yoga session together or whatever the latest exercise fad was. Dinner catch ups were usually accompanied by her latest fling and often a friend. She was glad there was no friend to be flung in her direction on this occasion.

Their server appeared by their table asking if they would like any drinks to start.

"Of course," Celeste beamed. Without looking at the menu she requested a bottle of pinot noir at the sommelier's discretion.

Abigail was seated to Celeste's left and Alexander was next to her. Abigail took Celeste's hand in both of hers and begged for an update, "How is Hinge working out? Tell me everything!"

"Well, I have to say you may have been right," said Celeste.

Abigail released her hand and clapped while she squealed like a teenager, "I told you! I mean look at this man," Abigail turned to Alexander and squeezed one of his cheeks then ran her hands through his thick hair. "You know we met on Hinge, right?"

Celeste did not know but continued, "I mean, they haven't all been great. But I will concede it was better than expected."

"What do you mean it was better. Does that mean you're off it already?" Abigail asked.

"I may be about to delete the app," Celeste replied wryly.

Abigail noticed the look in her eyes and pondered this response for a minute. "Wait a second ... Does that mean you've met someone?"

"It means I don't have a desire to be on the app any longer."

"Because you've met someone?" Abigail was sure she was right.

"Look ..."

Abigail squealed again and the table next to them turned around to see what the fuss was about.

"Shhhh," Celeste blushed as she lowered the decibels at the table. "I don't want to make a fuss just yet."

"Just yet," Abigail interrupted, implying there was hope for the future.

"Look," Celeste said again, shooting a look at Abigail that instructed her to keep quiet. "I may have met someone who I think has a lot of potential." She reached to touch Abigail's arm as if to hold her down, "But you know me, who am I to know if this one is a keeper?"

The server returned and placed large fishbowl sized red wine glasses in front of each of them. He showed them the bottle he had selected on their behalf, and pulling out a corkscrew from his apron, popped the cork off the pinot noir and smelled the cork bottom. Gently placing the cork on the table, he poured a small amount of wine into Alexander's glass. Alexander gave a cursory glance around the table and picked up the wine to inhale its aroma and taste. Celeste knew it was not a big deal to most; it was something that people barely considered in the moment, but her lips curled in the smallest of smiles as she recalled when Prince passed the glass to her to determine if the wine was what she liked.

After a nod from Alexander, Celeste smiled and thanked the server as he skilfully poured what she rightfully assumed was expensive wine into her glass.

She knew that whatever the price point was on that bottle, she couldn't afford it. But she was also accustomed to the game they played. Celeste had learnt long ago that Abigail had no interest in paying attention to the numbers on a menu and while she appreciated that Celeste was mindful about spending not just her own money, but Abigail's too, she also didn't want to have to haggle over the price. So, she would order what she knew the table would like, Celeste would offer her credit card to split the bill, and Abigail would tell her she could buy her a cocktail at the next bar. Occasionally she even let Celeste buy her one.

"So, tell me more about this guy and I'll tell you what I think," Abigail pressed.

"He's amazing. He is kind, generous, and funny. And kind. Did I say that already?"

"Someone has a crush," Alexander interjected and quickly apologised. "I'm sorry, I know I don't know you, but you just seem to really like this guy."

Abigail leaned over and kissed him, "Oh babe, I love you know my friends already." She turned back to Celeste, "He's right you know. This one is different."

"How can you say that? I've hardly said two words about him," Celeste contested. However, she could feel the butterflies at the recognition she was getting from her friend.

The server passed by, and Abigail called for his attention to order a bottle of champagne.

To celebrate she said; to which Celeste suggested there wasn't much to celebrate just yet and that they should stick with red seeing they had already started on that.

"Nonsense," Abigail replied. "The whole booze should go in some sort of order is not a rule I follow. And I think there is something to celebrate. Look at the two of us meeting the love of our lives on Hinge."

It was quite the statement to make in front of Alexander, yet he beamed from ear to ear, and his smile didn't fade after he kissed her. "It's true," he confirmed. "We are in love."

Celeste wondered if the two of them had been drinking prior to her arrival, but they seemed dead sober. Now that she thought about it, she hadn't really seen or heard much from Abigail in not just weeks, but close to three months. Was this why? Could it be love? *Good lord,* she contented with her own thoughts, *you've had a few good dates with some guy and now you believe fairy tales really can come true.*

"Well, well. When is the big day?" Celeste joked.

"Not until next year, but we are thinking around May." She had not expected Abigail to respond with a real answer.

Celeste sat back in her chair and looked from Abigail to Alexander and watched the way they looked at each other. For the first time, she realised she had never seen that look on Abigail's face before. She reached out a hand and placed it on Abigail's arm, "I'm truly happy for you." She meant it.

While she was genuinely happy for Abigail, she was also aware that Abigail had been engaged twice before with no weddings to speak of. Celeste did concede that she did seem calmer with Alexander though. She couldn't pinpoint what it was, but there was an ease between the two of them that she had not seen before. "I'm sorry it's taken so long for us to meet," Celeste said to Alexander.

He smiled in return, "Abi speaks about you a lot, it feels like I already know you." Celeste loved the way Alexander had affectionately shortened her name to Abi, in a way that seemed like he had known her for a long time.

"So, we need to meet this guy," Abigail interjected. Another part of her charm, she could really make someone feel like the centre of attention when she wanted to. And she was fixated on learning more about Celeste's new crush. "Have you met any of his friends yet?"

"Not yet, I don't know if it's too soon?"

"That's a big deal," Alexander agreed.

Abigail strongly disagreed, "Oh no it's not." She took her conquests to family dinners within hours of meeting someone she deemed either appropriately fun to play with, or someone who would create drama at a family gathering.

"I don't know. I don't want to read into anything and make bad decisions based on something trivial that I've blown out of proportion."

"She has a tendency to push away the good ones," Abigail let Alexander in on the secret. "And has a track record for dating fairly shitty guys." She turned her attention back to Celeste, "It's almost like you enjoy it."

"They're not all shitty," Celeste defended herself. While she was sure that Abigail didn't intend to insult her, her words sometimes felt like a hot knife through butter, slicing away at her confidence. Or maybe that was Celeste's own insecurity and possible jealousy that Abigail seemed to have the confidence of a thousand women.

"Fair. Average guys then," Abigail giggled at her lack of concession.

The server returned to their table and poured the champagne he had brought with him, taking their order at the same time.

As the drinks flowed, Celeste held court, fielding questions from both Abigail and Alexander about Prince. She hated to admit it, but she loved talking about him.

Even when their meals were served, rosemary focaccia and burrata to start, followed by some of the most delicious pasta any of them had eaten and a Tuscan kale salad so they didn't feel guilty about the carbs they were consuming, Celeste continued to gush about Prince.

By the time dessert was served, and by dessert they had ordered espresso martinis, the conversation had turned to how to behave in the beginning of a relationship.

"You know me, I don't buy into any of that crap," Abigail declared. And she didn't. Abigail also had an innate ability to do what she wanted without being judged by society. Or she simply just didn't care if she was.

Celeste on the other hand spent most of her time concerned with what people might think of her. And from her sessions with Nya, had become aware that she adapted her personality to please the men she spent her time with.

"Have you slept with him yet?" Abigail asked outright.

Celeste glanced at Alexander, and he gave her a look that said he didn't have a judgemental bone in his body.

"No, I haven't."

"Seriously? Wow, I'm impressed," Abigail stated.

"For starters, it hasn't been that long. And second, I like this guy."

"So not sleeping with him is your way of showing it?" Alexander chimed in with his joke.

"You're a guy, right?" Celeste waved her arm up and down, almost theatrically thanks to the drinks that were making her feel empowered.

Abigail leaned into Alexander and took his hands in her own. Together they rubbed their hands over his body as if to confirm he indeed was. Celeste could tell she wasn't the only one a little buzzed.

"I just mean there are rules. I have to play the game. I don't want him to judge me."

"Pfft, rules schmules," Abigail laughed.

"That's easy for you to say. You get to make up your own rules," Celeste replied. "I on the other hand have to follow these ridiculous rules that society has bestowed upon me as a woman."

"She's not entirely wrong you know," Alexander added.

Abigail almost spat out her wine before she replied, "You don't actually think she has to fit some mould, do you?"

"Of course not, but I'm just saying some guys expect the chase."

"If this guy is that kind of guy, then he isn't the one for Celeste," Abigail said defensively.

"I mean, he seems pretty progressive."

"But you never know ..." Alexander interjected.

"You are not helping," Abigail pointed out.

"Hey, I'm not saying it's okay. I'm just saying ..." Alexander was not trying to tell Celeste what to do. He was merely stating his lived experience with his own kind. While he didn't agree with arbitrary rules that applied to one gender and not another, he was also aware that societal norms were part of our world and it was going to take more time for women to smash the patriarchy, with the support of men like himself.

While Celeste pondered what she wanted to do versus what she should do, the drinks kept flowing. The more cocktails she had, the more she allowed her insecurities to creep into the dark corners of her mind. She knew Prince was a good guy, she believed he had the same values as she did, and she thought that he would not judge her as long as any decision she made was with conviction. She wasn't sure if she was making decisions with conviction, or if they were simply based on popular demand.

She had bedded men too early in previous relationships and had regretted the outcome later. She found herself wanting for a man that she didn't love for she had given all of herself to him. She struggled with these feelings to this day. She sexualised relationships to fulfil an expectation and a desire to be wanted.

Her head was spinning. She knew the alcohol was impeding her thoughts, but she let her mind wonder. She considered her relationship to sex and how it had impacted how she behaved. She knew she liked sex, she knew she enjoyed it and desired it. But what frightened her the most was that she couldn't confirm or deny whether she made love to be loved.

Her phone buzzed with the notification of a text message. Prince was wishing her a good night with her friends and was looking forward to seeing her soon.

What version of me is he looking forward to seeing? she wondered. We usually consider people as being able to have two versions of themselves. Two faces. Public and private. At work and at home. Celeste was sure she had not only two versions of herself to draw on, but very likely, three, four, five ...

She knew this was something she needed to remember so that she could speak with Nya about it at her next session. But her next date with Prince would be before then. So, she had to make a decision now. *Who did she want to be? Who did he want her to be? And why did she care?* It was a question she was afraid to answer.

Chapter 10: *Dark Clouds Cast Magical Spells*

The rain was coming down hard. It fell in drops the size of giant's tears. *Cry me a river*, Celeste thought as she watched it hit the windshield in front of her, each droplet making a perfect rounded shape before cascading down in tearful lines, picking up traction as it collected other bubbles of water that had come moments before. It had been a humid day, and they had predicted thunderstorms.

She turned to look out the passenger window to her right at the lush greenery. She caught a glimpse of a cricket jumping under the cover of a fern that was resilient in mother nature's lashings, swaying in the wind and throwing water from its leaves like a dancer discarding a partner to perform solo.

"Sorry about this," Prince said. As she spun around to meet his gaze, her hair fell across one eye and he reached his fingers to sweep it from her face. She lifted her hand to fix the loose tendril, and her hand skimmed his for the briefest of seconds. He smiled, and she looked away from his gaze.

They had driven upstate to Hudson Valley because Prince had wanted Celeste to experience the Walkway Over the Hudson. It was a scenic sight not to be missed; the pedestrian bridge spanning 1.28 miles connecting the Ulster and Dutchess counties. It sits 212 feet above the flowing waters of the Hudson River and is breathtaking in the right light. Unfortunately, on this day, the skies had opened and wept instead.

"You mean you didn't talk to the woman upstairs about the weather plans for today?" she joked.

"Woman?" he questioned.

"Obviously," was all she answered with a sweet smile. Reminding herself not to talk about anything untoward.

They were sitting in Prince's car, a 1970s blue BMW that had done a lot of miles, had seen a lot of sunrises and could do with a little restoration. Celeste shifted on the leather seat and hoped she wasn't sweating through the activewear she had pulled from the back of her drawers that morning. She had wanted to appear sporty yet sexy and was finally getting some use out of the overpriced outfit. It may have been raining but the humidity was still lingering in the fog.

He'd invited her for an action-packed morning of hiking, followed by a hearty lunch. However, as they neared their destination the storm clouds had rolled in, and they conceded to a change of plans. They drove by the Walkover Over the Hudson, and he pointed to where they *would* have gone and continued driving in the rain to what would have been their second stop enroute, the home of Franklin Roosevelt. The estate had been turned into an historic site and Prince promised that next time they would do the tour. But the drive through on its own was still an impressive sight. As they had a little over two hours to spare until their lunch reservation, he decided to park and take in the view for a while.

As he pulled into a car park, and the rain continued to pour down, he said, "Sorry about this. Are you okay sitting here a while? Or we could go grab a coffee if you'd prefer?"

He was concerned he had let her down and that she might not be comfortable sitting in his old, prized possession while they waited for their reservation.

"For once I was on time today and now, we have all this time to just wait around," Prince laughed. "At least it's together," he added.

Celeste looked over at Prince and her heart melted a little. She was coming to understand his mannerisms and expressions, and it was evident he wanted to make sure she was happy. "This is perfect," she reached over and touched his leg.

He took her hand in his and held it while they watched the rain fall for a little longer.

"We could go to a café if you'd prefer," he asked again.

Celeste couldn't think of any other place she would rather be. "We can wait here," she smiled.

They sat in the BMW and comfortably chatted about their week. She mentioned her night out with her friends and casually said maybe he'd like to meet them sometime.

Celeste was pleased at how quickly he accepted her offer and said he would love to join them next time.

Now all she had to worry about was making sure her friends behaved and didn't betray any of her confidence by telling Prince any of her past he might find unflattering.

After her conversation with Abigail and Alexander, she had allowed herself to imagine all the ways Prince might judge her should her past come back to haunt her. Not that she had many skeletons in her closet, by today's standards she probably had a lot of making up to do.

She couldn't imagine Prince being so antiquated given he had shown no signs of such outdated beliefs, but their relationship was still new, and she considered whether he might be so inclined to reject used goods, as she had so appallingly described herself in her head.

Celeste was aware of how close her hand was to Prince's groin. She was sure it was just because it was the most comfortable for the two of them, with her arm stretched over the centre console and where it had landed when he took hers in his own. But she was in her head now and moved her hand further down his leg just in case.

"Is everything okay?" he asked.

How does he know? Sometimes she felt like he could read her thoughts by how attuned he was to her shifting emotions. She looked directly in his eyes and paused for a moment before replying, "Yes."

He leaned over and kissed her. She wasn't sure if it was the look he gave her, the feeling of being seen without speaking, or the romanticism of the rain falling around them, but she kissed him back with more passion than she expected. She suddenly pulled back when she realised how heated it could become.

"Are you sure everything is okay?" He looked worried.

Celeste fumbled in her reply, "Yes, sorry. I'm just … getting to know you still."

"I'm not pressuring you, I promise. It was just a kiss."

"I know. I'm sorry." *Why am I apologising? What have I got to be sorry for? Good God woman, he doesn't need an apology,* she scolded herself for being so accommodating. "Well, actually I'm not sorry …" Now she felt like she was berating him. She took a deep breath and explained, "I just mean, I don't want to rush anything."

Prince was relaxed and laughed. Not in a condescending way, but in a way that suggested he understood her and wasn't bothered by her internal battle that he rightly took as one she was fighting alone and had not a lot to do with him. "I was always taught that good things come to those who wait," he said candidly, as if to reassure her she had nothing to be worried about.

Celeste smiled with a sigh of relief.

Prince continued, "Just because something isn't happening for you right now, doesn't mean it will never happen."

Celeste played along, "That's right."

"Patience is bitter, but its fruit is sweet." Prince bantered and continued, "Have patience with all things, but first with yourself … patience is not the ability to wait, but the ability to keep a good attitude while waiting … two things define you, patience when you have nothing and attitude when you have everything." Prince finally paused but Celeste wasn't sure if he was finished, so waited for more.

"Why so quiet?" he laughed at himself, and she laughed along with him.

"You seem to know a lot of quotes."

"I read a lot of motivational books."

Celeste was surprised. "You like motivational books, too? Like, self-help?"

"Not the self-help you are referring to," Prince jibed.

"Which ones are those?" she joked in return.

"You know ... the ones in the back of the bookstore where you find people in dark glasses and big hats ..."

"Rocking back and forth in a ball." Celeste mimicked what that might look like and they both laughed out loud together.

"When I say motivational, I mean books that teach you how to stay positive and see the world through optimistic eyes. For all the philosophy I read, I can get a little pessimistic. So it helps to balance things out," he paused as if considering the weight of the words on the pages he often read.

Prince continued, "They say to achieve your goals you should write them down, but only around twenty percent of people do that."

"I write down my goals. I have a vision board," Celeste stated proudly. *Is this impressing him?* She couldn't help but feel like she should have been handed a gold star for doing something that aligned with something that seemed important to him.

"Vision board?" Prince inquired.

Shit, is that not what he meant? While she considered this in her mind for a second, her genuine excitement about her practice overrode her insecurities about how he might see her. She wondered how she could bottle that momentum in future.

Celeste was feeling comfortable and herself. She relaxed and forgot about the need for her puritan act. She let herself just be. She didn't skip a beat before answering, "It sounds a little hippyish. Every year I put up pictures of all the things I want to achieve. And you know what ... it works."

"That makes sense. Maybe I should do one myself."

"Have you ever thought about writing your own self-help book?" she teased. She was curious about what motivated and inspired him. She was someone who loved to pursue an idea to the ends of the earth and her friends knew if you mentioned an interest to her that she might have a business plan written before they could end their sentence.

"Motivational. Stop making me sound crazy," he teased back. "Not necessarily a motivational book, but yeah I've considered writing something ... someday."

This made Celeste feel good. She pondered on that feeling for a second and recognised it made her feel like she was with someone who had his own dreams and didn't need her to come up with any for him. She made a mental note to talk to Nya about this.

"So, you're one of the special few who writes down her dreams. I'd like to see this board of yours sometime." Prince gently moved another tendril of hair that had fallen near her eyes and their eyes locked. She felt like she was falling into the deepest river with no bottom in sight. Her body tingled and her belly was in knots.

She started to feel like she was under a spell and pulled herself out of it. "So ... got any more quotes?"

He laughed and instead replied, "What's on your vision board for this year?"

"Travel, of course." Celeste was an avid traveller and had spent most of her adult life spending her time and money on travelling abroad. She was a firm believer that travelling made you a better human being, being afforded the opportunity to meet new people, see how they lived, how different their lives were to her own, but underneath it all, how they were all longing for the same basic needs in life.

"Of course!" Prince agreed. "Traveling is non-negotiable for me, so it sounds like we are on the same page."

Celeste's stomach turned over as a wave of expectation tightened around her. It was a familiar feeling, one of envisioning a future with the man she was dating, her hopes as high as the peak of Mount Everest. She did this regularly with the men she had invited into her life, her previous fixer-uppers. She had spoken with Nya about it, and it was why she was aware these feelings had been activated. She breathed in through her nose and casually let her breath escape her mouth. While she was excited about Prince, she wanted to make sure she wasn't leading herself astray.

Instead, she continued, "Study. Volunteering, I just need to find the right organisation. What else? ... Oh, dance classes. I hate to exercise ..."

"Whatever you're doing is working for you," Prince praised her.

Celeste's mind immediately went into overdrive. *Did he just look at my body? Was he being inappropriate? Did he like what he saw?* She wrapped her arms around herself and slightly turned her body away from him and any lingering gaze. *Aren't you worried about what he's thinking?* the little voice in her head asked. She knew she was overacting and chastised herself, *pathetic.* It was a harsh word, and it was not uncommon that the voice in her head would use such derogatory terms. Not that she realised—most of the time she took the abuse her insecure self doled out without a second thought. Had she heard someone say such things to any woman out loud, she would have been outraged and protective. She wouldn't hesitate to tell that girl to not listen. But when your own demons address you, it's funny how we listen on command.

"You must think I'm so old fashioned," Celeste blurted out.

"It's not old fashioned. And I respect it, I do," Prince was genuine in his response. He remembered conversations with his dad about doing what felt right for both people in a relationship, not just what felt right for him at the time. "Nothing wrong with waiting. Less chance to complicate the relationship if we take it slow too."

Celeste's eyes lit up and then he noticed a shadow cross over them. What he didn't know was that he was the only man who had made Celeste feel truly safe. It was a feeling she didn't recognise and her instinct was to refute her feelings, but she forced herself to conclude his thoughtful nature was sincere.

Prince lightened the conversion by asking, "So, you don't like to exercise?"

For a moment Celeste didn't understand the question and then realised he had circled back to their conversation about the vision board. "Oh yeah. I don't like going to the gym; but I love the idea of doing something like a dance class to keep fit. What about you?"

"I don't know if dance classes are for me," he joked. "Although I think I'd look great in a leotard. What do you think?"

Celeste was grateful he had shifted the mood into a lighter space and laughed when she replied, "I mean what would you put on your vision board?"

Prince considered this question and pondered it thoughtfully. "A trip to Italy. I would also like to study. Honestly, I'd love to go back to school and do a law degree." He paused as he seriously contemplated what he would like to achieve in the coming year. "Maybe if I win some money, a house upstate to escape to, you know?"

"Don't forget you'll write your own self-help book."

"Motivational book," Prince joked in return.

Celeste laughed, "Yeah, yeah."

Prince turned his attention to outside the car. It wasn't until that moment that she realised they had been looking at each other almost the entire time they were talking. Enthralled in each other's words.

"Looks like the rain has stopped," Prince commented. The sun was even starting to peek through the clouds as a few remaining droplets fell from the skies. "Looks like it's going to be a beautiful day after all." He turned back to Celeste and asked, "Want to walk around the estate a little?"

"I'd love to."

They opened their doors and stepped out into the thin summer air that only happened right after it rained. A few more cars had parked while they had been getting to know each other like teenagers with nowhere else to be. Other visitors were getting out of their vehicles, some stretching their arms, others taking off light sweaters they thought they would need due to the rain but had forgotten that summer rain doesn't mean fall temperatures.

They decided that given they still had time to spare, they would try to get tickets to tour the home. However, it was peak season and tickets were sold on a first-come, first-served basis, so had sold out for the next time slot. Instead, they walked through the public grounds and made their way over to take in the view of the Hudson River.

The water sparkled under the sun that had emerged from the rain clouds to shine upon them. Looking down at the river and across at the vast landscape of deep green trees and rolling hills before her, she was reminded how small she was in the world. She thought about those who had come here before her, what President Roosevelt felt when he too stood here. And more importantly, who were those that stood on this land before the white man came. She had looked up the area when Prince had told her they were headed to Poughkeepsie. She had heard the name before. She remembered it from an episode of *Friends* when Ross met a woman on the train who was changing trains at Poughkeepsie Station to keep going north. It's funny what words and sentences stick in your mind, even after many years.

When Henry Hudson sailed by the City of Poughkeepsie in 1609, it had been inhabited by the Wappinger people. The Wappinger lived along the east bank of the Hudson River from Manhattan Island to what is now known as Poughkeepsie, and eastward to the lower Connecticut River Valley. While the Dutch had settled and developed New York City first, it took almost a century for the same colonisers to realise the beauty and bounty of what is now known as Dutchess County. Around the same time, the English set about taking over what the Dutch had started.

"Penny for your thoughts?" Prince asked.

Celeste was pulled from her introspection and back into the moment. "Oh, I was just thinking about what this would have looked like before we were all here."

"I would think from this standpoint, the view would have looked much the same as now." Prince was right, as from their vantage point, it appeared it was endless land ahead of them. What lay beyond the hills was unknown.

They spoke about the history of Native Americans and Celeste was eager to understand as much as she could. She had realised not long after she had arrived in the United States that she knew very little of its history and after her quick Google search earlier in the week, had been reminded she still had a lot to learn.

Prince was educated and held steadfastly to his opinions on the wrongdoings of the past. When he spoke of those things, you could see the fire in his eyes. Celeste wondered if that anger ever flowed over. She had experienced enough in her life to know that even the kindest people have limits, and no matter how patient they are, those limits can be reached quickly.

She realised they were both passionate about righting wrongs and agreed that as humans we should be better. She loved the way he spoke with such conviction but delivered his message in a way that made one think they came to their own decision to agree with his point of view even if they entered the conversation in opposition. She loved everything about him.

She was doing it again. Staring at his face, into his eyes. He had been looking at the view and had found her gaze upon him when he turned to her. "Hungry?" he asked.

Celeste smiled and responded with a hearty, "Yes!"

Prince took her hand, and they walked back to the car. He opened her door for her, something he had done at every opportunity. She liked that he appeared to have two sides of him, one that agreed and supported women to be whatever they wanted to be, but a gentleman all the same.

Before she got in the car, Prince kissed her again. Softly, as if an extension of their conversation earlier. She blushed as she pulled away and took her seat on the passenger side.

It was a quick 20-minute drive to make it on time for their lunch reservation. She was surprised at how quickly two hours had passed by. Their conversation continued to flow with such ease, as if they had known each other for longer. They were comfortable with each other in a way she had never experienced before.

Lunch was the Mill House Brewing Company. They circled the car park several times before a patron had finished their brunch and was heading home with a full belly. It was busy, which was a good sign.

As they approached the door to the restaurant, he once again held it open for her. As she passed him, another couple came up behind them and Prince gestured for them to pass through as well. It occurred to her that Prince wasn't a gentleman in the traditional sense that one expects in response to how men and women should behave, he was simply a gentle man who was kind to all.

They were greeted warmly by the host when they arrived. She looked like she was in her early twenties, much like most of the staff, which made sense as they were in a college town with Vassar College, Marist College, and the Culinary Institute all close by.

They were shown to their seats and a server promptly appeared with menus and the offer of a drink to get started. It was a rustic venue with exposed brick and wooden beams, exactly the kind of bar she would frequent. Elevated pub-fare with house-brewed beers and flights of mimosas, Celeste gave Prince a ten out of ten for his choice.

It seemed fitting to try the mimosa flight and Prince opted to join her.

"About earlier," she said. "I don't know when the right time is to talk about this stuff ... But I just want you to know that I like you and I don't want to ruin anything by ... you know."

"I know. I really like hanging out with you. We'll figure it out." He leaned over and squeezed her hand to reassure her.

She felt shy and wondered if she should stop this conversation immediately. *May as well get this over with now,* she told herself. "I've ... I've rushed before, and I've been hurt. And I don't really want to go through that again."

Prince didn't let go of her hand or pull his gaze away. He stared deeply into her eyes. "No pressure."

And she was at it again, words spewing from her mouth without thought. "And then there is the flip side, what if I want to but feel like I'll be judged. I mean, you wouldn't feel guilty, right?" She didn't give Prince a chance to respond. "It's the twenty-first century and women still have this pressure." She gestured with her free hand as if weighing up a decision, "Should we, shouldn't we?"

Prince was silent and she took this to mean he was having his own conversation in his head about how this woman was all over the place and questioning why he was on this date with her. "I'm sorry. I do this – it's light-hearted one minute and the next thing you know you're knee deep into a philosophical conversation you didn't know you were getting into."

"Did you forget I studied philosophy? We could get much deeper if you'd like," Prince offered to show he didn't mind. The server couldn't have had better timing as he returned at that moment with their drinks order.

While they both thanked the server and referred to their menus again to remember the flavours the flight offered, Celeste was chastising herself. *He's lying. You're boring. And frigid. This conversation is a good way to ruin the mood.*

Celeste straightened her back and decided to change the subject. *Enough is enough.* "Which one are you going for first?" She asked in reference to the mimosa choices that lay before them.

"Left to right, I think", Prince responded.

"Practical. I like it."

Sipping on mimosas they studied the large menu that Celeste wanted to hide behind earlier.

"How about bang-bang cauliflower to start?" Prince asked. Celeste made a face that suggested she was not at all interested. "Have you tried it?"

Celeste had a unique pallet and while she loved anything spicy, at times you could hand her the children's menu and she'd fit right in. She was wary of vegetables and avoided them where possible.

"Come on, they're deep fried and covered in sauce," Prince encouraged.

"Please, don't let me stop you," she smiled, hoping he wasn't judging her.

"Okay, maybe I can get you to try just one," he replied.

"Maybe," she grinned back and meant it.

After a few short minutes, the waiter reappeared and took their order. Fish and chips for Prince and a cheeseburger and fries for Celeste.

Prince looked over at Celeste and their eyes held for a moment. She felt comfortable under his gaze and she wasn't sure why that frightened her more than feeling uncomfortable.

Prince broke the silence with a question, "If you could go anywhere right now, where would it be?"

"Quebec City," she replied without hesitation.

"That didn't take a lot of thought," Prince said.

"It's been on my list forever. I almost got there once, when I was visiting Toronto but I missed my ride and alas." She shrugged her shoulders, "I missed my chance."

Prince's eyes darted, looking like he was doing a calculation in his head. "It's only about a nine-hour drive, you know."

She did not know and waited for him to continue.

"We could take a road trip sometime," he suggested.

"I would love that! I mean, I'd have to get a few days off work, but I'm sure that won't be a problem." Celeste was beaming at the thought of not only going to the French Canadian city but accompanied by Prince.

"Let's plan it then. We'll figure out dates and go."

They talked about what time of year would be the best time of year, landing on November. It would be cooler but less tourists and they agreed it would feel like they had the city more to themselves.

Celeste couldn't believe they were making plans for November. *Is he serious?* She wondered. *Would he really still be around then?* Her inner voice questioned. *Why would he still be around then?* Her insecurity crept around her mind.

Prince interrupted her by asking, "November is still quite a while away though, how about another getaway sometime sooner?"

"I know you're not a huge fan of the beach, but what are the chances of getting you to another one for a couple of days? Maybe a trip out to the Hamptons?"

Prince screwed up his face and instead of fearing she had said the wrong thing like she usually instinctively would, she laughed and implied he was too good for the Hamptons, "My apologies, should I have said Lake Como in Italy instead?"

He laughed at her joke and replied, "We can go to the Hamptons if you'd like, but personally I'd rather take you to Rehoboth Beach in Delaware." She'd never heard of it but trusted his opinion, and quite frankly would go almost anywhere he suggested right now.

"I trust your judgement," she extended as the waiter appeared and placed their food in front of them.

There was silence between them as they unrolled napkins and took out knives and forks. She was feeling giddy with all this talk of holiday planning. She was allowing herself to fall into the deep end at this moment and would plan a trip for next year if he asked. *Maybe the mimosas are going to my head?*

She didn't realise how hungry she was until she could smell the aromas of the bounty that had been placed in front of her. She was still not used to the size of the portions in the USA.

They chatted over lunch, dipping fries into ketchup and drinking craft beers they had ordered after finishing off their mimosa flights.

Their conversation flowed just like it had been since they first met. They talked a lot more about travel destinations, favourite memories, worst airline stories, best food in which country, nicest people, best tours, favourite bars and must-see cities. They were animated as they shared their tales and opinions and shared an excitement about adventures yet to be had.

As they popped the last of the fries into their mouths, Prince circled back on their conversation about a beach getaway. "So how about next weekend then?"

"Next weekend?" Celeste wasn't sure what he meant.

"Rehoboth!"

Her eyes smiled before her mouth and she said, "Works for me." She wanted to keep her cool and keep it casual. She didn't want to read into it, but had anyone been listening into their conversation, they too could have been mistaken for thinking this was a long-term couple planning a trip like they would to the grocery store.

"Great!" Prince said, "If you can finish work early, I can pick you up around two o'clock and we can try to beat some of the traffic."

"Perfect," she said.

"Perfect," he replied.

And they both meant it in more ways than just their itinerary.

Celeste leaned back in her chair and placed her hand on her stomach. Prince mirrored her, "Tell me about it."

"Thanks for bringing me here. This was delicious and I feel absolutely stuffed." She rubbed her stomach again and let out a deep and happy sigh. "It's been a great day."

"It's not over yet, we still have to drive home," he reminded her.

It would take them around two hours to get back to Manhattan. She wondered if he wanted to stay for dinner. And whether that would lead to him staying over.

"I'll let you pick the music on the way back," he offered. "Seeing you let me pick on the way up."

"It's only fair, the driver gets first choice." She had enjoyed his music taste, and while they liked a lot of the same bands, he had a wider variety of genres that were new to her. "As long as you promise not to judge my choices."

It was a double-edged comment. As she said the words, she meant the music but realised it was a question she had wanted to ask all day.

Prince stood up from the table and held out a hand to help her up. He didn't take the comment in any other way other than how it was presented, "Your taste in music is just fine. You picked great songs when we were coming back from Jones Beach."

It made her smile to think how much she was in her head, a million thoughts a minute, meanwhile Prince is simply living in this moment. She decided to join him.

Chapter 11: *Conjured Confessions*

Celeste was sitting on the small grey sofa she had purchased from Wayfair when she had finally found her own apartment to move into. While it wasn't the most luxurious, it was comfortable enough and was the perfect size for her studio. She had made a mental note that if she signed another lease, the commitment to staying in her apartment meant she could splurge on the kind of sofa she saw at Roche Bobois. She would often visit the store that was barely ten minutes from her apartment and pretend she could afford anything in there. That meant she would allow herself to buy a close knock off from somewhere more affordable.

Celeste was frugal and watched how she spent her money. Every penny spent that was not spent on travel or shows was scrutinised. When pulling out her credit card, there needed to be solid rationale behind it.

She had been living in her apartment for almost a year now. Before her arrival in New York City, she had searched Airbnb for the appropriate accommodation that would support her budget. She found the perfect place to lay her head at night in Astoria, Queens.

It was a great neighbourhood that was well known for being the most diverse not only in New York City, but possibly the planet. Over 100 different languages are spoken and a walk down one of the streets or avenues could make you believe you were in another country if you closed your eyes. Back in the early 1800s, wealthy Manhattanites built mansions in the area and some of these grand buildings still stood today.

In a post-war apartment building, Celeste rented a room from a woman not much older than herself who occupied the second bedroom. It was her home, and she subsidised her rent by subletting her spare room, usually to short-term travellers coming through, just like Celeste. It was a common practice in one of the most expensive cities in the world.

Her landlord was chatty and quick to share anything and everything about herself. While Celeste was grateful she had found a roommate who was not a serial killer, she desperately missed having her own space.

Like most apartments in New York City, her new temporary home didn't have a washer/dryer. It was a luxury that Celeste didn't think of until she didn't have it. She now realised how lucky she was to have the convenience of the in-home appliance and begrudged having to take her laundry to the local laundromat.

You take for granted the carefree life you live until it's interrupted. Like when you realise you have run out of underwear and now need to sling on period knickers and trudge a block, or sometimes more depending on what neighbourhood you lived in, to wash and wait. These days she sometimes took the liberty of dropping off her laundry and letting someone else take care of it, but it's a luxury she could only justify on the odd occasion.

Celeste loved living in Astoria and keenly took in the architecture and the diversity. However, her dream was to live in Manhattan. She was lucky to only view a handful of apartments before she found the one she lived in today. She had heard of stories of people looking at 20, 30, 40 or more. So, when she found the almost-perfect-but-didn't-have-a-washer/dryer-just-like-everyone-else, she grabbed the lease with both hands.

Celeste was getting ready for her virtual session with Nya today. She had worked from home, and it was more convenient to have a video session than leave work early to make an in-person appointment on time.

Celeste picked up the fluffy grey cushion she had bought at Raymour and Flannigan after she had spent a considerable amount of time looking at sofas there. She had felt bad for taking up the associate's time without a large purchase to take a commission from. So rather than leave empty-handed, she bought two overpriced cushions instead. She chided herself for being so financially fiscal on one hand, yet on the other, her desire to be liked apparently spilled over to sales assistants at the expense of her bank balance. She placed the comfortable cushion on her chest as she wrapped her arms around it, almost as a protective shield to support her through her therapy.

Nya smiled at her through the screen, "So how have things been going?"

"Great! Not too much to report, I don't think." Although there always was. Even in those sessions that start out with 'nothing too much to report' she always ended up talking about something that had been hidden in the back of her mind, waiting for its moment to present. "I saw Abigail and her new boyfriend."

"Another one?" Nya asked. *She is good at her job.* Celeste often wondered how she remembered not only her clients' issues, but their wider circle of family and friends too. And she never appeared to be taking too many notes during their time together. Celeste assumed she must transcribe after their sessions and review before their next, but she still found it impressive that she could recall so much of Celeste's life.

"He seems sweet. And apparently, she is going to marry this one." She filled Nya in on her catch up with Abigail and Alexander, how happy

Abigail seemed and how life seemed easier for her than the rest of everyone else around her.

"Does wealth really make life that much simpler?" she pondered to Nya.

"I think Abigail probably has her own things to talk about with her therapist and as we've talked about before, her appearance on the outside isn't always what is happening on the inside," Celeste knew Nya was right.

While Abigail appeared to have it all, Celeste also knew people had a certain impression of her based on her outward facing persona.

Celeste also had personalities that shone and others that hid deeper down. While Celeste was never one to pretend to be someone she is not, the side most people saw was the strong and independent version she clung to with all her might. While she attacked herself often in her own mind, she also told herself she was strong and brave and that was often the persona most people saw. Or maybe it was simply that she was often caring for others, they were too busy to look beyond their issues to realise Celeste had any of her own. Her strength in their weakness meant she wasn't afforded the opportunity to be seen beyond that.

Celeste mentioned her dinner with Abigail and Alexander, and how she felt some sort of way when Abigail had told Alexander that she usually dated shitty men.

"What sort of way was that?" Nya was poised.

"I know I choose shitty men. And sure, Abigail and I talk about that. But to hear her tell Alexander, who is basically a stranger to me, made me feel ..." Celeste was struggling to find the right words and Nya patiently waited.

Celeste knew she could be, and had to be, honest in front of Nya. "I mean, I really don't like it when Abigail makes it sound like I'm an idiot."

"Is that how it made you feel when she said you chose shitty men?"

Nya pressed.

Celeste paused for a moment to really consider how it made her feel. She knew she didn't always pick the greatest men who would take care of her heart, but she also didn't pick truly shitty men who intentionally set out to hurt her. And there was a difference between those types of men. Although maybe that in itself was enough to establish that Celeste needed to extend her boundaries beyond 'not as shitty' to 'not shitty at all'. She dove into this with Nya for the next few minutes before she brought the conversation around to Prince.

"Things have been going really well with Prince," Celeste told her, and she sounded excited to talk to Nya about it. "He just keeps getting better. I keep waiting for the other shoe to drop."

"Tell me why it's going so well," Nya asked.

Celeste spoke highly of how Prince went to so much trouble to make their last date special. She reminded Nya that she hadn't had a man go to so much effort in a very long time. She gushed about his desire to travel and how his enthusiasm for it matched her own, and that this was an important trait she sought out in a partner. Celeste was never one to shy away from travelling alone and had done so for many years, but she was excited that she may have found a friend who would accompany her along paths not yet taken.

"I can see us exploring so much of the world together, assuming he is a good travel buddy. I mean if there is one way to test a relationship, it's to go on a long-distance holiday with them," Celeste laughed, and Nya agreed.

She recalled their conversations about his desire to continue his education and his motivation to continue to grow as a person and better understand those around him. "He just seems like such a good person, you know?" Celeste gushed.

She felt like she could keep talking about Prince all day. "He seems like he is just a good guy. Like ..." she paused looking for the right words. "Like he doesn't need to be fixed."

Bingo. That was why she felt out of sorts. Here was a man who appeared to have his shit together and she didn't need to rescue him and that was why she felt like a fish out of water.

Nya was already one step ahead of her, "And how does it make you feel that he doesn't need your help, in the way you have been used to giving it?"

Celeste pondered her question and dug deep to understand her own thoughts. "Scared," She finally answered.

"Why?"

"Because if he doesn't need me, why would he want to be with me?" Celeste felt her eyes tingle as if tears might be trying to find their way out.

She shifted on her couch and leaned over to pick up her teal green Yeti cup from her coffee table. It had been gifted to her from a corporate vendor as she would never spend that kind of money on a reusable cup. Although she had to admit she loved it and maybe it was worth the money she didn't spend on it. She took a sip of water and pushed away the tears.

"Are you okay?" Nya asked, peering down the screen. "It's hard for me to tell sometimes when we don't see each other in person."

"I'm okay," Celeste put her cup down and shook out her arms as if to loosen up. "Let me open the window, it's a little warm in here." She stood up and realised the window was already open and turned her small tabletop fan on instead.

Plonking herself back down on the couch, she continued, "I think he's perfect and it's freaking me out a bit. Or a lot. He can't be perfect, right?" Nya shook her head in agreement. "But he just seems to be. Or maybe he's just perfect for me."

"I think that is a good way to view it," Nya said. "No one is perfect, and I don't want you to categorise him as a perfect man. Because I also think that by using that language, it could be an intentional act of self-sabotaging."

"What do you mean?" Celeste knew she was possibly asking for some tough love answers.

"Based on how well I know you, you build your potential partners up in your head to a standard that even the best of us would find hard to achieve. And I think it's your way of protecting yourself. You set an unachievable goal because subconsciously you know they can't achieve it. So, when they let you down, you walk away with a broken heart but a mind that gets to say, 'I knew it'. Does that resonate with you?"

It was moments like this that made Celeste want to shout from her window that everyone should get therapy. Nya was spot on, but now Celeste needed to actively work on building spotters in her brain for this kind of behaviour. When she reflected on the men she had dated and the relationships she'd had, it was exactly how she viewed them. It wasn't that she didn't deserve someone to strive to be their best version for her, but she did explicitly choose men who would never be able to achieve that.

She chose men who required help managing their emotions, support in the form of a person who would shoulder their emotional baggage for them rather than have them resolve their issues due to the weight of their own load. She took their pain for them, and then when they were able to walk through their life seemingly indifferent to her self-destruction, without so much as a nod of acknowledgement to what she was carrying on their behalf, she blamed them for not being better men.

She positioned herself as the woman they needed in their life, through the dance of giving them what they wanted her to be. She gave wholeheartedly, and they took willingly.

But Prince seemed different. He seemed to see her and she didn't know how to handle that. So, she had continued to play the role she had always played and had dug deep into her toolbox of tricks when maybe he wasn't looking for someone trying to pull a rabbit out of a hat.

"I guess that explains the little game I was playing on our last date," Celeste offered.

"What game was that?"

"We haven't had sex yet, and I want to make sure when we do, it's the right time," Celeste shared.

"And how do you feel about that?" Nya asked.

"It's not that I don't want to, but I just don't want to move too fast," Celeste said matter-of-factly.

But Nya knew her too well and pressed on, "But?"

"Well why should we have to wait, you know?" Celeste felt a fire in her belly. "It's just ridiculous that in this day and age, women are still expected to be, well, almost sexless at the start of a relationship."

"Sexless is one way of positioning it," Nya added.

"Maybe not sexless, although I'm sure that's how they want to imagine us before we met them," Celeste knew she was making sweeping statements about men, maybe rightly so. She continued, "We are expected to act like sex is a gift designed especially for men's needs, and certainly not for ours. That when we bestow this gift upon him, we are giving a part of ourselves to him. And to make matters worse," she forged on, "it's also as if every time we give this gift, we give a little piece of ourselves away. Meaning the more I give, the less of me exists."

Nya agreed, as much as women had carved a path towards greater respect and equality, they still had a long way to go. And that came from both teaching men to be better and women understanding themselves more.

Celeste and Nya agreed on a lot, and it was what created a haven of trust between the two of them. It's always important that a therapist understands you culturally and for Celeste it was critical that she always connected on the same values and ideologies.

But instead of saying she agreed, Nya asked a question in return, "Why do you say you feel like you are giving away a piece of you? Tell me more about how that sentence makes you feel."

Celeste paused and considered her feelings. She was mad at the thought of the continued fight for women's rights, and she needed to calm down and come off the protestor podium for a moment to identify what was going on for her. "I think it's a couple of things," she finally said.

Nya waited patiently.

"Women do have needs and desires and that should be acknowledged and the same grace given to women as it to men. But I'm preaching to the choir here. So, I guess the other reason I feel so mad about it is because ..." She paused again. While she knew she was able to say whatever was on her mind, she wasn't always comfortable admitting a hard truth. "I guess with all this talk of my self-worth and attachment to being liked, blah, blah, blah ..." Celeste minimised what she was saying to force the pit of her stomach to stop feeling full of dread.

Nya continued to patiently wait.

"I really like him. I don't want to mess this up and I'm having a hard time trying to work out whether I'm not having sex with him right away because I'm trying to get him to want me more, or because I know if I have sex with him and then it doesn't work out, the damage will be far greater this time."

This intrigued Nya, "How do you mean?"

"I think what I'm recognising is that this deeper connection with Prince is making me feel more exposed than I ever have done. And can I really trust him not to hurt me? If this doesn't work out, I feel like I may just double down on my bad habits because the pain will be too much to bear. I may as well keep going out with dickheads because at least

I know what I'm getting myself in for," she was being one hundred percent honest. And saying it out loud was almost as scary as feeling it.

"We are going away for the weekend, and I don't know what to do." They had planned the trip to Rehoboth Beach that they had talked about upstate and would be staying in a small Airbnb a few blocks from the ocean.

"I don't think you need to make that decision now," Nya said. "And between now and then, I want you to focus on the vulnerability this relationship is making you feel." Nya always gave her homework to do, "And I want you to think about why you would feel so broken if this was to not work out."

"Will do," Celeste promised. "One thing I am becoming more aware of, I am less inclined to use sex as a tool or at least the promise of sex to win a man," Celeste proudly stated.

"Could you explain further?" Nya questioned.

"I think I'm now seeing that I used sex as a way to connect with the men I dated, but not in a responsible way. I think I thought that if I was desirable, that was a big part of the puzzle of getting him to stick around."

"A common misconception," Nya laughed.

"I don't think I'm ready to admit outside of our sessions that maybe I didn't know myself well enough. It never occurred to me that I continued the game of the chase well into my relationships. That if I kept up the persona he hungered for at the start, he would never want to leave. Why would he if he had it all at home ..." She laughed at her own naivety.

"I don't think we've really spoken too much about this in the past, so I'm interested to know how you're processing this and what you think it means," Nya asked.

"It's another act, right? Another tool. I don't think I told you about the guy I met on my Caribbean trip, did I?"

Nya smiled and seemed to prepare herself. She took a sip of her water and placed it back down in front of her on what Celeste assumed was the coffee table that her laptop was also positioned on, then she sat back in her chair awaiting the tale to be told.

Chapter 12: *The Forbidden Fruit*

"Alright, tell me about this guy," Nya seemed to get comfortable in her seat as if waiting for the show to commence. *I mean, it's a story alright,* Celeste thought. *I'm sure we'll have a lot to dissect after you've heard it.*

With mixed emotions, Celeste recalled it vividly.

***

She sipped her Hard Rock Cafe cocktail that looked like a child's drink in the colour of blue, the lemon floating on top attached to a twisted bamboo stick the only cause for thinking it may indeed be intended for adults.

Summer was approaching the Northern Hemisphere, but Celeste was impatient and couldn't wait. She was sick of her coats and scarves and had taken herself away on a beach holiday to the Dominican Republic to bask in the sun she so desperately missed.

Celeste had chosen the Hard Rock Resort as it was her guilty pleasure. While it may have been kitschy for some, she loved the loud rock and roll that blasted over the speakers when dining in their restaurants and the memorabilia she revelled in. It was her first time in one of their resorts and she was not disappointed that their rock theme stayed true throughout their vast compound, right down to the musical note embroidered on the fluffy pillows she fell into each night of her stay.

She stood alone at the beachside bar, drink in hand while she watched the ocean waves crash before her. It was early evening, and the tide was coming in. Beach chairs and towels that had been left unattended were at the mercy of the incoming waves and she watched a gentleman try to gather a stranger's belongings, so they didn't lose them to the Caribbean Ocean. By the time the group had returned to retrieve their beach essentials they were unaware of the kindness the stranger had bestowed upon them, as they casually packed up and left.

Journeys' 'Don't Stop Believing' was blasting out of small but effective speakers scattered around the bar and the beach that served only its patrons at that time. As she sang along to every lyric, Celeste imagined herself in a movie scene being played out on the big screen. She did this frequently during times she was alone. Assessing her surroundings and wondering what it would look like if her life story was being told to an audience. She had an active imagination.

Celeste checked her phone for a weather update, which was still set to Celsius as she was far from comfortable using the variation of the imperial system in the States. still used. It had cooled from its earlier thirty-four degrees Celsius, or ninety-eight Fahrenheit, and was a comfortable twenty-four degrees Celsius with a breeze. There was still humidity in the air. Celeste couldn't feel it on her sun kissed body, but she could in her hair that was becoming increasingly frizzy. She cared less than if she was at home. She was away and didn't have anyone to impress, at least that's what she told herself as she scanned the sun worshipers surrounding her. There were the usual holiday makers, a few elderly couples obviously retired and now living their best lives. You know the ones, who dance when no one else is because age has taught them life is too short to care what the rest of us think. There were the couples looking for a romantic getaway, some so close together they were almost one and you could tell they were still fresh into their relationship but also hoped that they were years in and still felt that way, meaning the dream existed. Some couples laughed comfortably with warm familiarity while sipping cocktails, and others stealing glances as they made friends with other couples. There was the group of twenty-something-year-olds with perfect eyebrows, buff bodies, designer shades and using the most recent iPhones. They fervently tapped away on their screens only to be interrupted to take a selfie or group snap to be immediately posted to Instagram. There was a large group of forty-something-year-olds who had either left their children with grandparents or at the resort day care and were taking shots as if they were twenty-one again. The girlfriend groups, the boy holiday groups; everyone had had too much sun, and the drinks were going down in a fashion that only applies on holiday. Drinks that are overpriced but worth every cent as you take in the view and forget about life for a while.

As Celeste continued to scan the crowd, soaking in the music, laughter, and serenity brought on by a few holiday drinks, she spotted him—a man, much like herself, sitting alone with his drink, watching the waves.

He wasn't much taller than Celeste, but his muscular arms filled his fitted black shirt. *Why a black shirt in this heat*, Celeste mused? She wondered how hard he worked out to maintain his physique. Gym junkies were not her type, at least not on the mainland. He had thick black hair that looked like it was due for a cut and a full beard that he carried well. He wore Ray-Bans, the kind that reflect your image when you try to look into his eyes. His smile was wide and welcoming as she watched him thank the waitress, dressed in a coral-coloured bikini top that emphasised her lovely large and natural breasts and a short spandex skirt, for picking up his empty cup.

As if he could feel her stare upon him, he turned his head to meet her eyes.

Celeste smiled and briefly looked away, before looking back again. He raised his glass as if to say cheers and she returned the gesture.

They both drank from their cups and a moment later, he was walking towards her.

"Hi," he said in a deep voice that had an accent Celeste couldn't quite pick. "How is your night so far?" He continued.

"Great," she flashed him her brightest smile that she hoped made her eyes sparkle. "Doesn't get much better than this." She turned to take in the view once more and he did the same.

They looked back at each other, and he reached out his hand, "Jay," he offered as she took his hand in hers.

He had large hands that easily wrapped around hers and she replied, "Celeste."

"What brings you to Punta Cana?"

Celeste always wanted to make up a story to tell strangers when she was travelling alone but honesty always got the better of her. "Just a quick holiday to escape the city. I'm from New York." He looked at her the way most people do when she delivers that line with an English accent. "Originally from London, but I moved there about six months ago."

"Wow, on your own?" It was usually the first question people asked when they learned of her move.

"Yes."

"That's brave." *There it is*, she laughed in her own head at the predictability of the accolade.

She always wondered why people thought moving overseas was brave. She had spent her youth travelling the world and had crossed many oceans. She took her rite of passage, applying for her working holiday visa to live in both Australia and New Zealand. She had backpacked throughout the countries, taking fruit picking jobs in remote locations. Bartending jobs in rowdy pubs and waitressing jobs she had no business doing. To her, moving to New York was a natural step when the opportunity arose. She was more worried about what she might be missing out on if she didn't go, rather than what she might be missing out on if she had settled down in London.

Celeste wondered if he called her brave because it seemed an appropriate response to offer to a woman and wondered if he would have made the same comment if she were a man. Her eyes wandered over him and she decided at that moment that she didn't care.

"And you?" Celeste turned the conversation back to Jay. People always liked to talk about themselves, unwittingly or not.

"Originally, I'm from Colombia, but I moved with my family to Philadelphia when I was twenty. The accent stuck," he said with pride.

Celeste found it was easy to befriend other immigrants as they usually bonded over not dissimilar stories of trying to assimilate into American culture. Or more often than that, stories of why they refuse to assimilate.

"And you're here because?"

"I'm actually working for the Hard Rock Café. I'm here for the week."

"Oh, what do you do?" She had always wanted to work for the establishment, romanticising a rock n' roll lifestyle that surely had to accompany even an administration role.

"Management," was all he offered, and she immediately wondered if he was telling her a mistruth. Or why he didn't want to share more about what his responsibilities were. She looked at the ring finger on his left hand instinctively and it was bare. *Doesn't mean anything*, she warned herself. *Rings come off.* But she had been given no reason to doubt him, even if it was only minutes ago they met, she decided to ignore any forewarnings, real or not.

"Do you get one of the fancier suites or have they got you in with the rest of us?"

He laughed, "It's not a suite but I've got nothing to complain about." He took a sip of his drink and looked at her over his cup, "Are you staying here?"

"I am," she answered as she felt a shiver run through her that was telling of her desires. She wondered if he could see it written on her face. "It's my guilty pleasure. And the pools looked amazing!"

"They're impressive," Jay agreed.

I bet you're impressive, Celeste thought and for a second wondered if she'd said it out loud. The cocktails, heat and anticipation of where this night might lead had made her feel a little lightheaded and somewhat confident.

Jay continued, "Want to look around the hotel? I've got insider access," he teased. She wasn't sure if arrogance lingered in the air, but she let it blow away with the breeze.

A million thoughts started flying through her head. *What did this mean, where will this lead, what does he want from me? Philadelphia isn't too far from me. Could we continue whatever this is back in the States?*

Please, you won't even go to Jersey, she mocked herself. *This will never work.* She always did this. She took herself on a journey within seconds of an initial thought that was far beyond what most can comprehend in a lifetime.

Stop it, she chastised herself. *Take this for what it is. You're on holiday, have fun. No strings. Don't expect anything.* She downed the last of her drink in one fell swoop, placed it on the table and said, "Let's do it."

They had asked for their respective checks and farewelled the busty waitress, who didn't bat an eye that these strangers were leaving together. Celeste wondered how many times she had watched this exact scene play out.

They made their way out of the beach bar along the blue plastic panels that acted as a footpath placed upon the sand towards the boardwalk. They reached the busy thoroughfare full of tourists walking to their hotels or the next bar and walked directly across to the grounds of the hotel.

They made their way to a bar indoors and Celeste excused herself to use the bathroom. She didn't really need to go, but she did need to view the state of her hair. Suddenly, she cared.

She had worn a green dress that showed off her small waist and fell in a feminine way. It was low cut and could be worn to reveal a little more. Celeste bent over and adjusted her breasts to fill the cups of her bra. As she flung her hair back, upon standing up she reviewed herself in the mirror. And once again, used her hands to push her cleavage higher.

My, my, don't we look like a tramp, she thought to herself. *Don't be ridiculous,* she cursed herself. If this was trampy, she'd love to know what they called the waitress who had been serving her moments earlier. *Don't judge other women,* she quickly told herself off.

They don't call them assets for nothing, she reminded herself. Quickly thinking he can go fuck himself if he didn't appreciate what she had to offer. The thought crossed her mind that she had just argued with her own self, but she quickly pushed it aside.

This too was not uncommon for Celeste. She would strive to be liked by a man and in the same breath be angry at said man for admiring what she had changed about herself for his pleasure.

She pulled a bottle of argon oil out of her beach bag that she had thankfully thrown in before leaving her hotel room. Pumping several drops onto her hand, she ran the oil through her hair to tame it as best she could. *It will have to do,* she told herself. She dabbed some face powder under her eyes, sure it hadn't made a difference but gave her a false sense of concealment. She always carried it with her for these just-in-case moments. And then applied some lip gloss.

She took one final look at herself in the bathroom mirror before thinking there was no going back now.

Celeste crossed the floor to the stylish bar full of music memorabilia. She spotted shoes worn by Chris Cornell of Soundgarden in a glass display and felt a pang of sadness that he had died too young.

She saw that Jay had found a table under an outfit previously worn by Dua Lipa. *Can't compete with her*, she thought. There were two champagne glasses on the table, filled with a drink that had bubbles but was a tinge of purple. He pushed one towards Celeste and picked up the other.

"What is this?" She didn't care, her mouth had become dry, and she badly needed a drink.

She saw the way Jay glanced over her body. As she sipped her drink and relieved her nerves with alcohol, she also let her eyes take in his body. She wondered what he looked like without a shirt on.

As if reading his mind, he asked "Do you want to walk with these?" indicating they take their drinks and make a move.

They strolled through the hotel and Celeste took in the musical décor and felt happy to be surrounded by items that belonged to some of her icons.

They bar hopped throughout the hotel and drank cocktails that were a multitude of colours, some in flames and others almost boring to look at but were saved by the eclectic glasses they were served in.

She was getting drunk. So was he.

"We should get food," she was sure she had said at some point. But after a few drinks the thought had passed.

"So how about this hotel?" Jay asked.

"I think we've seen it all now, haven't we?" She wondered if he would understand what she was trying to say. He did.

"Want to check out the rooms?" he invited.

Celeste had enough alcohol in her to feel brave enough to lean in and kiss him. It was a calculated move, after all, he had been putting his hands on her waist and his arms around her shoulders all night as the drinks wore on.

From that moment it felt like a whirlwind. They haphazardly made their way to the elevators and stepped inside one that was emblazoned with the words *Love in an Elevator*, lyrics to Aerosmith's song.

They kissed as it ascended to a floor high in the sky and tumbled out as the doors opened.

He took her hand and led her down the hallway to his room, his room keycard at the ready.

As he held the card to the door, she watched the light go green and heard the familiar noise of permission to enter. *Permission to enter.*

"Is that so?" Jay replied seductively.

Celeste had said *permission to enter* out loud. She wasn't sure if she meant to. She did know she was trying to be sexy in her drunken state; she was aware she was trying to impress him. Was this who she wanted him to think she was? She knew it was a part of who she was, she was playful and sexy, but she questioned if she was doing this for him.

Her thoughts were pushed aside with the swing of the door opening.

The room was large and spacious, with funky rock designs on the wall and rockstar lighting.

She stuck her head in the bathroom door as they were passing it.

"A jacuzzi!" she exclaimed.

"Maybe later," Jay grabbed her hand, and they continued into the hotel room.

Jay fell on his back on the king-sized bed and Celeste straddled him. As she leant down to kiss him, she again noticed the musical note embroidered on the pillow. *I feel like a rockstar,* she thought. *Or a groupie.* She didn't care at that point.

That night Celeste rocked his world. She behaved like a groupie in every sense and found herself enjoying every second of it.

He told her how much he loved her body, and it reassured her she was doing the right thing.

He seemed to be really into her, and this pleased her no end. *Could this be something?* She wondered in her haze.

I mean, this was the way to win a man after all. Sex sells and she was layering on the extras to get the contract signed.

He had fallen asleep and left Celeste alone with her thoughts. The voices were mocking her. *You're all in now, aren't you? You're screwed.*

She looked around the room and wondered if there were cameras anywhere. A stupid thought but you never know these days. *What would someone say if it had been filmed? Good effort? Hilarious to watch?*

Stop it, she chided. She looked over at Jay sleeping peacefully. It still surprised her at how quickly men fell asleep after sex. Even after the times when you'd done all the work, you'd think they'd run a marathon.

She too was tired, but her brain was in overdrive. She rarely had one-night stands, in fact she could only really recall one true one-night stand in her past. Usually, she took a full health history and family background check on the men she had even been casually involved with. It was just what she did naturally through her curiosity and line of questioning, and without knowing it they had always obliged.

She lay there wondering what he would think of her. Whether it mattered? Whether she would see him again? Whether she wanted to see him again?

Truth be told he wasn't really her type. Physical features aside he seemed like a man content with having a trophy on his arm in lieu of a good conversation. He had been fun and had served a purpose and yet that feeling of needing reassurance lurked.

You're just another girl on a different night, she told herself. *Maybe this was a mistake. Men don't get involved with their one-night stands. You'll never meet his family now.*

She wondered why she even wanted to meet his family.

She watched him sleeping, almost snoring. Oh god, don't let him be a snorer, she thought.

He woke up with a start and looked at her watching him.

"What time is it?" he asked.

"Late," she replied.

He closed his eyes, and she nestled into the nook of his arm, resting her hands on his chest.

You're pathetic, she thought to herself as she cuddled up to him, enjoying a feeling of intimacy he didn't.

When they woke the next morning, they took a shower together and enjoyed each other's bodies one last time.

Jay ordered room service, and they ate breakfast in bed together. He was due to fly out later that afternoon, so they lay together and watched a movie.

Jay was a gentleman. He wasn't going to be her gentleman, and she was under no illusion that this would become a grand story to tell at their wedding.

The cold light of day and a hangover eased by bacon, eggs and a can of coke had calmed her restless mind, however, every now and then the thought entered her head, *what could this be?* as she looked at his handsome face.

She was glad that she had been right enough in her senses that he was a decent guy. He wasn't an asshole and that made her feel better about her decisions the night before.

They politely exchanged phone numbers when it was time for Celeste to leave, and they thanked each other for a fun night.

It wasn't the last time they were in touch, but it was the last time they saw each other. Their text talk had dissipated quickly as she wasn't interested in sexting, and he wasn't interested in much else. *At least he messaged,* she had thought to herself at the time. She disliked that she felt let down after she offered herself up.She had a feeling of emptiness she couldn't explain and wanted to forgive herself for the mistake she felt she had made.

She was desperate to stop the voices in her head that kept asking her why she would choose a man who was wearing a shirt made of red flags when she met him.

***

"That's our time today," Nya wrapped up as Celeste had gone over their allocated forty-five minutes. It didn't happen often. Nya was a master at ending sessions on time without making you feel like she was cutting you off and left hanging mid-emotion. "Let's lock in our next session," she said as they both opened their calendars to find time.

"I'm going to be at a conference next week, so do you mind if we make our next session in two weeks instead?" Nya asked.

"No worries." Celeste gave some dates and times that she was available, and they confirmed their next appointment.

"And of course if you do need me urgently, please feel free to send me a message and we can see what we can work out," Nya reassured her.

Chapter 13: *A Mad Hatter's Tea Party*

Nya was at the American Counseling Association Annual Conference and Expo. She enjoyed attending conferences that expanded her knowledge and reinforced her career choice.

But she particularly enjoyed this one and she came every year. It gave her a chance to see old colleagues and friends that she otherwise wouldn't due to competing schedules and distant zip codes.

The conference schedule was comprehensive, and she was excited to hear about what was up and coming in mental health. While she kept up to date with most advancements, life still got in the way even for the attentive therapists, and it was the perfect opportunity to give undivided attention to her craft.

As she looked around the ballroom of the hotel that was hosting the convention, she recognised a couple of friends standing at the bar.

It always amused her to watch her colleagues taking advantage of the open bar which was often followed by loose lips. Therapists are not immune to their own vices and troubles and while a layperson may think they all have their shit together, one might tender a bet that often, a therapist is the last person to take their own advice.

One of the most therapeutic outlets, as far as Nya was concerned, was hearing patient stories from her colleagues that matched her own. They were able to talk about how it made them feel, sometimes shed a tear and other times laugh. It wasn't unsurprising to her to meet other therapists that shared her penchant for dark humour. It's a way to cope in the chaos. Dark humour has been associated with high levels of intelligence when used appropriately and some studies have shown that those who use dark humour tend to be less aggressive than those who do not. It's a complex topic that fascinates Nya who has read many psychological theories.

Being the lifeline to another human being is rewarding, but the demands of living with the secrets of hundreds of people takes its toll on you and can leave you seeking comfort from those who understand. That's why it's important that a therapist has their own therapist.

Nya knew better than to expect her loved ones to empathise with her, and the most she would accept was sympathy. Her years of training and her own sessions with her therapist taught her that it's not their job to feel your pain, but the acknowledgement was enough.

So, these conventions gave people like her a safe space to come together and empathise with one another. Mostly because they were already feeling a similar pain and could articulate where it hurt.

As much as they loved their jobs and helped their clients meander through this thing called life, therapists are people too, with their own pasts, their own issues and their own neurosis to work through. So, pile on top of that someone else's past, issues and neurosis and it's no wonder some of these conventions turn into frat parties. It was not uncommon to see grown professionals at these events, who spend a lot of time at the open bar, revert to carefree teenagers with the world at their feet.

This year it was being held in Toronto. Nya was thrilled at the opportunity to visit the Canadian city that she likened to a friendlier, albeit smaller, Manhattan. It has been many years since she had laid her eyes on Lake Ontario and she had gleefully sat along the harbour front drinking a coffee on her first day in the city. She had arrived two days early to spend time in the welcoming bustle of her streets and was a motivated tourist ready to get her steps in. Nya had visited the CN Tower and the Aga Khan Museum, joined a graffiti art walking tour and had wandered through St. Lawrence Market where she bought an assortment of cheeses. She planned a glutinous evening of devouring every morsel of cheese, along with a nice bottle of white she had picked up at a wine bar that sold locally produced wines. She planned to do so from the comfort of her king-sized hotel bed, with crisp white sheets and pillows, as she watched TV. The only time she ate in bed was when she was in a hotel room. She was sure she was not alone in that ritual.

She had fit as much as she could into her limited time and was now excited and ready for the expo to kick off.

She quickly scanned the large cardboard cutouts held by black easels that listed the schedule for the next two days. There were several items on the agenda. The keynote speaker opening the event was Susie Orbach: A feminist therapist and author, followed by a Q&A session. Nya was excited to be in the room with a peer she deeply respected and had learnt a great deal from. She had read most if not all her books that explored the relationship between feminism, body image, and social criticism. Nya had many clients that had benefited from the works she had digested and regurgitated over the years.

One of the sessions she was most interested in was the review of legislation regarding domestic violence, and particularly the impact on women. Her father's profession wasn't lost on her and over the years she had spent many hours with him in his office, drinking a cheeky port that he always had at the ready, discussing the inadequacies of our legal system and the direct impact it had on women and families. Men were also subjected to domestic violence of course, with one in nine experiencing some form of physical violence, however, the rate of violence against women was higher at one in four.

Nya was sure that if those rates were swapped around, we would be doing a lot more to reduce the rate of incidents. It was an uphill battle that women will likely continue to fight for a long time to come. Women have been fighting for equality for decades and while large strides have been made, they still had a long way to go.

Nya looked back over to the bar and saw her friends were still standing where she last saw them, but their circle of acquaintances had grown. She walked over to the bar to say hello and introduce herself to the two women who had joined. Everyone had glasses of sparkling wine in their hand, but Nya na asked for a glass of red instead.

She warmly hugged her two friends. Truth be told they were probably more suited to the acquaintance category than friends, but they always spent most of their time together at this convention and this was their fifth year sharing stories. A familiar face feels more like a friend when one is attending an event alone.

Jillian was around Nya's age and lived in San Francisco, while Nya estimated Julie must be at least twenty years older than her and was from South Carolina.

Nya had correctly guessed that Jillian shared her political views. The first year they met and forged their convention friendship, they found themselves charging drinks to their rooms while sitting at the pool bar after the first day of the event. Nya had brought up the upcoming election and it wasn't long before they were both complaining about the state of democracy and the lack of options to choose from.

Nya wasn't sure what Julie's political persuasion was. The USA had become a hot pot of this side or that and while it was not always the right assumption, Nya often found herself deliberately avoiding topics that could elicit such controversial conversations. For all she knew, Julie was a Bernie Bro who fought with her neighbours about their homes covered in obscene flags, the kind one would have assumed were once reserved for B-grade satire movies. Or maybe she was at the insurrection and is still claiming the election was stolen. Either way, she knew enough about Julie to know she was someone she enjoyed spending time with at these annual get togethers and she was happy to have this time in her life where she lived in a bubble with colleagues all seeking solutions to help those around them.

Nya knew she had work to do on herself when it came to her micro judgments of some people who crossed her path. She knew she gave one hundred percent to her clients, although she was also aware that almost all her clients likely sat on the same bench as she did. It was mostly due to the city that she lived in, the nature of her work and the fact that most of her clients were referred to her by other clients, that meant that they were all very similarly minded. But on the occasion where it had become evident a client had opposing opinions to her, if it wasn't a conflict of interest in how she cared for them, she was able to support them in a completely professional capacity.

Outside of work though, Nya knew she needed to apply more of her own advice to how she processed differing opinions. While she gave herself grace for being human, she also knew it was a topic that rotated on the agenda she set with her own therapist.

Jillian introduced Nya to Kelly from Austin and Chelsea from Kansas City. They shook hands and Nya said, "Sorry to interrupt your conversation."

Kelly said, "I was just saying I had a new client last week and she asked me whether she would ever find her fairy tale love?"

"Has that ever existed?" Chelsea said it in a tone while pitched as a question, one could argue was more of a statement that it did not.

"I'd have to say no, and I tell that to my clients," Julie interjected. Which made Nya want to learn more about what else Julie thought about relationships. Had it been lost on her that Julie mostly listened and gave Jillian and Nya the space to purge in her presence? She knew she was kind and thoughtful and had a wicked sense of humour, but somehow, they had truly avoided any of the big-ticket items that deepen a friendship.

Julie added, "The modern woman certainly doesn't need to be rescued anymore. Yet I am still surprised at the number of women who are still seeking it."

"Learned behaviour," the words slipped out of Nya's mouth without even thinking about it.

"However, I swear that while these women grapple with their own desire to be or not be rescued, so many of my female clients are still out there seeking to rescue someone else," Chelsea said.

"Ah, fixer-upper-syndrome," Kelly commented, as if it was a real-life diagnosis. The four women listening nodded their heads.

It was a common theme and often captioned as 'women who love too much'. In reality, 'women who didn't understand themselves enough' was a better definition.

"I've lost count of the number of times I've recommended my clients read *Codependent No More*," Nya offered.

There was a hum as all the therapists agreed in unison. It was a well-publicised book from 1992 that was still relevant today.

"The fact that we are still citing a book from 1992 says a lot," Kelly rolled her eyes as if to say she was tired that the actions of our society had not caught up with the research and recommendations on offer.

Lightening the mood, Jillian said, "Well we need to put out an APB on Prince Charming as I'm getting tired looking for him. I don't need to be rescued, but I wouldn't mind a good-looking man riding into my stable if you know what I mean."

The women laughed loudly with a shared appreciation of exactly what Jillian meant. Nya took the opportunity to share her own story. "Would you believe I have a client who, if a feminist trade school existed, would have graduated with honours, is now dating a man called Prince!"

The women laughed again, this time at the irony. While she was not breaking any confidentiality about Celeste's story, she was sure Celeste would also not have a problem with Nya speaking on the subject.

Nya continued, "But in all seriousness, his name was almost a gift in our sessions. It opened up this fairy tale conversation that we were just speaking of, and I have to say, even I feel like I've learnt from this experience. I think I had forgotten just how ridiculous most of the fairy tales we were told are."

"And toxic," Julie added.

"Yes!" Nya exclaimed. "I don't know that asking my clients to read and report back on Rapunzel is the golden ticket to unpacking their problems, but I have to say, it wouldn't surprise me if it was."

Nya considered some of her clients, past, present, and Celeste. She thought of the women who believed they could restore a man's sight through her own tears. And the depths she swam in after her tears became the waters she would merely continue to tread, exhausted in her choices.

"Maybe it could be a research project you can report back on at next year's conference," Jillian said as she turned to the bartender and pointed to her empty glass of bubbles with a smile.

Jillian joked but Nya wondered what the data showed about the impact fairy tales had on little girls, and little boys, and how they grew to see the world.

Her younger female client base continued to grow as quickly as any viral TikTok trend did. It was no coincidence. The journey of life and love these days is getting harder. It is getting harder to know fact from fiction. The magazines, the billboards, social media ... the crap we see and hear. Women are used as sacrificial lambs for brands and businesses to increase their market share and therefore shareholders bank balances; they are considered acceptable collateral damage, and no one was doing much to stop it. Until recently.

Several movements were taking place across the globe; women had started speaking up and men were being forced to be more accountable. This was progress, this was what was needed. And Nya praised every female and male feminist that weathered their shoes thin by marching in the streets and cracked their voices by shouting their demands.

However, Nya still saw the gaping void that corporations sat safely in, sacrificing their own sacrificial, usually white male, lamb to the masses that demanded justice. A gesture we all too readily accept as a victory. All the while policies or processes never really being updated within their systems to affect change. Maybe she was being cynical.

Nya, still lost in thought, said out loud, "We are practically Fairy Godmothers."

They all laughed as there was a lot of truth to what she said. "Now all we need are some magical powers," Jillian pointed out.

"Well, I could use some help, mamas," Julie said. "This digital age is killing me, and I am definitely going to have to get your advice on how to manage conversations about social media and dating apps. It was so much easier to manage this years ago."

"I'm not sure how much help I can be, I try to stay off it as much as I can myself," Nya acknowledged she should also better equip herself for those conversations with her clients.

"I need some help on how to stop scrolling," Chelsea admitted.

"I need some help to make better choices when scrolling!" Jillian exclaimed, referring to her how she should learn to control her thumb when selecting which man to swipe left or right on.

Julie was excited when she spoke, "I've been married since before the dawn of time but I'm dying to know what those apps are all about!"

"Tell you what," Jillian lowered her voice as if she was sharing a secret. "I'll let you swipe once I've had a couple more of these," she gestured to her glass and laughed.

"I want in on that!" Kelly exclaimed, keen to be part of the action.

A bell was ringing, and you could hear one of the convention coordinators asking participants to please move to their tables as dinner would be served soon.

Jillian got the bartender's attention and ordered another round of drinks, "For the road" she said, holding her half-empty glass in one hand and dropping a $10 note into the tip jar.

Their conversation continued as they made their way over to the large round tables that sat eight people, covered in white tablecloths and decorated with canary yellow roses in small vases.

"Have you decided which breakout sessions you want to attend this weekend?" Nya asked no one in particular.

"Did you see that session about toxic masculinity?" Kelly asked and an exchange of yeses resonated.

"The 'Building Resilience' session also looks good," Julie chimed in.

"And 'Failure to Launch' should be interesting. I've got a client who's 50 years old and still living at home with his parents," Jillian shared.

"To be fair, I've seen how much rent is in San Fran," Kelly's joke was well received.

"Wouldn't it be funny to see the breakout sessions named in light of some of the societal ridiculousness we have to deal with?' Chelsea pondered and piqued the interest of the others.

Chelsea continued, "Why should I wear pink if I don't want to?"

The women laughed together.

"It's my body but do I really get to make my own decisions?" Chelsea added, allowing her new friends to see the comedic side of her she normally refrained from sharing with strangers.

"How to keep a smile on your face at all times," Jillian joined in.

Their laughter got louder at each statement and Nya wanted to be part of it, adding, "Is she talking too loud?"

They roared with laughter together which turned the heads of some others making their way to their tables. It might have been the bubbles or simply the stress falling away by being absent from their everyday lives.

But Nya was sure that Kelly and Chelsea were going to be wonderful additions to her annual convention cohort of confidants.

Chapter 14: *Drops of Poison*

It was a beautiful fall day. The trees were considering when to start shedding their leaves and squirrels chased each other playfully, as if they were enjoying the warm weather before hunkering down for the encroaching winter.

Celeste was dressed in a bright orange maxi dress she had bought on a holiday in Spain years ago, with a light cotton scarf the colour of a summer sky. She had picked that up at a boutique store when she had spent a long weekend in Edinburgh. She finished off her look with her trusty though somewhat tired Banana Republic denim jacket. While she may not have been the kind of person to spend a lot of money on her wardrobe, she did indulge in buying pieces that told a story of the time she took possession of them. She loved reliving memories of her travels and sometimes that could come in the simplest of forms, such as pulling on a pair of pants. She had let her hair dry naturally, in part because she was running late to meet her friends downtown, but also because the natural wave lent itself to the look she was going for today.

She had taken the 1 down to Times Square and quickly switched to the N to take her further downtown to 8th Street. She had crossed over to Lafayette Street to walk past the Public Theatre on her way to meet her friends. It was a landmark building opening as a library in 1854 and over time the venue moved from the written to the spoken word. Home to emerging artists, the Public Theatre has developed and produced some of the most recognised theatre productions today. She was on their mailing list to make sure she didn't miss out on seeing their next hit show before it was the next big hit on Broadway.

Celeste took a left on 4th and crossed to the south side of the street. She spotted Abigail on her phone outside the pub they were meeting at for a late lunch and drinks. Abigail turned in Celeste's direction and wrapped up her call.

"Darling!" Abigail threw her arms around Celeste and embraced her.

"Someone's in a good mood," Celeste remarked.

"Oh, that was Alexander," she beamed. "He truly is the best!" While Celeste had heard Abigail speak this way before, the notes of sincerity that she had heard at dinner when she first met Alexander were still intricately tied to each syllable Abigail spoke about him. It was not familiar to either of them.

Celeste smiled and replied, "Ready?" as she pointed to the door of the Swift Hibernian Lounge. She had stumbled upon the pub not long after she had arrived in New York City during one of her many walks throughout her streets, simply taking in the mayhem, mess and majesticness of Manhattan. She had stopped in for a pint and it had reminded her of home. Much like NYC and the world over, London has its fair share of Irish bars filled with the Irish charm global citizens had grown accustomed to.

Swift had an authenticity that made her feel like the city that lay outside its walls could have been London. It had quickly become a go-to meeting spot for a quick drink or a Sunday session. Its exposed brick walls and thick wooden panels welcomed you in and made you want to stay, either perched on a dark green leather barstool at the bar that welcomed its patrons upon entering, or seated deeper into the pub, at the end of the hallway, past the stairs to the bathrooms and into a space that had a pulpit reserved for poetry readings held weekly.

As Celeste and Abigail entered through the heavy wooden door, she immediately saw Sarah and her partner Holland sitting by the large windows to her left. They had drinks in their hands and were deep in conversation, they didn't notice Celeste and Abigail until they were standing within their space. They placed their drinks down on the bench in the corner space they had secured and stood so they could all quickly hug each other the way close friends do.

Celeste offered to get the first round of drinks for the group, as she noted Sarah and Holland's were on the shallow side, and took her wallet from her handbag. It was comfortably busy at the bar, but there was enough room to be served without having to lean over patrons nursing Guinness's. She ordered a bottle of white wine as it was the easiest option to start with and handed over her credit card to open a tab. She immediately ordered potato wedges with curry sauce to share and knew she would be back for sausage rolls later. It was another reason she loved going there, the comfort food was another reminder of what she had left behind. While New York offered every possible cuisine one could ever want, she desperately missed a good chip. Not a French fry or their version of thick fries that still fell short of the real thing. And while Swift didn't do proper chips, their wedges and curry sauce was a close second favourite that she was forever grateful for.

When she returned to the girls, Abigail was standing while Sarah and Holland remained seated. Abigail was animated by nature, and you could see the excitement on her face and the smile that stretched from ear to ear. She was filling them in on her relationship with Alexander. Celeste was the conduit in the group, but they all knew each other well enough now to dig into their personal lives and share their thoughts and fears.

Abigail didn't hold back telling them about her feelings and about their sex life. Celeste had wondered if when the time came that Abigail ever found 'the one' she would possibly share less to protect the privacy of her lover, but she was as graphic as always. There was no doubt that

Abigail's libido was a source of aspiration for a lot of women. However, Celeste had also read once that libido is also tied to stress, and one could easily deduce that Abigail's life was of the most stress-free existences most of us only dreamed of. And she had realised it was not worth her sanity or self-esteem to judge herself against that of her friends' desires. As Celeste was mid-thought on her own sex life, it was as if Abigail was reading her mind.

"So, what about you and Prince?" she poked.

"What do you want to know?" Celeste asked.

Never one to back down to an open invitation, Abigail dove right in, "Have you shagged yet?" She loved using British slang when she was around Celeste.

The look on Celeste's face was all the three of her friends needed to confirm they had indeed taken that step.

It had been when they were at the beach for their long weekend away. They had spent the afternoon sitting by the water at a restaurant decorated for the Hamptons, but it was many miles from the decadence of where New York elites spent their summers. They had laughed at the irony of sitting in a Hamptons themed venue when Prince had made a definite stance that Rehoboth was his favoured destination.

While she had admitted to Prince that she was still keen to visit the Hamptons one day, she was not in favour of the cost. The Hamptons came with an outrageous price tag through the warmer months, but the rest of the East Coast wasn't far behind. It's the price you pay when you live in a region where six months of the year are spent protecting yourself from the brutal winter realities. By the time the sun starts to peek through, most people are ready to throw all their savings into a travel wallet if it means a few grains of sand beneath their feet.

Rehoboth Beach's price tag was also considerable, even for a cosy hotel, thanks to its proximity to the breaking waves of the Atlantic Ocean. But the convenience of a beach that was a few short hours' drive away, far enough away but close enough to home, meant they were willing to pay a little more than usual for a room that had not been updated in the last two decades. At least it was clean.

They ate cheese and sipped wine while drinking in each other. They were relaxed and anyone observing their banter would assume they had been together for a long time. There was a comfort between them that they both felt but were scared to admit. After dinner and cocktails, they had made their way back to their hotel where they discovered each other's bodies for the first time. Maybe it was the drinks, the abundance of sunshine, or maybe it was simply the safety that Celeste felt when she was around him, but their union felt familiar and they shared a night of discovery that felt both entirely new and eerily familiar, as if steeped in déjà vu. It was different to anything she had experienced before and she was working her way through her feelings. Both physical and emotional.

"I have no complaints!" was all Celeste was willing to share with her friends. But she glanced at Sarah, and they shared a look between friends who shared a connection and Sarah recognised this meant more to Celeste than she cared to admit.

"I'm happy for you," Sarah raised her glass, and they clinked and cheered.

"I'm happy for Prince," Abigail remarked. "You certainly made him work for it! My turn for drinks," and she skipped away to the bar to return momentarily with another bottle of wine.

While Abigail filled their glasses, Holland asked when they were going to meet Prince, "We've heard so much about him, so when do we get to meet him in the flesh?"

"Soon, I promise," Celeste wasn't sure she could keep that promise. Of course she wanted her friends to meet him, but something inside her told that she was making too much space in her life for him. *What would fill that void if he left?* She knew this was an irrational thought and that it was because she had had sex with him that she was allowing herself to consider multiple futures with or without him. She chided herself that she was letting these thoughts weave their way through her mind, like miners laying explosives waiting for the right time to detonate.

She knew her pattern of behaviour. She knew she felt out of control with someone she wanted to have full control of her own emotions with. She took a big gulp of her wine.

"Sooner rather than later," Holland continued.

"You don't normally keep them away this long," Sarah added.

"Is there something wrong with him?" Holland joked.

Probably, the little voice in her head said. Quickly followed with another thought that maybe there was something wrong with her. Another gulp of wine.

"Have you met any of his friends yet?" Sarah asked.

"Not yet."

No one said anything and they all swigged from their glasses. *Were they judging him?* Celeste wondered. *Did they presume he didn't think she was good enough to introduce her to his friends?* She went to take another mouthful of wine and realised her glass was empty. Instead of waiting for their reply, she hastened back to the bar to order more drinks. This time she came back with a tray of cocktails and a change of subject.

"There is a guy at the bar who looks like my ex," she informed her friends. They all leaned forward and peered in the direction of Celeste's head tilt. There were several men standing at the bar, but Sarah spotted him right away. "He looks like all of your ex's," she laughed.

It was true, she had a type. And he looked much like Prince.

"He's from California," Celeste continued.

"You talked to him?" Abigail asked.

"He started it," Celeste giggled.

"What's his deal, is he single?" Abigail wanted to know. While Abigail was indeed obsessed with Alexander, it was unlikely the thrill of the chase would ever leave her.

"I didn't ask," Celeste answered.

"No ring?" Sarah joined the conversation.

"I'm not sure," Celeste looked back over her shoulder at him.

"You always check for a ring," said Sarah.

"Should I go back over?" Celeste was playing a game she didn't want to participate in.

"I'll check when I go for the next round, you beat me to it last time," replied Holland.

"Let's not encourage her," Sarah was always the voice of reason. She also knew Celeste well enough that while she wasn't quite sure the game she was currently setting up to play, she knew it was not one Celeste wanted to win.

More people had poured into the pub, and the space was starting to get crowded.

It was getting louder, and they were having to raise their voices to be heard above the hum.

Sarah was talking about the new Mayor that had come into office and how hope had returned to her days. Holland added her own excitement about the new administration and what it meant for New Yorkers. Sarah, Holland and Celeste were incredibly political and more often than not their conversations led to current affairs both locally and abroad. Abigail on the other hand was not as concerned with world events and very often spent time on Instagram during these moments. It always surprised Celeste that Abigail didn't care to get involved in the conversation, but at the same time, didn't care to try to change the subject to one she could participate in. She happily let the girls take their turns on their soap boxes till they had exhausted themselves. Celeste wondered what it was like to be in Abigail's mind and the simplicity of her life. She also hoped that maybe by osmosis, Abigail took in at least some of what they were saying.

While Celeste saw Abigail checking out and checking in on Instagram, she took out her phone to see if there were any new messages. There were not and she felt the slightest weight in her stomach that Prince had not connected with her that afternoon. He knew she was meeting her friends, and the rational thought would be he was giving her time with them. Instead, as the drinks warmed her body, her thoughts turned to insecurity that maybe he wasn't thinking about her at all.

The game in her mind had been set into motion and rather than reach out to him herself, she decided to base his interest in her on the time it took him to reach out. *Shouldn't he be worried I might meet someone else that would take away my affections?*

That thought should have been enough to snap her out of her mindset. The last thing she wanted was a man who allowed jealousy to interfere in their relationship.

The spot at the pub the girls had secured was big enough for at least another two or more people to comfortably fit, and Celeste wondered if her new friend from the bar might want to join them later. Maybe that would put something out in the universe that would trigger Prince to ask how her day was going with her friends. With that in mind, Celeste slipped away to get yet another round of cocktails

The handsome man who looked like her ex was nowhere to be seen at the bar and she wondered if he was still in the venue or had he left out without her seeing. She looked around at the patrons who had flocked in. There was usually an eclectic mix of people at Swift. They were near NYU so it wasn't uncommon for the bar to be packed to the brim with college students, however, just as common were the groups of friends in their 30s and 40s who had come for a few drinks and then decided to stay for dinner and then more drinks.

She pulled her phone out of her pocket while she waited for her cocktails and there were still no new messages.

She looked around at the heaving crowd again and noticed no other potential suitors in her line of sight. *Why am I even looking*, she questioned herself? She knew she wasn't really interested in meeting another suitor to complicate her already complicated thoughts. Why was she being complicit in this irrational behaviour?

When the bartender returned, she casually added tequila shots to her order.

When she returned with the tray, Holland berated her. "It was my round," she reminded her.

"Next one, next one," Celeste shooed her comments away and handed them all a cocktail each, along with salt and lime for their guaranteed hangover.

"Oh, this is not going to end well," Sarah added.

"Already," Abigail had looked up from her phone and spied the shots. She was never one to say no to reckless behaviour.

Once again, they clinked their glasses, shot their shots, and contorted their faces as they tasted the harsh liquor pouring down their throats.

Celeste was feeling alone. She hated that she was feeling reliant on the attention of a man to make herself feel better. Instead, she relied on the cocktail in her hand to resolve any loose feelings she could tuck away.

Abigail was answering a message on her phone and by the look on her face, it was Alexander she was responding to. And Sarah and Holland were having a moment together, lost in their own conversation as they held each other's hands.

For the third time, Celeste checked her phone.

She started to replay her relationship with Prince to date, scrutinising their time together. One might say she was bordering on obsessive, but that seemed too extreme. Obsessive is a word used for someone who has no self-control and Celeste was fully aware of the repetitive nature of her thoughts. Surely if she recognised her obsession with Prince, it wasn't a problem. But deep down she knew it was a problem. It was something she had spoken to Nya about and wanted to delve into how she could stop the cycle she often finds herself in.

The voice in her head was taking control and Celeste was allowing it. She was finding comfort in the familiar feeling of feeling not good enough. Creating a battle in her own mind to see who would win.

It's going well with Prince. Celeste tried to reassure herself in what was often a losing battle when alcohol was involved.

If you say so.

Well, I think it is. I've got this, I know I have.

You sound confident. Are you sure you should be? Have you seen yourself? What have you got to be confident about? How do you think he sees you? Does he see you at all?

He's different from the others.

No, he isn't.

Maybe he isn't?

What should my next move be?

A woman walked into the bar and Celeste felt a wave of jealousy wash over her. She was at least ten years younger and looked like sex on a stick. She was sure she never dressed like that when she was the girl's age. Although maybe she should have. She wondered if she would have had better luck with men if she had just leaned into her sexuality instead of being afraid of it like they teach you to be.

Instead, she had leaned into everything else she was taught to lean into. With the occasional sprinkling of sex to tie the package together.

You do talk a lot. And I mean a lot. You can be very tiresome. She scolded herself.

Should I talk less? Did I look pretty enough the other night?

I think I looked good.

Maybe I should be more like ... she looked back at the girl who had taken most of the men's attention after she walked in.

I don't think I really need to do all that though do I? Why can't I just be me?

Because being 'you' just isn't good enough. Your next move better be good.

"Are you okay," Sarah interrupted her poisonous thoughts.

Celeste felt her eyes prickle, as if tears were about to force their way out and expose her.

"Maybe the shot wasn't the best idea," Celeste tried to laugh it off, although Sarah wasn't convinced.

She knew better than to broach whatever was playing on Celeste's mind now. A busy bar and multiple drinks down the hatch is never the right time to really uncover any emotional baggage that needs to be carefully sorted, laundered, folded and put away.

"I think it's time for sausage rolls," Sarah declared. She rubbed Celeste's arm in a way that spoke volumes.

"Thanks, I'm just going to duck to the loo," Celeste excused herself through to the stairs that took her down to the toilet.

Luckily there was no line. It was still early, and bladders were not at bursting points. She quickly used the first stall and then washed her hands. As she used a paper towel to dry them, she stared at herself in the mirror. The voice continued in her head

You'll never escape me. You just make it so easy. Like pulling a puppet's strings. It's so easy to get you to loathe yourself.

Do I have any self-worth?

Do you think Prince is going to give you some sort of a fairy tale happy ending? Your nightmare is just beginning and you know it.

Celeste shook her head. How drunk was she? God, she really needed some food. She was grateful for good friends and that Sarah was already onto it. Celeste took a moment to stand up straight, put her shoulders back and lift her head a little higher.

"Pull yourself together," she said out loud. Then quickly turned to make sure she was indeed alone. She shook her arms, took a deep breath, and was about to check her phone again, but decided it was best not to. She thought she had felt it vibrate in her pocket, but she decided she should wait to check it until after she had eaten her sausage rolls.

***

The next morning, she woke with a mouth as dry as someone lost in the desert, dreaming of mirages and pools of water that were never there, and a headache that felt like the pounding would break through her skull.

She rolled over to pick up her phone, glad she left it where she normally does on her bedside table. She didn't quite remember getting home but as she looked around the room, things seemed to be in order.

Prince had sent her a message late into the previous evening that she had missed while sending multiple messages to her friends that she had indeed arrived safely home. He had written to say that he hoped she was having a good time with her friends. A second message was received about an hour ago, asking how her night had been. *Destructive.* Not because she had crossed any boundaries or made any bad decisions, other than the additional shots she insisted they all drink. But because she had driven out the voices in her head by drowning them in distilled drinks. *And for what?* She wondered. He had messaged her after all. And because she had been too drunk, she missed what she'd been hoping to see all evening.

Sounds about right, she thought. Can't wait to tell Nya all about this.

Before answering Prince, she dragged herself out of bed and grabbed two CVS branded headache tablets from the large bottle she had purchased that now sat under her bathroom sink and retrieved a bottle of Gatorade from her fridge. Shuffling back to her bed, she theatrically threw herself back down on it as she let out a groan.

First, headache tablets. Second, finish the whole bottle of Gatorade. Third, order McDonalds. She knew it was bad for her and would likely not taste as good as she was anticipating, but the hangover was too substantial to give too many fucks about anything other than deep fried food at that point. Four, she would reply to Prince.

She was seeing him again tomorrow morning. She was aware she had less than twenty-four hours to recover and pull herself together. She was acutely aware that she didn't bounce back as quickly as she did in her 20s.

The pain of her hangover didn't allow much space for her to consider why she drank as much as she did the night before. But deep down, as she tapped on her phone to reply to Prince, she wondered what he would have thought about her behaviour. *What will he do once he sees the real me?* Celeste didn't consider that possibility he already had, and that was why he kept coming back.

Chapter 15: *Entwined Imaginings*

They had met at Grand Central Station at 7 am. They had taken the Metro North Hudson Line to Cold Spring as Prince had invited her to hike through the Hudson Highlands which on a clear day, had views of New York city.

They had decided to take the train rather than drive as Prince had secured a car park right outside his apartment and he didn't want to lose the spot. It was a ridiculous notion to own a car then not drive it thanks to limited street parking. But it afforded one the chance to brag about securing a park that people would kill for and almost do if you've ever watched two drivers lose their minds when fighting over a 10-foot asphalt space they had been driving possibly hours around to find.

"I'm really glad you were happy to do this today," Prince said.

Celeste was rarely up at this time of day on a Sunday unless it was to take an early flight to explore distant lands. But she had agreed to the hike not so much because of her love of hiking but her fear of missing out. Plus, he had seemed eager to share this with her because he used to spend time with his dad here when he was a child.

"Me too," she replied and meant it. While she was never enthusiastic about hiking, she never turned down a big walk, as she considered most hikes people went on were no different to walking from the Financial District up to Times Square. She wasn't sure why but hiking sounded so much more serious and strenuous, and people used the word loosely to sound more adventurous and athletic than they actually were. She also figured if they asked her to go for a big walk instead of a hike, it would make her much more responsive to such an activity. While pebbles underfoot in sneakers seemed more rugged, keeping an eye out for what you might step on and the creatures you might encounter along your path in the wilderness were not so different to a trek through Manhattan.

Did he think I wouldn't do something like this? She questioned silently in her head. It might not have been her first choice, but she didn't want him to think she wasn't open to new adventures.

"Did you think I wouldn't?" She asked, trying to keep from sounding out of breath as they reached their destination.

"I wasn't sure. I didn't know if you were the outdoorsy type."

You're not, she heard her inner voice say. Instead, she replied, "Well I am. I just love hiking."

"Well, that's good then!" *Is that the kind of woman he was looking for?*

"I mean, a taxi would have been an easier option," she joked in hopes her sense of humour would remind him why he invited her.

He laughed, "Don't you feel good now you made it to the top?" The hike was indeed more than a walk through the cobblestones of the Meatpacking District, being a little over a three and a half mile round trip, and while she wasn't much for this type of activity, she had surprised herself at how much she had enjoyed the Bull Hill short loop they had journeyed upon. The views of the Hudson River and the valley were breathtaking, and thanks to their early morning start, they were able to focus on the lush greenery and feelings of being one with nature before the sun assaulted them in the hours ahead.

They were halfway through and it would be another 90 minutes and change before she was back on the Metro North southbound platform.

She took a deep breath and exhaled, "Yeah, sure." She realised that may have come across as a little lacklustre. So, she raised her pitch and said it again, "Yeah, sure, it feels great. So how often do you come up here?"

"Not as often as I'd like. The first time I came up here was with my dad. I guess it kinda used to be our place." Prince paused in thought, and she wondered what his dad was like. *Would he like me? Approve of me? Am I good enough for his son?* She felt a weight on her chest ever so slightly. It was a familiar feeling she had slowly started to recognise as insecurity. She wondered how many other girlfriends he had introduced to his dad. What were they like? She was curious to know if they were like her or completely different. Thoughts started to enter her head about who these women might be and how she matched up to them.

"How special! And now here we are! Maybe it could be our place too?" He turned and looked at her and she felt awkward at that moment. *Did I say the wrong thing?* How would he construe her words? The weight on her chest got slightly heavier.

"I mean, not 'our place', even though I said 'our', I meant," she faltered and felt she was making a fool of herself. "So, you came up here with your dad?" Celeste took several deep breaths to calm her nerves. Why were the words of her friends ringing in her head? She should be pulling on her expensive therapy learnings and not the remarks of her drunken cohorts, or worse, her alter ego.

"A lot of memories up here. Dad and I are tight, like best buds. I used to joke that Mom was his annoying girlfriend, always hanging around."

Celeste laughed a little too loud and questioned if she sounded manic. "I'm really close to my mum. I tell her everything," she said.

Prince smiled and with a cheeky grin asked, "Everything?"

"Everything!"

"About me?" Prince enquired. She wasn't sure if he was genuinely interested to learn if she had shared whatever this was, with her family or if she had made a terrible mistake admitting that she had told anyone anything about whatever this was, in case it was indeed nothing.

Either way, she continued, "Yes about you. That I've met this amazing guy."

"Amazing?" Prince asked, seemingly chuffed at the compliment.

Celeste dug deeper into learned behaviour without thinking twice. *Make him feel good.* She was sure if Nya was present, she'd have a thing or two to say about it. "I may have used the word extraordinary."

"Extraordinary! That's quite a word to live up to. So ... you've told your mom about me."

Panic swept over her. She had said too much. She had taken the relationship too seriously. She had considered it to be more than what it was, and he was going to freak out now that he knew she was telling people about him. She wasn't sure that she wanted to hear the answer when she asked, "Is that okay?"

His casual reply made it impossible for her to read him. "Yeah, sure ... why not."

What the hell does that mean? She weighed up the many possibilities in her head. Feeling scared she had opened up too much without any guarantee he was feeling the same way, she had to know, "Have you told anyone about me?"

"Anyone?" He casually answered again. She was slow dancing with distress at the fact she couldn't hear his thoughts.

"You know ... people, family, friends."

"Maybe."

She was sure he was teasing her now, but she wasn't sure if it was with good intentions, or if he was using it as a tool to avoid the subject, "Maybe?"

"How about the view from up here?" Prince quipped.

"Are you changing the subject?"

"Maybe," he laughed and put his arm around her as they took in the view. She snuggled in and as she did, he leaned in closer and whispered, 'yes' in her ear.

The knot in her stomach came undone and she felt calm for a moment. *It's a really good sign he's telling people about me,* she thought. *But why did he change the subject and not just tell me right away? Or was he just distracted by the view, or the thought of his dad? Or is lying and hasn't told anyone about me at all?* She could feel the knot slowly twisting back into place again. She took several deep breaths again, acknowledging she was looking for any reason to plant a seed of doubt. *He's telling people about me and it's a good sign,* she reassured herself.

"Remind me, did you say you were a pet person?" Prince asked her, pulling her out of her anxiety ridden thought process.

"Come again?" She asked, even though she heard the question. One she always feared given she wasn't overly fond of any animal that made her eyes itch and water and caused her to descend into sneezing fits. While she appreciated them, she preferred to appreciate them from afar at this time in her life.

"Pets. Do you like them?" he pressed.

Unsure of how she should answer, because she never knew what judgement she might receive if she were to tell the truth. *Do I have to like them?* "Yeah, sure. Why not?"

"I'm not convinced." Prince countered.

"I mean ... I don't know." He almost looked disappointed in her answer. At least that was how she perceived it. *Wrong answer. Wrong answer. Make a joke.* "You know what, an ex of mine had a dog. I swear he paid it more attention than he did to me. Always fussing with that damn dog. Then I cooked it for dinner."

"What?" Prince had the look of someone who didn't correctly hear what she had said and someone who perfectly understood. He looked confused and weary at the same time.

"I'm kidding. Oh, the look on your face! Don't worry, I wouldn't ever actually kill anyone's pet." She thought she was on a roll with her comedic special unleashing in the hills. "There are better ways to get revenge," she laughed and realised she could possibly pass as being disturbed. *Crazy woman in the woods.* Her mind was racing after the words had poured from her mouth.

What kind of dumb shit was that? She rightly questioned her not-so-funny one-woman show. *He thinks you're serious. That was not funny.*

Is he reconsidering taking me on this hike now he thinks I eat dogs? She watched him watch her. *Do I look pretty enough?*

She wondered if he was waiting for an encore as he hadn't spoken another word.

She took stock of the situation and acknowledged just how many thoughts could run through her mind in a moment of milliseconds. The voice in her head returned with scathing criticism. *You are so lame. You can't deliver a good joke, and you're so far off a punchline it feels more like a punch in the face. What are you going to do to fix this?* She knew she didn't have much to offer because any hint of comedic talent, if she had any at all, was already on an express train back to the city where at least the noise could have drowned out the current thoughts in her head.

She shrugged, smiled as sweetly as she could and simply said, "You're a pet person then?"

"I am. Dogs."

Her friends' voices ringing in her ear to never admit you're not terribly fond of animals. No one likes someone who doesn't like dogs. "At least you're not into cats." She joked and he laughed. *Phew.*

"I could have a dog, I guess. If that's what you wanted." Not knowing when to stop, she added, "They just don't really fit with a studio in a fifth-floor walk-up."

"People work it out though, right?" He countered. "You wouldn't want a dog that needed a lot of outdoor time, that's for sure. But there are plenty of parks nearby, you'd make it work."

"And bring them to a place like this," Celeste offered. She wanted to contribute and appear open minded to the possibility of owning a dog one day. Although the mere thought of it made her cringe. It wasn't that she didn't like dogs, she did! It was true they set off her allergies that would often make her want to rip her head clean off her shoulders just to stop the insistent itching of her face, but she truly did see the joy they could bring. She had grown up with pets her whole life and had fond memories of loyal dogs who had meant more to her than some people. But at this time, the last thing she wanted was the responsibility of an animal. She often felt she could barely take care of herself, had a hard time keeping a plant alive, and therefore had little to no chance of providing a good home to a living creature that depended on her.

Luckily for her, Prince interjected into her consciousness and said, "But I feel like, at least at this time in my life, I'm not around enough to really take care of a dog."

She wasn't sure if he had just thrown her a bone, a pun she wanted to share but didn't or he had shared an honest thought. Either way, she took it and ran.

"Agreed," Celeste replied. "I'd be a terrible dog-mum. I'm never home and that poor puppy would be so lonely."

"Maybe one day when we've got a place upstate to take it to?" Prince replied. He said it so matter of factly that it took her by surprise. *Want to read into that,* she pondered? *Of course,* but she gave herself some space to pretend she could be rational about such a bold statement and quieted the voices for now.

"You want a place upstate?" She held the words *with me* in her mouth. She realised she was holding her breath as she watched him walk a few steps away and turned to take in the view again. *Please say with me, please say with me.*

"Wouldn't it be great?" Prince asked. "It was going to be on my vision board, remember?" Prince laughed at the memory in a way that implied it was just a dream.

Celeste felt stupid for not remembering he had told her that. *Idiot. He won't want a house with you if you don't even remember what he says.*

She didn't want to say the wrong thing and mess it all up.

"Oh yeah, of course! A big old country home, or maybe a little cabin - either would be great!" She conjured and he smiled. So, she added, "You, me and the dog." That was a risk she wasn't ready to take but she had thrown caution to the wind in her derailment of expectations. She wasn't sure if she said the right thing or not. She didn't want to mess up whatever this was that hadn't been discussed thus far. She waited for his response.

"Do you want kids?" His question came from nowhere. She stood staring at him for what felt like forever but in reality, was only a few seconds.

She contemplated what the right answer was. "I don't know," was her honest answer. "Do you?"

She held her breath as she hoped he didn't want to fill a large country home with a large family. It had been her dream when she was much younger. She always envisioned a large family for herself, just like the one she had grown up in. But the older she got the less inclined she was to bring children into the world. It was complicated for her as she always thought she would want a child with the man she would want to spend the rest of her life with, but now she was standing in front of the man she thought could be the one and she wasn't sure she wanted to give him that. Even if he wanted it.

"Not particularly," he answered in his casualness that was starting to drive her to madness. She could not get a read on him, and it was making her crazy. She recognised she could try taking him at face value and that just because he was not melodramatic, it did not make him monotone. She had become so accustomed to drama and despair in her relationships, did she not recognise a healthy response that was just the truth of the matter, with no hidden agenda or deception. "Unless you wanted to," he added, which left her reeling.

Did he just leave the ball in my court? Was he really not making any demands of me? Was he being truthful with himself and would he one day take it back and say I took from him what he really wanted, and he would leave me for someone half my age? She shook her head to stop the barrage of uncensored thoughts punching in her mind.

Celeste had been so used to saying what men wanted to hear that she was not used to hearing what she wanted. Prince had no reason to make up a narrative to get into her good graces at this point in their relationship and she didn't believe he was that kind of guy anyway. The more time she spent with Prince, the more evident it was that he spoke with honesty and was not laying any groundwork that would take advantage of her. He was of kind spirit and genuinely seemed to care about her. She had made many assumptions and accusations in her own mind of the man she presumed he would turn out to be, but at every corner, he appeared to continue to be who he presented himself to be at the beginning. And that frightened her. *Is he too good to be true? Did I miss a red flag?*

She didn't know how to respond and was struck with fear that if she allowed herself to believe in him, then she would only end up being hurt. She was reaching for familiar falsehoods. She was sure he would eventually want her to be a better version of herself than she was right now, to maintain his interest in her. That he'll never truly care about what she wants, when he has his own needs that require tending to. That he is broken and will not be able to love her the way she wants, and therefore she should plan for the end of their time together. That he ultimately wouldn't love her because he simply couldn't. Just like the rest of them.

She was a thousand steps ahead when she should have been spending time standing still to notice the difference.

She battled her thoughts in her head. The good, the bad, the ugly, the indifferent. The truth she knew was in there somewhere.

"I'm sure we'd have beautiful kids," she blurted out.

Prince laughed. She wasn't sure if it was at the thought of them having children or if he just thought she was joking. She wasn't entirely sure why she said what she said. *More to talk about with Nya.*

Scrambling to gain some control back over her words, she said, "Oh. Whoops. Let me just put those words back in my mouth. Wouldn't be the first time I put my foot in it."

Prince smiled, "What do you mean?"

Was she appearing as erratic as she felt?

"Are you okay?" He seemed genuine.

No, I'm not okay, she thought. *I'm losing it and by it, I mean you and I can't stop myself from being a bumbling fool.* Instead of saying what was on her lips, she replied, "Oh, just ignore me."

Prince wasn't sure what was happening with Celeste but knew well enough to not pry and decided de-escalation was the best plan of attack. "Are you ready for the trek back down?"

"We have to walk down?" she joked. She had taken her hair out not long after they had arrived at their destination and her hair tie was on her wrist. She pulled her hands through her hair and went to pull it back into a pony for the walk back down.

Prince was watching her as she did this and she felt shy under his stare. "Your hair looks great. I love long hair," he said.

"You do?" She was never sure how to handle a complement. "Well, I'd never cut my hair short. If that's what you like. I'd keep it this way." As the words came out of her mouth, she thought, *that is not the way to handle a compliment.*

She was sure that while Prince took almost everything anyone said with a grain of salt, it was moments like this that even he wasn't sure what to say. Instead of addressing her comment, he simply said, "We can take it easy on the way down if you like."

"Oh, I don't mind. Whatever you want." She silently kicked herself for being so compliant, where was that fierce woman she knew was inside of her? She should be stronger and take the reins more often. *Don't let him call all the shots*, she heard the voice in her head say. *Was he calling the shots?* Celeste was too comfortable with the noise in her head and recognised she needed to turn the volume down. Now was not the time to digress as she already had several times today. *Or was it?*

He was a few steps ahead of her as they started away from the view, and she saw him pull his mobile phone out of his pocket. His pace was slow, and he didn't appear to be hiding anything, but she wondered who he was messaging as she saw him tapping on the screen. She hurried her steps to be beside him.

"What are you doing?" She questioned, looking at his screen while wondering if she was giving away her insecurities. He quickly shut down whatever conversation he was having and put his phone back in his pocket while he took her hand with his free hand.

"Just replying to a friend," was all he offered.

What friend? Her inner voice questioned and continued. *Probably another girl. You can't be the only one. I wonder what she looks like. Is she prettier than me? Funnier? What if he likes her more?* She felt herself starting to spiral again, recognising the many paths her mind was ferociously careening down. *Do you think he's sleeping with anyone else? Where is this even going? You really like him but he's going to break your heart. You better figure this out quickly, don't be stupid.*

Prince was quiet and had picked up the pace.

"Hey, look I didn't mean to freak you out about the beautiful kids' thing," she wondered if she had upset him. His demeanour had changed, and she wasn't sure why.

He seemed distracted and agitated when he replied, "It's fine."

"Are you okay?" It was Celeste's time to ask.

Prince seemed to come out of his preoccupation and back to his usual self. "Yeah, I'm good," he said with a warm smile.

"I guess I just wondered where you see this going?" She blurted out. She realised her sentence made no sense and she was accosting him in the middle of the woods with no exit strategy for him to manufacture.

"This?" She wasn't sure if he misunderstood her question or was buying himself some time. Either was acceptable under the current circumstances.

"Us." Celeste answered with a hard stop.

He breathed an audible sounding 'ah' like he was definitely buying himself time to create an appropriate response to the crazy lady who was asking for answers so soon into a relationship that maybe he couldn't give.

She knew she was on the verge of being reckless and this conversation most likely should have been had in a more comfortable environment. But she forged on. "I don't mean to put you on the spot," a laugh resounded in her head as if to acknowledge that was exactly what she was doing. And that she was quite possibly sabotaging herself with full knowledge of her actions. Surprise attacks were the backbone of relationship destruction, and she was well versed.

"I guess I just kind of need to know. Not need to. But would like to. Are you dating other girls?" *Shut up, shut up, shut up. You're terribly close to the edge of that cliff, he'd probably rather throw himself off it than stand here having this talk with you.* "That's okay if you are, well." *It is not okay, why would I even say that?* "Well, not really."

She finally stopped rambling at him, let's be honest, she wasn't talking with him, and there was silence between them.

Prince looked at her for what felt like forever. She felt uncomfortable under his gaze, terrified of what he was about to say in response to the episode she was having.

"I'm not. Are you?" He replied.

"It's just that I saw my ex-boyfriend the other day and it got me thinking." Why she decided to say this, she'll never know. She hadn't seen any ex-boyfriend, and she was grasping at straws to shock him into loving her. Another tactic she had learnt over the years, which made her wonder exactly when and where women are taught this behaviour. Afterall, it wasn't uncommon, but she didn't have a clue as to where she acquired such a useless knack.

Make them jealous to desire you more.

How utterly ridiculous, she heard a voice in her head say. How she wished she listened to that voice more often.

If she took a moment to get out of her head, she would have seen Prince was genuinely trying to understand her thought process, "Okay," he replied with an edge of curiosity or anxiety, she couldn't tell, as to what she was going to say next.

While she hadn't seen any such ex-boyfriend recently, she had plenty of bad experiences to draw on and she delivered her story using the memories of previous pain. "Nothing like that. It didn't end well. I thought things were good and we were great and then the next thing you know, BAM, it all turns to shit." She was on a roll, the largest boulder gathering speed quickly as it flew down the steepest hill. If someone called her unhinged at this moment, she wouldn't have been able to argue her way out of it.

"You know, you've been there, right?" Not letting him answer, she continued, "Anyway, I didn't think it was going to end and then it did, and I thought I'd found the one, but he wasn't. And then I met you and I started to wonder if you're the one, but how the hell am I meant to ask you if you feel the same way." She laughed and even she had to admit it sounded like the laugh of someone who needed Valium to calm down.

"So, then it all just starts to turn over in my head again and again and now I sound ... I sound ..." She was stumbling over her words.

Prince tried to interject, "It all sounds a bit c ..."

Before he could finish his sentence, she cut him off, "Crazy?" she asked if that was what he was about to say?

"I was going to say complicated. But if you want to go with crazy ..." he trailed off.

There was an awkward silence. Celeste shuffled her feet as Prince turned his eyes from her and to the view and then pulled his phone from his pocket again. She watched as he read a message and sighed with what seemed to be frustration, before roughly putting his phone back in his pocket.

He turned back at Celeste and stood waiting for her to say something. Afterall, she had been throwing words at him for the last however long her show had lasted, and he seemed braced for whatever was to come next.

He opened his eyes a little wider and raised his palms up, as if to say, *Well?*

"Well, what?" Celeste asked as if he had said it out loud.

"What do you mean, well what?" His tone was almost abrasive and she realised she was seeing a different side. One she hadn't seen before. She tried to name what she thought he was feeling. Frustrated, cranky, impatient. She wasn't sure. *Have I upset him?* she wondered. *Who was that message from? Did the text upset him?*

You know you could always ask. Instead, she put on her happiest face and her biggest smile and conjured up as much self-confidence she could find in one of her weaker moments. "You know what, never mind," she reassured him. Another trait women had been taught since they were young, smile and the world smiles with you.

Prince looked confused. Like he was being tricked into thinking he wasn't required to respond and that this would later come back to bite him.

She grabbed his hand and pulled him in the direction of the pathway back to the carpark.

Prince looked tired and didn't argue with her decision. "Sure. Right. Okay. Let's go then."

"I'm not crazy," Celeste laughed as she squeezed his hand. She could feel the tension in Prince ease. She leaned over and kissed him quickly.

"If you say so," he joked, seemingly back to his relaxed self.

Chapter 16: *The Troubled Looking Glass*

It was 5:15 pm on a Thursday and the evening sun beamed into her apartment. The warm September weather had continued into October, and the city was alive with autumn jackets and ankle boots. It was a beautiful time of year, right before the leaves were about to change and Mother Nature left you guessing as to whether she would bless you with warm kisses. It was the time of year that wardrobes in small apartments were swapped out, where summer dresses and tank tops were carefully placed into vacuum sealed storage bags and last season's wardrobe was pulled from the back of the closet. She had commenced the ritual the night before and was halfway through the process.

As she had been pulling out fluffy jumper after fluffy jumper, she was reminded of what lay ahead. For the last several months, light linens, 100% cotton and Lycra cut into a two-piece had replaced any memories of the brutality a New York City winter can unleash upon you.

While she opined that winter should, without doubt, run its course a lot quicker, she also saw the beauty of it. She enjoyed the cosiness one felt wrapped up tight in endless amounts of wool, the way footsteps in heavy boots sounded on the pavement, how the fairy lights seemed to twinkle brighter in the cool evening air, the shared experience of red noses as the cold whipped at your face, and the dance of removing layer after layer once inside a warm retreat.

Celeste was sitting on her couch, with her laptop open on her coffee table, awaiting Nya's call. She looked around her apartment and took stock of what was left to pack up and unpack. Her bed askew with clothes that she really should have waited till the weekend to attack but her impatience and inability to sit still saw her rummaging through closets far later into the evening than she should have.

She had a forty-five minute call scheduled with Nya and was to meet Prince forty-five minutes after that. She had been feeling on edge since their last date and worried her behaviour must have set off warning bells for him. Thoughts, endless thoughts, had been coursing through every corner of her mind and she was not unaware that her anxiety was the likely cause for her midnight desire to clean out her closet. She would have done anything to stop the incessant voices in her head.

Her thoughts were interrupted by the familiar tone of the incoming call jingle of Nya ringing. She answered and saw the friendly face of her therapist. They greeted each other with warm hellos and Celeste leaned back and placed a throw cushion across her belly, something to hold for stability.

"How are you?" Nya asked. "What's been going on?" It was a standard start to their calls, Nya opening the door for Celeste to start where she felt comfortable. And in that moment Celeste unloaded, she told Nya about her date with Prince, the things she had said, her interpretation of how Prince had responded, him appearing to get upset with her, or at least at something, and her irrational fears since.

She told her that since her date, she had focused on her failings and decided she simply wasn't good enough for Prince. How could she be? She was far from perfect, and she was sure that was what he was seeking. Though she had never heard him speak such words, she assumed he longed for an easy relationship. One that was not fraught with arguments from loose lips or opinions that differed too far from his own.

Celeste spoke from previous experiences and Nya tried to remind her that her past was not indicative of her future, and that Prince had so far not shown similar signs of what Celeste had become accustomed to. Men whose stories were more important than her own.

Celeste admitted that he appeared to listen to what she could only imagine others would describe as ramblings, and initially he was quite calm. But she didn't like that he had grown bothered by her or, she had conceded, possibly by whoever it was he was texting. And that while he had recovered quickly and returned to his usual self, Celeste had done what she does well and held onto what she considered was now a problem.

"Talk to me about that, you said you felt he was bothered and in turn, that made you feel some sort of way." Nya probed.

Celeste thought about it and gave the question the consideration it deserved. She finally answered, "I felt like I had done something wrong."

"And had you?" Nya asked.

"I don't think so."

"I don't think so either," Nya reassured her. "You don't even know what upset him."

"Well, it was either me or whoever he was texting. And I just don't think it was appropriate for him to get so cranky," Celeste said straightforwardly.

"And what if you had upset him? People are human, he is imperfect, remember. Is there no space for him to be that way?"

It was a good question, Celeste thought as she analysed, again, what had happened that day. "If my behaviour was testing him, I would hope for some sort of patience. I'm not usually a psychopath," Celeste added with a shrug of her shoulders.

"I don't think he thinks you're a psychopath," Nya offered, and Celeste received her support with open arms. She had said it as a joke, but it had come with a side of insecurity she had been feeling since their date. "And it's reasonable to ask for patience," Nya reassured her.

"I wasn't there so I can only take your word for what happened, and how you felt in the moment," Nya knew Celeste wasn't a liar and she admired her transparency. It took some clients much longer to get there, and some never quite did.

"So, this feeling of doing something wrong is tied to my perceived impression of his lack of patience with me, right?" *Nailed it.*

"How cranky was he?" Nya circled back on the language Celeste had used.

He wasn't. But after the interaction, Celeste had increased the severity of his behaviour into a much bigger deal than it was. "Well, whatever it was, I could feel the change in his mood. And he could have talked to me about it, whatever it was, but he didn't. So, something must have been going on in his head that he didn't care to share with me."

"And you wanted him to share it with you," it was a statement from Nya, not a question.

"How can I help him if I don't know what the problem is? And here we are again, another guy needing my help."

Here we are again, me looking for a problem to fix.

"It seems he didn't ask for your help though," Nya delivered what felt like a blow. Celeste felt the weight of her words land on her and forced their way into her psyche. He hadn't and maybe that was why she had been at a loss. *What was her purpose?*

"It's a good thing you know. He's a grown up and whatever it was, he can deal with it himself. That's the kind of guy you want, remember," Nya said, like a warm hug keeping her safe in a cold room.

"Well, sure. But ..." Celeste wasn't sure how she should feel. It was true, she was looking for a man who could take care of himself. But then what was her worth if he wasn't going to ask her to help.

It was as if Nya could read her mind when she said, "That doesn't mean you can't support him, when he asks for it."

Celeste moved uncomfortably in her seat. She was feeling anxious, and she didn't like it.

Nya continued, "What are you thinking about?"

Celeste really didn't want to talk any more about the fact she had categorised Prince as problematic based on one small moment in time. And instead mentioned her new belief that Prince's expectations are too high. "I think that he has this idea that relationships are easy and perfect."

Nya was surprised at this statement, "How so?"

"I remember on our first date he said it was perfect," Celeste offered.

"Okay ..." Nya waited.

"I was perfect on that first date. Who isn't on a first date? So, when he gets to see not-so-perfect Celeste, he doesn't like it." *There, I did it,* thought Celeste. She had managed to tie a bow around her mixed emotions and triggers and was holding a flame too close to the fuse she had also hung from the package.

Instead of leaning into the reality of what the situation might be, it was easier to slide back into old habits of finding a reason for the end before Prince could prove otherwise. Most of her relationships had ended in disaster or heartbreak or a combination of both. Her previous lovers were never going to live up to the expectations she had placed upon them, which was allowing her to make him whole again, and in the absence of Prince needing any obvious rehabilitation, Celeste assumed he was seeking a woman who was as content as he was, and not neck-deep in therapy.

Would he really find me worthy? She doubted it.

She wanted to be the woman of his dreams, however her actions on the trek only served as a reminder of the nightmare she could be.

He was looking for the perfect woman and she was not it. Not only was she not perfect, but she also knew this could be her leverage to be on the offensive. Prepared to retaliate at any moment when he exposed himself as the man, she expected him to be, rather than the man he was.

This story she told herself became her truth and she leaned into it like you would a strong headwind. She pushed back on any rational thought and embraced the struggle of taking one step forward and many steps back.

Nya tried to gently guide Celeste to a place of self-understanding. She asked her to reflect on her actions that day on the trek. Was she feeling anxious before they met? What had triggered her insecurities.

Celeste recounted her night out with her friends, and how with the help of a few shots, which were never a good idea, she had spiralled into an insecure tailspin that she hadn't been able to get out of since. She told Nya she felt embarrassed by how she had spent the night constantly looking at her phone, hoping to see his name appear in the notifications, or that she kept thinking she'd felt the vibration to alert her that he had reached out. How her friends had teased her about being needy and while she could have taken their words as harmless jibes, she had taken them to heart. She hated how much she wanted his attention and instead, sought it from other men in the bar to try and prove to herself it wasn't Prince she only wanted. She admitted to crying in the bathroom alone before pulling herself together, or at least she thinks she did.

She knew what Nya must be thinking, another drink down the hatch leads to another thought bubble that blows up in her face. It wasn't uncommon for Celeste to tell Nya tales of drunken nights out that led to a river of tears. The causes of such downpours were usually moments in time that would normally have passed by with the clouds, but certain words turn into claps of thunder and before you know it, faux alarm bells enabled by alcohol are ringing and one finds herself in a hysterical encounter.

"If it's hysterical, it's historical," Nya reminded Celeste.

This was one of her favourite lines from Nya, and Celeste repeated it with fervour. It meant that should one find themselves in a somewhat hysterical moment, or enduring emotions that are not at all equal to the degree of the situation one finds themself in, then one has been triggered by something historical. It had served her well ever since hearing it, and with time and practice, Celeste had been able to start applying that rationale in real time.

However, on some occasions when she had drunk a wine or two or three, the lubricant of intoxication that permitted her to lose her inhibitions also allowed for words of wisdom to be lost.

She told Nya how happy her friends were in their own relationships and how happy they seemed to be that she had found someone herself.

"What is wrong with that?" Nya questioned as Celeste seemed sceptical.

Instead of answering with honesty as she usually would, telling Nya she was afraid that she would get hurt if she allowed herself to continue the relationship with Prince, she dug deep for her defensive dictionary and used the words she had curated so well over the years.

"I don't need a man to make me happy," Celeste stated.

"What's wrong if a man does make you happy?" Nya countered.

Without thinking much about her question, Celeste answered, "I'm independent and being in a relationship is not the be all and end all."

Nya had heard this narrative before, when they had first started their sessions together. Celeste was, without a doubt, an independent woman and had forged her own path, however, her past, as does everyone's, was still lurking in the shadows and unwittingly, Celeste was making decisions based on those feelings.

Celeste looked at the time and realised she had little left with Nya. "We've only got a few minutes left," she said, and Nya nodded.

"How are you feeling about your date with Prince tonight?" she asked.

Celeste brushed aside any real feelings she may have been having at that moment and simply said, "Fine."

"Maybe you could take a rain check if you aren't up for it?" Nya offered. She was worried that in the state Celeste was in, she may regret any actions she was about to take. "I think that we should set some time for us to talk again soon. And in the time being, I ask that you don't make any rash decisions."

"What does that mean?" Celeste asked, knowing exactly what she meant. She just needed to hear it out loud.

Nya knew that Celeste was asking her to spell it out so that she could determine later whether she agreed with Nya's findings. It was the nature of her work. She provided the pieces of the puzzle, and the client was to put them together in their own time. "I think you are feeling vulnerable, and maybe even exposed right now."

Nya was right. Celeste felt like she had shown all her cards to Prince and he held on to his too tightly. She wanted to know what he was thinking, and in lieu of that, was taking it upon herself to deduce.

"I'd like you to spend some time thinking about the feelings you had throughout your last date. What was coming up for you as you were seeking to understand his feelings? Also, this notion of perfection. Dig into that and again, write down the words that come up when you think about what that means," Nya prescribed.

And Celeste thought that surely what Nya had handed out was enough, but apparently there was more, "Consider how you immediately thought that you had done something wrong when he became bothered."

"That's a lot of homework," Celeste joked.

"Think it all through, write it down, so we can talk about it when we next speak."

And with that, they made their next appointment in one week's time.

Chapter 17: *A Crack in the Mirror*

"Shit," she said out loud to herself. Celeste was running a little late.

She had decided on a last-minute wardrobe change after spotting a dress she had forgotten she'd bought as the seasons were changing last year. It was at one of those 'last chance' pop ups down in Soho with brand names she didn't recognise and had questioned if this was a tactic to get people to buy clothes that were marketed as expensive styles you were lucky to get your hands on, when in fact they were just as cheaply made as what we have come to expect from fast fashion. She hoped not.

She hadn't had a chance to wear it before it was packed away for the winter, and she had somehow not worn it throughout the warmer months this year. It was unlike Celeste; she didn't often buy clothes that she didn't frequently wear. Her rule of thumb was to wear each item in her closet at least once a year.

Well, she thought, *this counts as my once a year*. Meaning she didn't have to pack it into a charity clothing shop bag.

She had quickly pulled on the black dress with gold spots and fashioned the two buttons at the back of her neck together. It was made of material she always thought resembled papier-mâché, with long sleeves that cuffed at her wrists and an elasticised waist she wasn't sure she liked. The skirt swayed around her hips and sat slightly above her knees. She threw on a pair of gold strappy sandals, the only pair of shoes she owned that she thought matched the dress. Recognising she was at risk of a cool night breeze; she grabbed her trusted denim jacket that had also not seen the light of day for several months and flung it over her arm.

She raced out of her apartment and down into the subway. The next train was only two minutes away and she silently thanked the MTA Gods.

She was meeting Prince down in Greenwich Village and was hoping she might only be a minute or two late if the stars and connecting trains aligned.

Celeste was feeling anxious. She had butterflies in her stomach, and not the good kind, and she felt like she needed a good shake of herself to throw off the discomfort that lingered upon her. Or a strong drink. *I'm sure Nya would not approve of the latter.*

As she sat on the train heading downtown, her conversation with Nya kept repeating in her head. She put in her ear pods and found a British rock play track to help calm her, hoping memories of home would settle her. Instead, she found herself reminiscing of past boyfriends who had let her down and the songs played along as the soundtrack to her disillusioned love life.

The butterfly wings increasingly hit harder in her stomach.

Celeste replayed her time with Prince. She retraced their steps, she recalled when he made her laugh, she remembered the moments she had felt shy, she revisited their first night being intimate with each other. She reminisced about when she first met him, and it was the start of something new.

But what Celeste could do best was repurpose past hurts into current events. Her anxiety led her to recreate her time with Prince. She questioned why he would go to great lengths to make her smile, assuming an ulterior motive. Were his text messages late into the evening to her alone, or was she one of many? Was his casualness carelessness and how long would it be before he took her for granted? Had he told anyone about her?

Celeste was a storyteller, and her imagination could run wild, and her fear of being hurt allowed her to recreate her relationship with Prince into a love story gone wrong before it had even had the opportunity to form a single crack.

Deep down she believed he would let her down like everyone else and she would be the one standing with the broken pieces of her heart that she had just put back together, albeit with tape.

'Stand clear of the closing doors please' the speaker announced. Celeste had almost missed her stop, and she made a quick dash to exit the train, apologising as she brushed past a woman holding several shopping bags who was stepping inside as she rushed out.

The express was pulling into the station, and she boarded for the short trip from Times Square to 14th Street. She looked at her watch and realised she wasn't going to be as late as she expected and was grateful for that. Being late would have only added to her already anxious state.

She stood on the subway for the short journey and tried to calm herself as she got off at her stop. She took her ear pods out as she climbed the stairs to the street and looked up and around to get her bearings. She had come out on 12th Street and only had one block to walk to get to the restaurant he had picked.

She took a right onto 13th Street and after a short stroll down the block she came upon Alice. Prince had been wanting to try it out since seeing its participation in Restaurant Week earlier in the year and after a quick search online, she too was excited to see if it offered all the reviews had promised.

She stood outside and caught her breath before entering through the heavy curtains that hung in lieu of a door. As she entered the outdoor dining space, she immediately forgot the streets of New York as she looked around at the beautifully decorated intimate tables. She took two steps down and entered the restaurant which made her feel another world away from the noise of the city.

The host greeted her warmly and she gave Prince's name. "He has not arrived yet but please, have a seat at the bar and we will show you to your table when he arrives," and she followed him to a dimly lit nook that separated the restaurant into three sections. The space created a sense of hidden treasures yet to be discovered. The ambience enveloped her as she took a seat and the bartender handed her a menu.

Celeste pulled out her phone and saw it was seven oh five. He was five minutes behind schedule and had not sent her a text that advised of his late arrival. Lateness was one of her biggest gripes and she took this opportunity to add his tardiness to her list of reasons why it all went wrong. She scanned the menu and ordered a cocktail called Viva Amor. She couldn't read much Spanish, but it wasn't lost on her that she ordered a drink called *Long Live Love*, yet she was seeking ways to avoid it.

As the bartender created Celeste's drink made of vodka, pomegranate molasses, lime juice, agave and orange blossom, her phone lit up. It was Prince, apologising for being late due to a stalled subway car. While she knew it was a reasonable excuse, she cursed him for not allowing more time to be on time.

Without haste, her drink was placed in front of her and Celeste took a long sip. The flavours ignited her taste buds with summer romance sensations. The drink was what she needed to calm her nerves, the sensations a reminder of what she could lose in the next few hours. She had a feeling this night was not going to go well, and she had put Nya on mute for the evening. Celeste was comfortable immersing herself in the misery of love lost and she wore it like a badge of honour.

Better to end it now before the war drags on for longer than it should.

Prince arrived halfway through Celeste's drink. *10 minutes late*, Celeste clocked.

He came strolling through the restaurant, smiling when he spotted her at the bar. "I'm so sorry I'm late," he leant in and kissed her quickly on the lips.

Celeste was curt in her reply as she considered his apology along with this casualness of entering the room, "It's okay."

"Is it?" Prince asked, half joking but half serious.

She had become accustomed to his knack of reading people very well. She had never met someone who so quickly and innately understood when someone was off kilter. He might not know the reason right away, but he was sure of it when something was awry.

"I sent you a text once we got moving again, did you get it?" He asked. It must have gotten caught in the ether of the next tunnel and by the time it had arrived in her inbox, she had already put another red cross against his name.

The bartender interrupted the moment and asked Prince if he wanted a drink. He often asked for them to make their favourite, his way of trying something new, and he did it on this occasion too.

"You look beautiful," he said. Celeste still wasn't comfortable with compliments, and she simply smiled.

Don't let him fool you, she heard the voice in her head say.

Celeste sat quietly, not saying a word. There was enough running through her head. She was afraid if she opened her mouth they would all come tumbling out.

"Are you okay?" Prince asked.

"Fine," Celeste answered.

Prince laughed a knowing laugh. "Fine never means fine," Prince smiled at her, waiting for her to open up.

She looked at him and felt agitated that he was suggesting he understood her better than she understood herself. Even if that were true at times, while she was not comfortable with compliments, she was even less comfortable with vulnerability, and knowing Prince could see right through her made her feel exposed.

While she sat in front of him feeling his eyes upon her, expecting her to open up, rational thought slowly let itself out the back door of her mind and the music started to play in her head. She started the familiar dance of destruction. She knew the steps by heart.

Her instinct was to attack. *Don't let yourself get hurt by him,* she thought. Her pre-emptive strike was bound to leave her hurt, but at least it was by her design and not his. This gave her what she perceived as a measure of control over the situation. She positioned the conversation in a way that would end how she saw fit.

"It just would have been nice if you'd left your place at a time to be here on time," she told him.

"I did. The train was delayed," Prince countered.

The corners of her mouth barely lifted as she smiled with condescension dripping from her lips. "That's why you give yourself extra time. So, I don't have to sit here alone, waiting for you. Again."

"I said I was sorry. But thanks for the lecture," Prince's tone had shifted, and she could hear the terseness lingering. He had taken the bait.

Perfect, her inner voice was saying. *Look at how he is ready to fight you instead of just being sorry.*

"Well, it's not the first time and you know it's my pet peeve," she dropped his shortcoming into his lap.

The host appeared and interrupted their conversation. "Your table is ready, if you'd like to follow me," he said as he spun on his heel and led them to the back of the restaurant.

The bartender handed Prince his drink, confirming it would be added to their check, and they followed their host, holding their cocktails and their tongues.

Celeste and Prince took their seats and silently drank from their glasses. Their server arrived and they quickly ordered another round.

Prince looked at his phone and seemed to send a text before turning it upside down and placing it on the table to his left.

Celeste's eyes closed in on him, and she asked "Anything important?"

"No, it's nothing," he said and she could tell he wasn't pleased with whoever nothing was.

Sure. But important enough to let it interrupt our conversation.

Celeste was quiet and that made Prince uncomfortable. "How is your drink?" he asked.

"Good, that's why I ordered another one," Celeste answered sarcastically.

"What's wrong with you?" He didn't seem to be in the mood for playing games. On one hand, it reinforced Celeste's nonsensical belief that he was just like the rest of them and was on the verge of showing his true self. On the other hand, she acknowledged she wasn't making the evening pleasant, and he was behaving like any rational person would.

Fine, give an inch, she thought.

He'll take a mile.

"Sorry, I've just got a bit of a headache. It's been a day."

"Can I get you something to take?" he was prepared to pop out to a drugstore if he had to.

"No, but thanks," his consideration made her uncomfortable.

"Well, if it makes you feel any better, I've had quite the day too," he offered.

"What happened?" Celeste asked.

"Ah, I've been having this ongoing conversation, if you can call it that, with an old work friend. He is beyond frustrating with some of his opinions with everything that is going on in the country right now, and I've somehow wound up in an ongoing battle of the beliefs over text." Prince sounded fatigued just sharing this titbit of information about his dilemma.

"Tiring?" she asked.

"Exhausting," he replied. Prince continued, "So forgive me for being a little on edge these last few days. I feel like my frustration at him is overflowing and I don't know what to do with it."

"Is that who you were texting the other day, on our trek?" Celeste asked.

Prince thought about the timeline and confirmed, "Probably, it started the night before."

Celeste remained quiet as she considered his reply. She wondered if he was telling the truth. She had no reason to disbelieve him.

Except most of the other men you've dated affirms you shouldn't trust what he says.

You know that's not true, she told herself. *Not all men are liars.*

If one can be, so can the rest, the voice in her head countered.

They sat in silence and drank their drinks, a little too quickly.

Their server appeared and went to fill up their water glasses, realising that they had not been touched. Instead, he offered them another round and without hesitation they both replied 'yes'.

Celeste spoke first, "So anyway, if you wouldn't mind, I'd appreciate you being on time in future."

Prince appeared agitated that she hadn't let it go, and she was sure he was wondering why this was still a discussion.

However, instead of conceding to making some sort of peace, his own anxiousness got the better of him and he doubled down with his reply, "You know I'm not the best at being on time. However, this time it wasn't even my fault. As I explained to you." To Prince, it seemed it was expected that he should have to understand her needs and not receive the same in return.

"Fine," was all Celeste said about his defence. A years-old method of saying that everything is not fine, as he respectively understood earlier.

"I'm not sure what's going on here, but I'm pretty sure this isn't about me," Prince stated.

He had called her out for creating a fire that had no connection to the kindle that started it.

The server returned with their drinks, and they reached for them like reaching for water in the desert.

"Would you like to order?" The kind server asked, too busy to be aware of the tension between the two.

Celeste and Prince asked for a few more moments as they both picked up their menus. The server walked away to give them time.

Once again, there was a silence between. And not the comfortable type. They both drank from their glasses while holding their menus.

Celeste spoke first, "What are you thinking of having?"

"Definitely the scallops." He knew she hadn't tried them before and added, "You should try them."

Don't tell me what to do.

"Maybe," she replied. "I was thinking of either steak or pasta. What do you think?"

"The pasta!" It was Prince's second choice.

"Hmmm, do you think so?" Celeste asked, unsure. "Don't you think they'd make a great steak here?"

"So have the steak then," Prince replied bluntly.

"But don't you think the steak would be better?" she asked again, and Prince didn't reply.

The server returned to take their orders. Prince ordered the scallops and Celeste ordered the steak.

"Anything else? Would you like any wine?" the server asked.

Before Celeste could answer, Prince ordered a bottle of red, and the server was gone.

"Luckily I was also in the mood for red," she said.

"You could have ordered a glass of something else if you didn't like what I chose," was his response. "Besides, you ordered the steak."

Of course, it made sense to have the red wine with her steak, but she wasn't convinced he only did it for that reason. *Is he pissed at me?* She couldn't tell. But she knew for sure he wasn't happy.

She danced harder, two-stepping with ease, and with an air of indignation asked, "Have I done something wrong?"

"I don't know, have you?" Prince appeared to have found his own rhythm in the dance she had invited him to.

"Apparently so," was all she said as she finished her cocktail.

"I don't know why you asked for my opinion and then ignored it. You know you do that a lot," this was the first time Celeste had heard of his quandary.

"Just because I ask for your opinion, doesn't mean I have to take it," Celeste replied.

"I didn't say you did."

Sounds like it.

Prince continued, "But you quite often ask for it and then when I don't tell you what you actually want to hear, you give me more reason to tell you what you are looking for. How about you just don't ask in the first place."

Celeste felt the weight of his words on her sensitive shoulders. She immediately felt hurt and undesired. She immediately felt like she had done something wrong. *That explains everything,* she thought. *Of course you were being too much for him. How annoying.*

Celeste responded the only way she knew how. "Clearly you think I've got issues, so I'm not sure why we are doing this."

The server arrived with their wine. He showed Prince the bottle and she watched him nod his head in approval. The server took out his corkscrew, used the knife to pierce the foil capsule to reveal the protected cork, and promptly set about opening the bottle. They did not make eye contact with each other and kept their gazes on the bottle opening performance.

A mouthful of deep red wine was poured into Prince's glass. He lifted the oversized chalice, swirling it to allow the aromas to fill his nose, then finally took a small sip. "Thanks," was all he said with a smile as he placed his glass back down on the white linen. The server filled Celeste's glass before topping up Prince's.

Prince was glad the server had interrupted their conversation, as her words had left him speechless for a moment. He didn't understand what was happening. All he knew was that she seemed out of character and his own emotions were on high alert. He wasn't completely unaware of the choreography of a relationship, but he was stumbling on his feet and didn't like it. His head was starting to feel light from the cocktails and he realised he hadn't eaten much that day.

Prince took a long drink of his wine before he spoke. "What do you mean?" he asked in response to her words that were still floating between them.

"The other day on the trek, you were going to say I was crazy," she told him.

"No, I wasn't! I said complicated. You were the one who went with crazy."

Perfect, she thought as she heard him defend himself.

"To be fair, you kind of were," the words slipped out of Prince's mouth. And to be fair, she had been. She knew it and had kept that thought to herself. He knew it and just decided to say it out loud now.

They were on a downward spiral, and she could feel herself gathering speed in their combined recklessness.

"Well, you could have handled it better," Celeste wanted him to prove her wrong. She deeply wanted him to say everything was okay. She knew she could stop this charade right now if she wanted, but she didn't know how. Once she had hit the fire alarm button, there was no going back until someone came to save them.

"I'm just saying, you got shitty at me at a time that I just needed you to, to ..." Celeste couldn't end her sentence.

"To what?" Prince asked and she appeared stoney in her silence.

Celeste had caught herself off guard. She was about to say that he could have told her she was important to him in that moment. Reassured her that she had nothing to worry about. That he loved her.

Loved you? So pathetic.

The words rang louder than the alarm in her head. *Do I want him to love me? Do I love him?* She knew she was falling for him. *He is different from the others.* Is that why she felt so frightened?

Not worthy.

"I can't read your mind," Prince interrupted her thoughts. "And frankly, you can't expect me to." Prince took another large gulp of his wine. Celeste did the same. Her head was spinning. She realised she had had too much to drink. She considered whether the alcohol was clouding her judgement but decided it was allowing her to speak her truth. Deep down she knew tomorrow she would regret most of what she was yet to say.

The server appeared once more and placed their food in front of them. Neither of them was hungry at this point and they picked at their meals that others would have oohed and aahed over. They were missing out on the experience they had both been so excited to share.

After quite some time of moving their food around their plates, Celeste said, "I've been thinking and maybe we are just in different places right now."

Prince looked at her and then around the restaurant before turning his eyes back to hers. "I think we are in the same place."

Celeste wasn't sure if it was an olive branch to diffuse the situation or if he was agreeing with her. The voices in her head were not having it.

End it now. He thinks you're crazy and he knows how messed up you are. End it before he dumps you.

"Look, it's not you, it's me." She knew it was a weak line, but the hook was strong.

Prince threw the rest of his wine down his throat. "Fine," was all he said. She felt like he had given up on her.

Why wasn't he fighting for her?

He lifted his empty glass in the air and asked Celeste, "More?"

"May as well," Celeste accepted his offer and for a moment the air cleared, although the tannins from their wine steadfastly gripped their tongues and their coarse words.

"I thought we were having fun?" He explored her eyes with his own.

Always with the fun. You're the fun girl to play with but never to settle down with. He's going to hurt you and you'll be left sad and alone. Take the power back.

"I did too, but I just ... look, I can't explain it."

"Can you try?" It was a reasonable request. But her answer was quite the opposite.

Celeste took aim. "I thought you were good at reading people. But if you don't understand then I don't know what to tell you."

It is funny how fights work. The nuances in words, tones and expressions. Just when you think you have recovered, someone says something that untethers the rope that was holding you together.

Celeste's words were all it took to derail Prince's thoughts. They pierced his senses with their sharp edges, and he felt attacked. Real or not, the combination of the cocktails and wine had altered his perceptions.

"I don't know how you think I'm meant to understand," Prince shifted in his seat. She could tell he was irritated, and she wondered if he was about to get up and walk away from her.

"Maybe we just aren't so good for each other after all." Prince wasn't sure if he was actually agreeing with her or was just being spiteful in return.

His words stung.

More silence and Prince stared at the wine he was spinning in his glass. Celeste looked around the restaurant and wondered if anyone noticed them. Did anyone else see the tension, the unease that was radiating from their conversation. She looked around the room to see if she caught the eye of someone watching. Instead, she saw a room full of people who were smiling as they sat at their tables, talking with their loved ones, glasses clinking in celebration. Everyone looked happy.

"I thought we had something going?" Prince said more to himself than to her.

Deep down Celeste wanted Prince to be everything she thought he could be, and likely was. But she wasn't willing to risk the pain of disappointment later.

Please he says that to all the girls, the voice in her head said.

"Do you think we moved too soon?" He continued, searching for an answer to what was happening between them. He didn't think they had but he was also aware women were often forced into questioning their decisions based on archaic societal expectations. They had talked about it earlier on during their courting and he thought he had expressed his progressive stance that women have the same choices as men and should be viewed as equals. Had he not made himself clear?

I knew it! The fact he was bringing it up meant he thought they had moved too soon. That she had given it up too easily. *You know he'll never see you more than anything but a slut. What were you thinking?* She took another long drink.

"You know what, yes. I think we moved too soon," she answered.

"You do? Well, I don't mind if you want to slow things down.

He is not going to be happy to slow things down. Don't listen to him.

"Maybe we need to take a break?

Prince contemplated her response and took a beat before replying. He was wavering between resolution and revolt. He didn't like conflict within his relationships and truth be told, he hadn't learnt how to navigate footing that was not solid. He was aware she was upset but his own emotions had been taking priority throughout what was not quite a fight but was more than just a conversation. "Look. I don't know if I believe a break is the best way to resolve an issue."

Celeste wondered if this was the moment he was going to fight for their future. Instead, he said, "Maybe you just need to sleep on it and see how you feel in the morning? I don't know what's gotten into you, but it seems you're being a little erratic right now."

"I'm not being erratic, I'm just trying to tell you how I feel," she retaliated and continued. "You know what, I think that you don't really understand me at all then."

"Oh lighten up," Prince took his chances at being light-hearted but a voice in his head questioned if his dismissiveness was intentional. He wondered if he was throwing petrol on the fire.

Her eyes were wild, and she pulled herself deep into the back of her chair. "I've been trying to tell you who I am, and you just don't listen."

"I do listen to you."

"I don't know that you do."

Prince shook his head and opened his eyes wide with bafflement, "I'm not exactly sure how we have gotten to where we are tonight. This is crazy."

Celeste was angry and she raised her voice, "I'm not crazy!"

"I never said you were!" His patience had run dry, and his tone had also lifted an octave. He heavy handedly put his glass down on the table.

Prince took a long breath in and exhaled, and Celeste finally picked up her water glass and took a sip.

Prince spoke first. "What do you want to do? I mean, I thought things were going pretty well. But if you're saying otherwise, then I guess that's it then."

Celeste felt a pain in her heart. *Was he not going to fight for her? Was he really giving up?* While it seemed like he was about to give her the ending she wanted, she wasn't prepared for the hurt she had caused herself.

"Look, I was having a good time," he told her.

She could have taken that statement in many ways, but the pain she was feeling was real and she didn't want to experience it anymore. She was already too exposed, and her vulnerability fed her sensitivity, and she created an elaborate story to the seven words he just spoke.

"Oh, I bet you were! Particularly the other night! Was it a 'good time'?" she played on his words in hope that he would react. She wanted any excuse to follow through with her plan.

Prince almost sounded confused when he answered, "Well, yes, but that's not what I meant."

"What? You don't like sex? Or is your problem an 'easy girl'?" She was off the rails and her words were loose in their air between them.

No going back now, I guess.

"No, that's not what I meant."

"What do you mean then? Exactly what are you looking for in a girl?" Celeste taunted.

Prince weighed whether he should answer, "A woman who ..."

Celeste clapped back, "A woman who ... Do you want a lady? Or a whore? A simple girl? An intelligent woman?" Exasperated, she continued, "What? What do you want?"

She was flabbergasted that he considered her question and answered, "All those things!"

Celeste responded sarcastically to mask the inadequacy she felt, "She sounds like the perfect woman!"

Prince appeared to have conceded to the battle he was in and let off his own warning shots, "She does, doesn't she."

For a moment, Celeste broke the character in her own play and asked, "Do you believe that?" The storm had subsided for a moment, allowing them to catch their breath.

"Believe what?" Prince genuinely had lost track of this production he was starring in.

"That a perfect woman exists?" Celeste reminded him.

"Maybe? Yes. I don't know." Prince felt like he was caught in a trap, and he understood at this point in the game, he was losing no matter what. He allowed himself to feel agitated. He also knew he could have diffused whatever this was that was going on, but his own anger that had been within reach all week was growing and he toyed with the idea of just letting it envelop him and to feel the sweet release of uncensored rage.

The thunder roared again in her head. "Do you believe in love at first sight too? How about fairy tales?" She was trying to belittle him, and he wasn't having it.

"Can't I?" He threw back in her face.

Celeste laughed as if she didn't have a care in the world. "The perfect woman. Fairy tales. Sounds delightful!"

She watched Prince drink his wine, not saying a word in return. *You're not good enough. May as well double down.* "You should look for that. You deserve it. And if she can't give you all that; she's clearly not good enough."

Prince may have been dragged into this fight, but he caught the weakness in Celeste's voice and the sadness that poured from her eyes. He understood she meant she was not good enough. "I'm not saying that," his anger subsided but his patience was still a thin morsel of what it usually was.

"Yes, you are! You expect perfection!"

"Well, I thought you were pretty perfect," he spoke honestly, and she felt an arrow pierce into her heart.

Celeste didn't know what to say. She was confused by his words and while he had been complicit in the latter part of their battle, he seemed to be waving a white flag.

Don't be pathetic, you're not perfect.

The words assaulted her mind and swelled like the ocean. If she paused for a moment, she could have allowed herself to recognise he was being genuine. He was not playing any games and was speaking his truth. But instead, she let the scarred child who was scared she wasn't good enough take the lead.

"Well, I'm not perfect. And you can't expect perfection. Are you perfect? No, you're not. So, stop expecting perfection from everyone around you. Stop expecting it from me," Celeste realised she had raised her voice again and some of the other patrons had turned their heads to see what the commotion was about.

The server approached and asked if everything was alright. Prince smiled and handed over his card, "All good here, but we'll take the check thanks." The lightning had struck, and the damage was done. The dark clouds remained, and neither could see any signs of a rainbow through the fog of their inebriation and their egos.

And just like that, Celeste got what she had set out to do. As Prince scribbled on the receipt and put his credit card back into his wallet, he mumbled and shook his head, "Okay ... I tried ... but ... I can't do this." And with that, he stood up.

They looked at each other for the briefest of moments and a thousand words could have passed between them in those seconds. If you looked closely, you could see the sadness in their eyes that lay behind the armour they wore. Prince walked out.

She wasn't sure if he had said anything to her while he stood before her. It was a blur. She wasn't sure if he was angry or sad or just fed up. And while she got what she wanted, she found herself wanting a different outcome. She realised she had indeed wanted him to fight for her, whatever that meant. She wanted him to calm her nerves and reassure her everything was okay. But he hadn't. Instead, he had left.

So maybe her historic pattern of behaviour had saved her disastrous heartbreak, and his name was another to add to the list of men that lived up to her low expectations.

Celeste felt the harsh prickles in her eyes as tears threatened to escape. It took everything she had to not allow herself to cry. She sat for a moment, looking through the empty space he had walked through seconds ago and instead of sadness, forced herself to find anger.

"Typical," she said out loud as she stood and gathered her belongings.

Chapter 18: *Beyond the White Horse*

"Where are those self-help books you read, sounds like you need them," Prince's dad joked, and Prince rolled his eyes.

"Okay, for the last time, they aren't self-help books."

"Don't knock it till you try it," his dad replied. "So, you had a fight, I'm sure it's not that big of a deal."

"I thought it was going so well but then she flipped out and said she needed time, and something about me not understanding her," Prince shared. He was perched on the edge of his old brown leather couch that he had had for years. He had picked it up at a second-hand store in the East Village and while not as cheap as it could have been given it was used, it had worn in all the right ways over the years, and he loved it as soon as he sat in it.

Prince continued, "I thought I made it clear I liked her? What more could I have done?"

His dad had walked over to Prince's bookcase and was looking at the bookbinders without really reading the labels.

"Dad?" Prince asked.

"Oh, you're actually asking me?"

Prince slouched back on his couch.

His dad pondered his question before he replied, "I wasn't there, so I'm not sure I can give you all the answers you are looking for. But I can assume that the two of you were not really listening to each other by the end of it."

"What do you mean?" Prince enquired.

"Look, all I know is that when your mom and I first got together, we had some whopping big fights that usually stemmed from a lot of stuff that had nothing to do with each other."

"Like how big? I don't remember you guys ever really fighting when I was growing up. I can't imagine you having any sort of serious argument." Prince seemed genuinely surprised and his dad laughed.

"Oh, we are human and just like most other couples. We've certainly had our fair share during our time together. Still do," he offered. "You must have noticed the fights your mother and I had over the years. I'd like to think we were that perfect, but I know we aren't."

"Well of course I knew when you had spats, but I didn't think it was anything big. I mean, you guys always just got along."

"We did. We do! But just because you didn't see what went on behind closed doors doesn't mean it didn't happen. We were good at only letting you see the rainbow and not the storm."

Prince fidgeted with the cushion he had put on his lap and seemed to be taking in what his dad had just said, "I guess I just always thought of you guys having this perfect relationship."

His dad laughed again, and Prince considered his memories, holding firm on his stance that his parents had projected that a real-life fairy tale was possible.

"You always say each mistake leads to the perfect person."

"You know what I mean," his dad replied, like he always did when he spoke about finding the perfect mate.

"Actually, no, I don't," Prince waited for clarification.

"Perfect for you." His dad said matter-of-factly like Prince should have known already.

"What does that even mean?" Prince asked.

"It means if you're looking for 'the one' then you're probably not going to find it."

"Gee, does Mom know you don't believe in 'the one'?"

"Come on son, did we really lead you down some yellow brick road? Are you telling me you believe in fairy tales?" his dad pressed. "Look, it's not that I don't believe in happy endings – actually I'm a big fan ..." he paused for effect and grinned at his son.

Prince had a soft spot for his dad's inappropriate dad jokes. "Yes Dad, I get it. Continue please."

His dad looked pleased with himself and went on, "But the reality of relationships is that they can be hard work. Your mom and I love each other, but love doesn't give you a lobotomy. We were still two different people trying to work as one. And that takes compromise. The so-called fairy tale you see in the two of us came much later when we really understood each other."

"So, what am I meant to do now?" Prince asked. He had exchanged only a few text messages with Celeste since their fight, and they were polite bordering on professional. He wasn't sure where they stood and whether they were even in a relationship anymore.

While he may have appeared confident on the outside, inside he was spinning. Prince had realised it was the first time in his adult life he felt a piece of himself was missing since their altercation and her absence. He had spent much of his time going over that night in his head trying to understand when it all went wrong. What she said. What he said. What had he done that he shouldn't have. He had concluded that walking out on her probably wasn't the right decision. But he had admitted to himself he didn't know how to react in the moment, and instead of facing the music, he ran to a quiet place.

"What are you scared of?" His dad interrupted his thoughts.

"Huh?" Prince didn't understand the question.

"When you guys are fighting, or whatever you want to call this, what are you scared of? What scares you the most?"

Prince sat in silence for quite some time and truly digested his dad's question. This was not an unusual question from his dad. He got his philosophical outlook from him, and they have spent many hours over the years peeling back the layers on every topic imaginable. Just not quite enough time on love, Prince considered at this moment.

Probably because there had never been anyone who had gotten under his skin the way Celeste did, and he assumed it would just be easy when the time came.

He thought back over their conversations, her reactions, their mild disagreements, and their final blow-out. The age-old answer was the first to pop into his head, that he feared being hurt. That was a no-brainer and while not everyone can admit it, Prince wasn't ashamed of that. But that's not what his dad was asking. He wanted him to go deeper into himself and put the pieces of the puzzle together. Find the broken parts of himself, the same brokenness everyone who has experienced life has, and feel the rough edges.

How did he react in those moments? What was bubbling inside that he ignored? What was he truly feeling?

"I'm scared I'm not good enough," Prince answered honestly. His dad looked at him and didn't say a word, giving him space to think through his words.

When Prince contemplated how he felt when she was around, how she would sometimes put herself down and in the moments she would speak her truth and open up about her insecurities, he would often find himself feeling agitated that she didn't see herself the way he did. But the more he thought about it with his dad by his side, he realised his agitation was a reaction to his own insecurities. He knew he had his own flaws. He had his perceptions of the world that made him act in ways not understood by all around him. He could be short tempered and critical. He knew he wasn't perfect, and deep down was afraid others viewed him differently to how he wanted to be seen.

He was no different to most people walking wounded through the world. Their hurt and inner frustrations assailing those around them. Prince often felt he should be better. For his family, his friends, his loved ones. For Celeste.

He understood how perfect she was. Perfect for him. And in her absence of understanding her own self, it made Prince more acutely aware of what an extraordinary woman she was.

And this frightened him. Because what did he have to offer in return? And if he was unable to help her see past her own demons, what good was he? If he couldn't banish her demons so she could live freely, he embraced his own in solidarity. That was why he walked away.

His thoughts assaulted his mind and swelled like the ocean. If he paused for a moment that night, showed her he was genuine, and truly listened to what she was saying, could he have changed the course of their evening?

As he sat reflecting on what might have been instead of what was, his dad's voice broke through the silence. "And what do you think she is scared of?"

"Probably the same thing," Prince thought out loud.

"Humans are not as complicated as we like to think we are," his dad gently said. "But we manage to complicate our lives all the same."

It was true. Prince had watched people wreak havoc on themselves the world over. Through his travels he had met many people from all walks of life, and the great lesson learned was that we are all the same. We are complex creatures with emotional trigger points and often, we are not equipped to manage more than mild turmoil.

It's not part of our school curriculum to learn the mastery of self-help. And it's not part of our everyday conversations to better understand ourselves. 'I'm good, thanks' is an acceptable answer that makes everyone feel comfortable.

Most of us move so quickly to build up brick walls to protect ourselves and wonder why we feel pain when they occasionally come crashing down upon us.

Every time, we pick up each brick and build the wall again but forget to clear the fragments that have remained behind. This leaves it more unstable than the last time it was built.

"Most of us just want to be seen," his dad said. "But we fear showing too much of ourselves, as that leaves us vulnerable."

"Unfortunately, we live in a world where vulnerability is sometimes seen as weak," Prince interjected.

"Which is ridiculous," his dad countered. "Vulnerability is beautiful. We should all try it more often."

"So, what are you saying, Dad?"

"I'm saying it won't kill you to open up to each other. Communication is key, kiddo."

"So, I hear," Prince said.

Prince had played his part in their fight, and he knew it. But acknowledging it out loud was another story. No one wants to be the reason why something went wrong.

"And apologising won't kill you either," his dad added.

"Hey, I've got no problem saying sorry, her on the other hand ..." Celeste had even admitted it herself, so he wasn't speaking out of turn.

"Don't let a simple fight ruin something that could be great. Or it might not be! But you won't know if you don't give it a try."

"I mean, she is pretty great. You'd really like her."

"I trust you've got good taste! I mean, you're your father's son, right.

"Yes, Dad," Prince laughed.

"Just remember, you've got to let each other be heard."

Prince smiled at his dad. He was lucky to have such a close relationship with him. Their bond ran deep and he was grateful he was able to be so unabashed with him. He really wanted to introduce his father to Celeste.

As if he could read his mind, his dad said, "I'd like to meet this woman who has gotten under your skin."

"Soon Dad, soon," Prince stood up and stretched. He felt like he was stretching away his angst and the unease that he had been feeling for the last few days. It felt good to unload his thoughts and regurgitate them into some semblance of order.

Now all he needed to do was find out if Celeste had had the same opportunity and whether she was open to walking down the path they had started on together.

Prince's tummy grumbled, "Want to head out and grab something to eat?"

"Sure!" his dad rose and felt his pockets to make sure he had everything.

Prince grabbed his keys from the old glass ashtray where he kept them, which sat on an entryway table. He had bought both at yet another second-hand store, that time upstate.

"Let's go," Prince said as he made room for his dad to walk out of the apartment first before closing the door behind them.

Chapter 19: *Flee the Wicked Woods*

Celeste jumped up from the couch when she heard the buzz on the intercom. "Pizza's here," she called out to Sarah who was in the bathroom.

"Coming," she heard Sarah reply.

Celeste took a moment to familiarise herself with the intercom buttons and pressed the one labelled door. She had been in Sarah and Holland's apartment a thousand times over, but she wasn't often charged with door duties.

Celeste swung open the door with several locks that Sarah never used, and patiently waited, listening for footsteps on the stairs or the hum of the elevator. Sarah and Holland lived on the third floor of an elevator building in Greenpoint in Brooklyn. They had flown the coop and left the island a few years earlier when they secured a rent stabilised apartment in the up-and-coming neighbourhood. Since then, seemingly overnight, high-rises appeared along the water as well as trendy restaurants and bars selling cocktails at the same price you'd expect to pay in the West Village. Gentrification was real and they were grateful their rent increases were secured.

The third floor was just two flights of stairs, given the ground floor in the United States was classed as floor one. So, it always sounded a lot worse than it was when talking about walk up buildings. At least in Celeste's mind.

She heard the door of the elevator open. Celeste was always curious about the people who chose to take the lift over using their legs, and as the thought entered her mind she smiled at the dishevelled but grinning delivery man who appeared before her a moment later. She didn't blame him for taking the weight of the world off his weary legs by taking the short elevator ride, as she wondered what his step count was at the end of each shift. She always tipped delivery drivers well, especially in extreme weather. It was not lost on Celeste that someone was willing to work for minimum wage to allow her to be too lazy to collect her own order.

She had cash at the ready and thanked him as she took the huge pizza box and handed him a handful of bills.

Closing the door behind her, she walked back into the living room where Sarah had laid out napkins and glasses of water beside the carafe of red wine on the coffee table.

They didn't use the dining room table, instead they sat comfortably on the couch.

Opening the lid of the pizza box, they each grabbed a New York slice and dug in. In all seriousness, New York pizza was quite possibly Celeste's favourite thing about living in the city. At least in her top five favourite things. She admitted she might even miss it more than her friends here if she were to ever leave.

Sarah had invited her over for pizza and wine, and to debrief about her current relationship status. Holland was at an exhibition opening at a gallery in Chelsea with friends from college and it was a good opportunity for her and her old friend to spend some time together.

Celeste asked Sarah how her day was, and Sarah rolled her eyes. She worked at a studio that rented its space for rehearsals and auditions, mostly for the musical theatre industry given its proximity to Times Square. Sarah was in charge of operations and coordinated the rentals to aspiring actors and demanding producers. It was where Sarah had met Holland eight years ago, when Holland was auditioning for a part in a new musical that she didn't get. But Sarah liked to say that Holland got an even better part that day, as she became Sarah's leading lady. It was corny and it was an old joke, but it still warmed Celeste's heart whenever she heard that story. She loved their love story.

"So how is Holland? How's things? How is work going?" Celeste asked Sarah, right as she took another bite of pizza.

"Busy," was all she could offer with a mouthful of food.

"Any new shows coming down the pike?" It was a funny saying that Celeste had never heard of before she moved to the US. Down the pipeline yes, down the pike, no. But she had picked it up and liked how it sounded in her British accent.

"Enough about me, what is going on with Prince?" Sarah had quickly moved on to her interrogation.

Celeste dramatically rolled her eyes as she fell back on the couch. She sat back up and grabbed her glass of wine.

"I don't know how it spiralled the way it did," Celeste told a half-truth.

"Sounds about right," Sarah offered. "Got to love those fights that you reflect back on and can barely remember how they started."

"Right! Well, he was late for a start," Celeste said.

Sarah shook her head in solidarity with Celeste. "How hard is it to be on time?"

"Right!" Celeste said again.

"I get you, I mean, you and I are the same when it comes to that," she paused to let Celeste continue.

"I don't know," and she felt like she really didn't. "I was already feeling jittery on the way there, picking holes in him and looking for red flags."

Sarah nodded and drank her wine.

"And I started thinking about past relationships, and how they've turned out. And then I started judging myself and thinking maybe I had got it all wrong and that he didn't really like me." The words fell out of her mouth before she could stop them.

"And then he was late," Sarah was coaxing Celeste to open up.

"And then he was late, so that was it, confirmation he wasn't such a great guy, because how could he be late if he really cared about me?"

Celeste listened to herself and knew she sounded exaggerated. She put her glass down on the coffee table and defeatedly buried her head in her hands. She looked up at her friend who had picked up her wine and handed it back to her.

"I'm pretty sure he thinks I'm crazy," Celeste stated.

"I doubt it. And if he does, fuck him." Sarah didn't mince her words, but she softened them. "You know I'm on your side, so if you tell me he's no good then I believe you. But can I say," Celeste braced herself for some hard truths, "you do have a tendency to self-sabotage."

"And on that note, I'm pretty sure I said something along the lines of 'do you want a lady or a whore' or something like that."

Sarah almost spat out her wine and laughed out loud. "You sure go in for dramatic effect."

"I think the cocktails went to my head," Celeste tried to make excuses. "I just wanted to know what kind of woman he is looking for, am I it or am I doing something wrong?"

"You don't need to do anything or be any sort of someone," Sarah smiled.

"I know, well, rational Celeste knows that. Irrational Celeste seems to have thoughts of her own."

They both drank their wine and took a beat while Celeste processed her thoughts before she continued. "Speaking of voices in my head," Celeste started.

Sarah laughed and interjected, "How have they been lately?"

"I will say, at least now I have a better understanding of why they are there. Nya is an absolute legend," Celeste used the term she picked up while living in Australia.

"Isn't she! I'm so glad you like her. She's a master at what she does. So just how messed up are you?" Sarah joked.

"Where do I start," Celeste joked in return. "I'm not looking forward to having to admit to her I took a few steps backwards."

"Ah, that's what she is there for. But how frustrated do you think therapists get with their clients? What do you think they're saying about us to their other therapist friends?"

"I don't even want to know," Celeste laughed. "But I'm going to give her a lot to complain about at our next session when she finds out I threw all her good work out the window with this stupid fight." She turned to look straight at Sarah and asked, "Have I totally fucked it up?"

Before she let her answer, Celeste continued, "You know he didn't even stay to work it out. He just left. Just like that."

Sarah considered what her friend had just said and tried to piece together the story she was telling, along with the thoughts and feelings she knew were bubbling up inside her. "What do you mean he didn't stay to work it out? What did you want him to do?"

Celeste didn't need time to think about her response, "I think if he really cared, he wouldn't have left and would have stayed to work it out. I was ready to talk about it if he was. We could have worked through it and fixed it." She had dropped the magic word, and it didn't go unnoticed by either of them.

"Fix it?" Sarah asked and Celeste knew where their conversation was headed. Sarah has had front row seats to Celeste's past relationships and behaviours, and the topic of fixing a man was not a new one. They had spent plenty of nights eating too many slices and drinking too many glasses of wine as they dissected what was wrong with him and how Celeste was going to address it. "Or fix him?" she asked.

Celeste thought about her friend's question and whether she was indeed trying to find fault in Prince so she could endeavour to resolve his problems for him. "The thing is, I don't know that there is anything to fix," Celeste said with some hesitance.

"Well, I'm sure that isn't true," Sarah didn't mean to imply Celeste should dig deeper for grievances she could uncover. She meant that no one is perfect.

"Don't worry, he might not be as damaged as you are used to, but he has still got his own set of issues just like the rest of us," Sarah added.

Sarah was right of course. Celeste felt unsettled at the fact that Prince was not as broken as the other men she had allowed in her life. She perceived him as whole which meant she questioned what she could possibly offer in return. If she was unable to provide a service of repair, then what was she good for?

Celeste had always considered herself to have high self-esteem but as she confided in her friend of the thoughts that indiscriminately steamrolled her, and her sessions with Nya, she wondered if that statement was true anymore. *Has it ever been?*

"I think I just wanted to be perfect for him," Celeste admitted.

"What does that mean?" Sarah asked. "Is there such a thing?" She knew there was not, but she knew this was not the time to lecture and Celeste needed to work through this herself.

"I tried to be the woman he wanted," she answered.

"And what woman is that?"

Celeste laughed a small laugh as the absurdity of her actions was becoming clear. "I truly have no idea," and she didn't. When she thought about the words she carefully crafted and the personalities she tried to project, she realised she had once again allowed her self-doubt to influence her behaviour in ways that made her feel embarrassed.

"It's not that I did anything truly regrettable," she confided in Sarah, "but I am not proud when I think about how I would change who I was if it meant making him happy. It's pathetic."

"It's not pathetic," responded Sarah. "And I won't have you talking about my friend that way."

"If you only knew some of the things I tell myself. The voices in my head … I'm not very nice to myself sometimes," Celeste admitted.

"We all go there. And honestly, I think that crazy voice in our heads isn't all bad. I think most of the time it is just about trying to protect our hearts."

"Well, it hurts more than helps."

"And that's what Nya is there for," Sarah said objectively.

"Ain't that the truth."

"You know, he isn't perfect either," Sarah commented. "Two things can be true simultaneously. He can be flawed and whole at the same time."

Sarah was right and Celeste recalled her first date with Prince, and how afterward she lay in bed considering what kind of man he was. She had observed a man who appeared to be genuine and who might be her match, rather than her usual expectation.

But that voice in her head had been quick to remind her that she could still end up being hurt and had continued to ensure the exit sign was illuminated in her mind. It was a safety mechanism she had learned a long time ago and deployed at the slightest hint of disaster. Real or not.

"Why does this keep happening to me?" Celeste asked.

"Isn't that what you pay Nya for?" Sarah teased as she got up.

Celeste watched as she walked over to her bookshelf and spent the next minute scanning the many books crammed against the wall. An explosion of literature that was not orderly and Celeste wondered how she would possibly find what she was looking for.

"Here it is," Sarah rejoiced as she pulled a book from the shelf and held it up high as if for all to see. She walked back over to the couch and handed the book to Celeste as she sat back down.

"Codependent No More," Celeste read the title out loud and laughed. "Um, thanks …"

"I'm pretty sure I've told you to read this before, and frankly, I'm surprised Nya hasn't."

Celeste's memory was sparked, and she recalled one of her first sessions with Nya where she had indeed told her to buy the book and read it. Now that she thought about it, she had even gone as far as looking for it online at The Strand bookstore. She had met Prince not long after and for some reason, the book had slipped from her mind.

When she thought about the last few months, she knew she had acquired a new set of armour by way of Nya. She had been trying it on more frequently to see if it fit her better than the one she had been wearing for so long. She had an easier time giving away a favourite dress she hadn't worn in a year than she did giving up the battle gear that she felt had protected her since she was a child.

Celeste had approached her therapy the way she approached most things in her life, head on and with sincere certainty that she would excel at what she had set her mind to do. However, as she sat across from her friend, unloading her sadness and fears, she was beginning to understand that while she had addressed many relationship obstacles with Nya, she was not cured of her triggers.

On more than one occasion, Nya had reminded Celeste it would take time to overcome her instinct to react when faced with an undesirable interaction. Once again, the words 'If you're hysterical, it's historical' rang in her head.

Celeste had hoped she would progress as quickly as a New York minute in resolving hidden trauma she carried with her, but therapy takes time and while she had started to heal, she knew she had a way to go. Her old armour was within reach, but she liked the way her new suit felt on her. When she considered how much money she had spent on therapy to date, she realised she had her own designer outfit hanging in the closet of her mind.

She turned the book over in her hands as her eye scanned the words on the cover. 'Is someone else's problem your problem?' she read and laughed out loud.

"Fine," she said to Sarah. "I'll read the book."

"Good! I think you'll get a lot out of it. And be sure to tell Nya it was me who made you read it."

"Maybe you should talk to Nya about your need for recognition from your therapist," Celeste laughed as she slid the book into her oversized handbag that was sitting on the floor beside her.

Sarah poured the last of the wine into Celeste's glass and stood up to get another bottle from the small wine fridge that was her pride and joy in the kitchen.

"Thanks," Celeste said as she raised her glass and took a sip. She let the bold red swirl in her mouth and tried to taste the flavours the label had promised.

She thought about how much she still had to learn about herself and began to mentally prepare to read the book. She wondered if one ever truly understands themself and if relationships could really ever be easy. She asked Sarah as she walked back in the room holding a different bottle from the last.

Without skipping a beat, Sarah replied, "Yes and no."

"Lucky I'm not paying you as my therapist," Celeste jibed.

Sarah laughed, and clarified, "No, I don't think we ever stop learning about ourselves, but yes, I do think it gets easier. Nothing is perfect my friend, and the sooner you realise we are all perfectly imperfect, the better."

Perfectly imperfect. The words swam around her head and she wondered if that was a reality that existed.

"All right, enough!" Celeste exclaimed. They had talked at length about Prince and she needed to change the subject. While she appreciated the support and knew that Sarah would continue to listen for as long as she wanted to talk, Celeste was sick of the sound of her own voice and frankly was tired of saying Prince's name. She would take what Sarah had imparted and reflect in solitude later.

Celeste changed the subject, "Tell me about your holiday." Sarah and Holland had returned only days earlier from a week-long trip to Bordeaux and Celeste wanted to hear every detail.

Chapter 20: *Bullet Proof Slippers*

Celeste waved the book in front of her laptop camera and announced, "So, I finally read it!"

She was excited to share this news with Nya. After Sarah had unceremoniously thrust the softcover book into her hands, Celeste had been unable to put it down. 'This Melody Beattie really knows what she's talking about', she had thought of the author, time and time over as her eyes drank in her words. While she had found a lot of conversation starters for her inner voice, she initially thought she was reading literature about a subject she found she knew a lot about, but she didn't feel applied to her.

However, her lightbulb moment came upon her when she was reading the chapter on loving yourself. Celeste had always been proud of what she considered her high self-esteem. Or at least in how she defined it. She was a high achiever and a self-starter, she flaunted her impeccable ability to multi-task and the fact that no matter how busy she was, she always found time to take on a new project or help someone in need. She could do it all, just ask her.

She didn't relate to the words on the page that spoke about how a codependent didn't like how they looked, couldn't stand their bodies or thought they were stupid.

Celeste rarely felt that way about herself, at least not, outside of a relationship. However, the sentiment of feeling unlovable weighed on her. She liked being loved, she knew that for a fact. But the word unlovable cut right through her and she couldn't define how it made her feel in that moment.

But as she continued reading, different words on the pages jumped out and figuratively slapped her in the face.

Melody's statements swirled in her head and ignited feelings she recognised immediately. She spoke of only feeling worth something when we are helping someone else; of constantly putting oneself in situations where we have no choice but to feel badly about ourselves; being a perfectionist and a workaholic; and the self-destructive behaviour of constantly picking at ourselves.

It made Celeste consider the ease in which she entered relationships with someone who was not good for her, as their words were never as critical as her own.

Celeste had sat wide-eyed reading the chapter and felt the sting of tears she didn't hold back. She had laid the book on her lap as she digested it all.

Melody's words cried out to her.

Celeste reflected on the men she had chosen to initiate relationships with. They were almost carbon copies when surveying their behaviour. They weren't bad men, certainly not. But they were damaged, maybe as much as Celeste was, possibly more. They were projects that Celeste threw her heart and soul at, most likely in a vain attempt to fix unresolved problems of her own.

Celeste was confirming what she had already started to realise through her sessions with Nya. She had learned over the years that it was better to hurt herself before she let anyone else hurt her. She was much harder on herself than she was on others and had regularly caused herself harm by choosing men who would break her heart.

It gave her a sense of control.

She shared these thoughts with Nya who had been listening intently to Celeste.

"I'm not sure where to begin, or how I'm meant to start fixing myself," Celeste shared.

"Well, you have already started that journey," Nya comforted her. "We're here aren't we?"

Celeste shrugged her shoulders, "I guess so," she smiled.

"You're being too hard on yourself," Nya said.

"Sounds about right," Celeste joked. "I just don't understand how it could be this way. How did I not recognise this about myself till now? I've spent so much time recognising it in others, but here I was falling apart this whole time."

"Tell me how you're feeling right now? Use whatever words come to mind."

Celeste didn't have to think long, and she knew from previous sessions it was sometimes better to let the words fall quickly from her lips rather than analysing them first.

"Once I let someone in, I'm no longer free," Celeste said. She was sure this should be defined as a major breakthrough.

Even Nya seemed surprised, replying, "That's quite a statement. Can you elaborate?"

This time, Celeste allowed herself a moment to craft her words into a statement that truly meant what she felt. It was a bold declaration, but she stood by it.

"On one hand, I'm trapped being the person I pretended to be to get here," Celeste summed up what her declaration meant to her. "Being bound to another person helps me define myself. I'm the caretaker, I'm the rock, and I'm the one who will make things better."

"And on the other hand?"

"Deep down, the real me is still in there. Caged. And I complain about it. I don't want it to be that way, I say I want to get out. And eventually I do. But really, it's where I'm most comfortable, just like the book says," Celeste hated she was a textbook case. "And then I do it all over again."

She paused and Nya remained silent, giving her time to ponder some more. "It's a safe space for me. While I look after someone else; I don't have to acknowledge that no one is looking after me."

"You want to be looked after?" Nya pressed.

It made Celeste's stomach turn over to admit it. She felt weak. She didn't want to be seen as a woman who needed anyone.

"So why choose men who can't?" Nya asked her.

The pieces of the puzzle were clicking together for Celeste, and Nya was eagerly awaiting the moment she would see the whole picture. It wasn't Nya's job to tell her clients how the story ends; it was her job to guide them there. "So, you're not free in these relationships. How else does that make you feel?"

"Unseen."

"Okay …" Nya trailed off and patiently waited.

"I want to be seen as the woman I am."

"And you don't think they do see you like that?"

"Somewhat, but not really. They see the parts they want to see, but not me as a whole person."

"Why do you think you have never dated someone who does see you?" Nya pointedly asked.

"Well, that would require dating someone who doesn't need fixing," Celeste had started to despise the word fix.

"I'm sure you've met those men before. Did you give them a chance?"

Celeste reflected on the men who had come and gone throughout her life, and it was true. There were a few that she recalled who probably had more to offer than she realised at the time. The 'nice' guys who she 'just didn't have a connection with'. The ones she said felt more like friends to her — rather than the foes she tended to fall for.

Nya interrupted her thoughts by adding, "and it seems like you are dating one of them now."

She was right, of course. Celeste had found a friend that she was falling in love with and it frightened her. Friends were given the keys to your house. They were who you called when you needed help. They celebrated with you at your best and held out their hands to you at your worst. They accepted you for who you were and loved you unconditionally.

"Yes, but ... I don't know if he really knows me. The real me." As the words came out of Celeste's mouth, she knew that wasn't true. She knew that Prince had been privy to the woman her friends saw, but she had also made sure to slap on some lipstick and conceal as much of herself as she could. "So, maybe he's seen pieces of me," she concluded.

"Why not let him see the whole of you," Nya asked the most terrifying of questions.

Is she out of her mind?

"Because if too much is revealed ..." Celeste wasn't sure she could finish her sentence but the silence in the room called for it. "Will he leave me?"

"Why does that make you afraid?"

"Because I don't want him to," Celeste admitted. Prince had flown under the radar and had broken the protective defence system she had so carefully placed around her.

Dammit.

When her other relationships had ended, it was inevitable, and Celeste was comfortable amid the cacophony of regret mingled with self-righteousness.

But if Prince were to leave her, she was sure her self-doubt would explode and her feelings would be written in the sky, for all to see. Full view. No facade to hide behind.

She would be exposed and raw to the world and she was not sure she could recover.

"Feeling unloved by someone who doesn't love themselves isn't so bad. Feeling unloved by someone who has their shit together ..." Celeste trailed off to find the right words. She couldn't find them.

Nya told Celeste, "You have your shit together."

Celeste laughed out loud and replied, "Me? Look at me, look at all the things that are wrong with me."

"You have your shit together," Nya repeated. Adding, "Everyone has flaws."

Nya was trying to make a point that Celeste wasn't as damaged as she was allowing herself to believe she was. She wanted her to find in herself that she was worthy.

"I just want to be loved," tears streamed down Celeste's cheeks. She felt exposed and ridiculous. Saying out loud she wanted to be loved felt like taking a bullet. This wasn't the projection of a strong woman she purported to be.

"And yet you chose men you knew would not change and could never put your needs above their own," Nya reminded her.

"I'm my own worst enemy. I sabotage myself. I'm too comfortable ignoring my own needs. As if I don't deserve them to be recognised. But deep down, I desperately want them to be."

"It's your self-protection." Nya tilted her head to the side, and Celeste knew it was her way of saying it's okay. "It's how you protect your heart."

Celeste knew that to be true. It was a well-worn playbook, and she knew every move.

"So, when they let me down, I can say I knew it. Not that the pain isn't real but now I question where that pain was coming from. Them or my past. I'm comfortable in it either way. It's familiar," Celeste took a tissue and blew her nose. "When I walk away, it's with some sort of feeling of control, when in reality, I don't have as much as I'd like to think I do." She took a deep breath and exhaled loudly.

"How are you feeling?" Nya asked.

"Like I'm a cliché. Just like that bloody book says, I do this to myself because I think I deserve it."

Celeste continued, "I wish I could control that voice in my head. Sometimes she's standing beside me and other times it's like she's pinning me down."

"If you could sum up what that voice says, what do you think that would be?"

It was a difficult question as that voice in her head was both ally and enemy. Although for the greater part, she felt attacked more often than supported.

"If I date someone who is not broken, what if I'm not good enough?"

"Once you let someone in, maybe you'll be free." Nya used Celeste's expression to help her navigate to another journey she hadn't opened up to the possibility of.

"What do you mean?"

"By fully realising your own worth, you'll find a freedom you don't understand yet," Nya answered. "Regardless of any outcome in life, once a woman finds herself, she can be unstoppable."

"Are you referring to another cliché ... you've got to love yourself before anyone else can love you?" Celeste smiled as she asked Nya when she already knew the answer.

"Hey, some clichés ring true," Nya replied.

Celeste pondered what Nya had just said and understood the gravity of what it meant. If she didn't allow herself to be who she was, would she ever find the happiness she longed for?

It scared Celeste to allow herself to fall in love with a man that she deemed whole. She would be leaving herself wide open to take the kind of hit she didn't think her heart could withstand should he ever leave her. But how much longer could her heart withstand her leaving herself over and over again.

When she met Prince, she knew right away he was dangerous. While not flawless, he was different from the rest of them. *He's too good to be true*, she had told herself often. But she had no statistical data to back up that old wives tale, and he had done nothing to prove otherwise. In fact, he had done quite the opposite.

What frightened her the most was when he would look at her when she was speaking. He didn't look through her like many past boyfriends had done. Instead he seemed to see her. He truly listened and for the first time, she felt heard.

He seemed genuinely interested in her and she found herself being put first. It was a peculiar feeling to her, having never had a partner who put her needs above their own.

However, instead of embracing this newfound feeling, Celeste had panicked. She was unaccustomed to a man who might remove her role as caregiver.

What scared Celeste was her unbound feelings for Prince, but what scared her even more, was that she thought that he might feel the same way about her in return.

Nya knew Celeste well enough by now to know that Celeste didn't have the confidence to declare he felt that way about her, even though from everything Nya had heard to date, it did indeed appear that way.

Nya needed to get Celeste to admit she wasn't comfortable being seen and had spent years ensuring she wasn't by choosing men who stole the spotlight, allowing her to remain in the shadows.

Celeste was faced with the fact that she only let herself be exposed with her explicit permission, which was rare with the men she dated. She mostly spent her time allowing their emotions to occupy hers. She took on other people's pain in an effort, she believed, to help them. However, Nya had pointed out that in fact, she felt if she burdened herself with their trauma, it allowed her a place in their life. What use was she otherwise?

The only time she laid herself bare was in her darkest moments by herself when she questioned why she wasn't worthy of more love.

Her role in any man's life was to make his heart sing, meanwhile she felt she was bleeding from hers.

"You've dated a lot of pricks," Nya said candidly, cutting the tension that had been running through Celeste's nervous system.

Celeste laughed out loud at the bluntness of Nya's comment. "Yes, I have," she agreed.

"The right man will accept you for who you are," Nya offered. "And from everything you've told me about Prince, he seems like a good guy. I say that because I've gotten to know you and while we both know you've made some questionable decisions," they both laughed at Nya's honesty, "I think you should trust that uncomfortable new feeling you're having when it comes to him."

Nya never gave advice like this lightly. She had to be certain when she made such judgement calls, and it was only because she had felt Celeste was ready to take that next step; and she would be there to hold her hand along the way.

Celeste felt her stomach flutter. She was thrilled Nya was giving her what she felt was permission to write her own story from here on in. Although she was still frightened at the possibility of getting hurt, she wanted to be brave and was ready to stand up and be courageous.

"Do you think I'll get my fairy tale ending?" Celeste asked with a grin on her face suggesting she was kidding.

"I mean, do we believe in them?" Nya didn't and she didn't think Celeste did either. As far as Nya was concerned, it was a dream sold to little girls that recklessly continued into adulthood. The commercialisation of love had too many women skipping down that dollar bill road and it was one of the biggest causes of the self-destruction she saw in her clients every day.

"I've got to stop listening to that little voice in my head," Celeste said.

"Don't give up on her just yet," Nya countered. "You just need to fine tune your radar and realise when it is that voice is helping you, or if it's just white noise."

"You're right, as usual," Celeste was grateful for Nya. Without her she wondered where she would be, or maybe more to the point, knew exactly where she would still be. She knew she had a lot of work ahead of her, but she had come a long way in an already short amount of time.

"I've got some homework to do," Celeste intended to work on all they had spoken about today.

"I think you might find Prince could play a different role in your life that you didn't think possible, if you let him."

Celeste smiled, "You really think so?"

"That's not to say you won't have challenges and compromise will be required," Nya reminded her. She had no intention of creating an illusion of romanticism that only existed in a Hollywood movie. "Anyone who tells you relationships aren't work, aren't truly in one."

"I guess you really have to love your job then," Celeste replied. "We're at time, right?"

"We are, so let's put some time on for next week."

They both looked at their calendars and scheduled their next forty-five-minute session at the same time, on the same day the following week.

"I just want to leave you with this," Nya offered. "That freedom you're looking for, it's already in you."

She didn't need to say any more. Celeste heard her loud and clear. It was time to break the mould, turn the page and start rewriting her story. Like all little girls, she had been raised on fairy tales, but from today on, she decided she wasn't going to let anybody sell her on a dream that isn't true. It was time to accept her flaws and time to love herself. There was nothing that she couldn't do ... with a little help from Nya.

"Thank you, I'll speak to you next week!" And with that Nya disappeared from her screen.

Chapter 21: *The Enchanted Forest of Truths*

Celeste sat nervously on her couch before standing and looking at herself in the mirror, then sat back down again, anxiously wringing her hands in her lap. Prince was due any minute.

It had been almost two weeks since they last saw each other. Almost two weeks since Celeste had lost her sensibilities and two weeks since Prince had followed suit and walked out of the restaurant.

It was Prince who had been the first to reach out, two days after their fight. It was a simple text asking how she was. He had not mentioned the fight in his four-word message. She wasn't sure how she should respond. In a new relationship it was always difficult when the first wave of reality crashed over you. Often, you are left without a life raft and struggling to stay afloat. They had both been in uncharted waters and felt like they were learning to swim.

She had responded politely, saying she was good and asking about his wellness in return.

They were aware of the weight of each word that fell on the eggshells under their feet.

After some messages back and forth about the weather and world news, Prince had asked Celeste if they could meet. Celeste was glad Prince was more courageous than she was. She was not convinced he was without his own hesitation. She had wanted to ask him herself, but her fear had kept her lips buttoned tight. She knew that hope burned within her consciousness, and she was longing for the possibility of a 'happily ever after'. This new realisation rested uncomfortably upon her shoulders, but Nya's voice echoed in her head, and she needed to try and not only accept, but embrace, her own vulnerability and the possibility of happiness.

The buzzer sounded. Every cell rushed through her veins, as if sending out an alert to her entire nervous system and vital organs. Celeste took a deep breath, stood up and crossed over to her intercom in the kitchen. She pressed her finger on the button that would allow Prince into the building and into her being.

She opened her apartment door and nervously waited. *Will he be okay with the real me? All of me?* She could hear his footsteps, steady and resolute. At least that's how they sounded in her head.

For Prince, he lifted his feet dubiously, uncertain of her forgiveness.

Within moments Prince was at her door, standing before her at the threshold. "Hi," he smiled. His voice, now so familiar to her ears, made her feel safe.

"Hi," was all Celeste could manage as tears stung her eyes.

Prince immediately took her in his arms and embraced her. They were silent as they clung to each other and for once, the voice in Celeste's head was silent too. Minutes passed without words. Prince felt a sense of relief and Celeste felt a sense of calm. Together, they felt they were where they belonged.

Celeste lifted her head from where it was cradled on his chest and looked into Prince's eyes, "Want to come in?"

They shared a quiet smile as Celeste stepped aside and watched him walk into her home. She closed the door and followed Prince to the living room, where they sat next to each other on her small couch.

"I'm so sorry," Prince was the first to apologise. He had taken her hand in his own and looked directly at her as he spoke. "I should never have walked out on you like that."

Celeste felt her tears start to swell again. She felt the familiar rise of insecurity and it took all her strength to let him see her cry. She wanted to apologise in return but the words were caught in her throat. She had never been good at saying sorry. Not because she wasn't. In fact, she felt sorry almost all the time which was part of the problem. But saying the words out loud felt like an admission of her vulnerability. And in this instance, acknowledging she had something to be sorry for meant she had done something wrong, and in her mind, that meant she was unlovable.

Don't start. Just do it!

She looked at Prince and he looked back at her.

Do it!

"I'm sorry too," Celeste's words fumbled out. She felt sick and exposed. But she had to trust what she had learnt about herself. Prince was different to the rest and that was why this moment was so much harder for her. She was giving hope a space in her heart, and it almost hurt. *What if he lets me down?* She remembered Nya's words, that she already had her freedom inside her. That if he did let her down, it wasn't because she wasn't worth it.

Tears streamed down Celeste's face, and she was embarrassed she couldn't make them stop. But when she looked into Prince's eyes, she saw he was crying too.

"Would you look at the two of us," Prince joked, and Celeste was grateful. He reached out and wiped her cheeks. Celeste returned the favour.

"Ugh, I'm sorry," Celeste said again, wiping at her own tears. But it was one apology Prince wouldn't accept.

"Don't ever be sorry for this," he told her. His words wrapped around her stronger than any hug and right then, she understood that he truly saw her.

They spent hours together that night, coming back together. They talked about their faults and flaws, and their scars and wounds.

Celeste knew that it was the first time in her life that any man had truly seen her. It was a sensation so new, so unfamiliar, and so unchartered, it terrified her. Yet, in that moment of freefall, she knew with Prince by her side she would always land softly.

Celeste could trust Prince with her heart and that's why she was daring to give it to him.

And Prince knew he could trust Celeste.

***

That night, Celeste had brought up an idea with Prince and she was unsure how he would respond. Couples therapy. It could seem an outrageous suggestion to even the most seasoned relationship. Would he think her crazy to suggest this pursuit after such a short-lived romance? She had decided it was worth a possible rebuttal.

She had been surprised when he readily accepted the invitation. *He really is different,* she thought at the time.

In contrast to Prince, it had taken not one but two solo sessions with Nya to coerce her into agreeing. Nya had told Celeste when she first made the request that she didn't think it was appropriate. After all, Nya was *Team Celeste*, and her role was to champion Celeste's needs. However, over those two sessions, they made some long strides in better understanding what happened during her fight with Prince. Spent time discovering more about Celeste's triggers, and Nya felt she was getting a better understanding of what Prince's triggers might have been too. Before she made any more assumptions about him, she had finally agreed to a one-time-only session with the couple.

Ultimately, Nya had agreed to the couple's session as she truly did believe in Celeste and Prince's relationship. She rarely made exceptions unless she honestly believed she could be impartial when required and when she thought she could objectively help.

With Nya at the helm, they reflected on their courtship, the end of the first act at the restaurant that night, and the encore showcasing their apologies to each other. Celeste and Prince could see they had both reached for behaviours that had kept them afloat for most of their lives. It was natural to go to what you have always done. Which made it so much harder to break those habits in future.

Nya had made them dig deep. With kindness, she exposed them to each other in a way they hadn't before, even more than the night they had laid themselves bare to each other. Neither knew that there was still more lying dormant. She pulled from them their worst fears and forced transparency saved for only your most trusted confidant.

Celeste admitted her fear that Prince would see her as she saw herself. That she was broken and unbridled.

She spoke of her pain in her imperfection.

Her desire to be well-received.

Her need for control, because she was never allowed to be reckless.

Her pride in never letting people down and her shame in wishing that she could.

Her desire for someone to look after her.

Her guilt for such a desire.

Her anger when she saw how comfortable Prince was within his own skin

Her fear masked as anger that she will never be as comfortable within her own.

Her need to lose herself in another to avoid finding herself.

Prince spoke of his fear that Celeste would see past his confident facade and find him disillusioned and wanting.

His pain in his imperfection and of those who revelled in it.

His need to appear strong when he just wanted to be held.

His grandiose illusion of love to avoid the harsh realities of life.

His desire to be loved amid a world full of hate.

His voice in his head that told him he wasn't worthy of her affections.

Celeste admitted her fears of being unlovable.

Prince admitted his fears of never being good enough for her.

Their time with Nya allowed them to be seen by each other, flaws and all. They had each stood under the brightest spotlight on the darkest stage and when the curtain fell, they embraced each other with acceptance and forgiveness.

Nya had not spoken lightly of what was yet to come. She knew the road ahead was likely to be rocky and there was more work to be done. She reiterated the importance of vulnerability and of turning towards the other when one felt themselves retreating. Of the time it would take to replace the old habits and swap them with new ones that only spoke the truth.

They took what they had learnt from the session and continued to let it all out. Communication was key and they continued to talk about everything. Nothing was off limits, and when it was said with respect and love, it was easier to listen to.

Celeste still didn't believe in fairy tales, but she was starting to believe in herself in a way she never had before. And she was confident that she would write her story with honesty and with love.

Chapter 22: *Ever After*

Celeste smiled from the couch as Prince walked into their living room, holding a bottle of red wine he had taken from their wine fridge.

Two large round wine glasses and a decanter sat on the coffee table they had purchased six months ago, when they first moved in together.

"That was such a heavy talk," Celeste was referring to their first real conversation with each other after their fight at Alice.

After their reunion and their conversation with Nya, it had only taken them six months before deciding to take the next step in their relationship and live under the same roof. It made sense. They were already at each other's places all the time, and both of their leases were about to expire. And while it wasn't lost on them that combining expenses in one of the most expensive cities in the world would also be of great benefit, it wasn't the reason they wanted to live together.

There had been a lot of soul searching since then. Celeste and Prince had agreed it was important to keep working together as a couple, but equally important, as individuals.

As predicted by Nya, there was still work to be done. Old habits die hard, and they reared their ugly heads at every opportunity afforded. It wasn't unsurprising that throughout the forging of their relationship they were susceptible to triggers being pulled and arguments here and there. One couples session was not the golden ticket to happily ever after.

Celeste continued her solo sessions with Nya. Her sound board and trusted adviser enabled her to be comfortably unsure of what was yet to come, yet confident in her approach.

And a request from Prince led Nya to refer him to his own 'sidekick' as he liked to call her. Celeste was proud of Prince's willingness to seek help. Afterall, men asking for mental health support still wasn't as common as it should have been, especially when it came to talking about feelings.

Nya was Team Celeste and now Prince had his own comrade in his corner. Ultimately, that's what therapists are meant to be, your advocate, your ally, your defender, but most importantly, your mirror. They are there to support you to better understand yourself. Therapy requires a willingness to know more about why you do what you do, when you do it. And for Celeste and Prince, they were lucky enough to have found the right people to catch them in the moments they fell.

Now they sat in their apartment on the Upper West Side, celebrating their official one-year anniversary, and Celeste wondered how the time had passed so quickly. They had only moved a few blocks from her studio apartment to a building on 76th and West End Avenue, but it was a true one-bedroom apartment that had the kind of space New Yorkers dreamed of. She looked around at the new furniture they had purchased together. Aside from Prince's worn leather couch, which Celeste agreed was one of the most comfortable she had ever sat on, most of their furnishings had been brought together. Some were new, some from online markets, and others from antique stores where they overpaid for items they fell in love with.

And the eclectic artwork that hung on their walls had become a favourite pastime they indulged in together. They were delighted to discover they mostly agreed on the same style of works, and on the occasions they didn't, it always led to rich conversations long after they had seen the piece, often over a glass of wine.

The stories that covered their walls spoke of their travels together, artists they had met, and memories they had made. It showed glimpses into their personalities through the stroke of a brush.

Celeste continued, "That was the night, I think, we really got to know each other."

"I agree," Prince said. "Even though I felt like I had known you forever already." They smiled at each other. It was true, they had a connection from the get-go, but it had not taken long to realise even the strongest of bonds can be broken when tested.

Celeste was grateful she had had Nya by her side before she even met Prince. She knew that without her guidance, she likely would have made the same mistakes she had made in her past and lost the best relationship that ever happened to her.

While Prince felt more assured they would have worked through their differences, he too was appreciative he had his own outlet to reflect on himself. He was determined to contribute in a way that made sure Celeste understood how much she meant to him.

"I never thought this was possible, you know," Celeste said to Prince, who nodded his head and held her hand as he listened to her.

"We just clicked, right away," she remembered out loud. "Even though I didn't know you at all, it was like I had met you before."

Prince looked at Celeste and smiled as he watched her lost in thought. He too hadn't thought it was possible to feel the way he had felt about her, especially so quickly.

"I never thought I'd find anyone I could really just be myself with," Celeste grimaced as the words came out of her mouth.

"I'm glad you did. We've come a long way," Prince said as he poured the bottle of wine into the decanter.

Celeste smiled as she watched him. "I like who we are today," she said.

"But you're still that girl I met on our very first date," Prince held up his glass to cheers. "Salud!"

"Cheers," Celeste said as they leaned toward each other and kissed.

"And I see you," Prince added.

'I see you' was their mantra. Throughout their ups and downs, and their learnings about themselves as individuals and as a couple, they had come to know that truly seeing your significant other was a fundamental pillar in any relationship.

They had become more comfortable being so exposed to each other and their insecurities were respected. And communication was key. Celeste and Prince had learned they had to talk through their feelings before reacting to them. Not that it was always possible to do in that order, which meant they still had their fair share of quarrels — often over the most ordinary things.

"Even with all my flaws?" Celeste made fun of herself.

"You're just perfect ..." Prince said and before he could finish his sentence, Celeste did it for him.

"For you."

Celeste and Prince were proud of the time they had dedicated to themselves to be better, and their efforts to be the best version of themselves for each other.

They were aware they had become 'that' couple who openly spoke about therapy when out to dinner with friends, or at a bar with strangers they had just met. But their intentions were sincere. They felt that happiness lay within reach and it was something they believed everyone deserved.

However, happiness is relative, and Celeste often found herself considering what that word really meant.

In her childhood fairy tale books, happiness was Prince Charming rescuing the damsel in distress, and that narrative had weaved its way into the fabric of society. While women are much more powerful today, she also knew they were still miles behind. For every step forward, there were whispers from those in the past who called for women to return.

Celeste understood, better than ever before, why she felt the way she did about herself and her past relationships. She was giving herself permission to be the woman she was and not be the woman she thought she had to be. She knew she was still a work in progress, as was Prince. She knew she wanted to continue her journey with Prince by her side, as was her choice and not her destiny.

Celeste took the last sip of wine in her glass and placed it next to Prince's as he refilled their chalices.

Never one to miss an opportunity to say cheers again, Prince raised his glass and said, "To us!"

"So far, so good!" Celeste quipped with a swelling heart.

"I guess it really is possible," said Prince.

Epilogue: *Beyond Midnight*

Celeste's story is not unique, but it is her own.

Her feelings are singularly hers.

Her truths are hers alone to live with.

Her future lies in her hands.

I often wonder, if I had a magic wand to wave, would I use it to fix my clients problems? In theory, that fairy tale sounds idyllic. However, like all fairy tale stories, I don't believe it to be sustainable. Human beings are flawed and while we learn from some mistakes, we inadvertently perpetuate others.

We are designed to survive but it takes us, the brave, asking for help to thrive.

We are not perfect.

But imperfection is the closest thing we have to it.

– Nya, Therapist

Acknowledgments

Thank you to my wonderful friends Chelsea, Jodi, Ariel, Kate and Esther, for reading my draft and giving me their honest feedback. You have all championed this process and given me the encouragement I needed to keep going. I'm so lucky to have women like you in my life and I love you all.

A special thank you to Chelsea for not only reading the book but for the many hours, and I do mean many, you poured into it for me – line by line, word by word – to make sure I got the story to where it is today. Chelsea, you really should consider a career change to editing! I will cherish those hours we got to spend together while working on this project. You are amazing!

And a special thank you to Ariel for also dedicating so much of your time to reading, editing, supporting, encouraging and being a shining star of encouragement. You have inspired me in so many ways and I am so grateful you came into my life. My world wouldn't be the same without you.

Thank you to Alana for helping me understand myself more than I knew possible.

ACKNOWLEDGMENTS

Thank you to my mum. Thank you for reading the draft, but more importantly, thank you for always being my safe harbour. Thank you for making sure I have always felt loved. And thank you for continuing to grow over the years. Your guidance and wisdom is never taken for granted. I love you.

Thank you to anyone who has listened to my ideas, helped me craft my pitch, supported my crazy dreams and made me feel like I can do this.

And to my husband, Vladimir. Your constant encouragement and belief in me reminds me every day of what I can make possible. My respect and admiration for you is boundless. Thank you for seeing me. I love you beyond any words I could put on a page.

About the Author

Angela Monteagle is a writer, lyricist, and storyteller based in New York City, originally from Brisbane, Australia.

With a career spanning nonprofit marketing and communications, she has always been drawn to person-centered storytelling — work that puts human experience at its heart and ultimately exists to help people.

After showcasing her original musical Flaws and All at Adelaide Fringe Festival, she relocated to NYC where she reimagined the show with a new composer — reworking the music and retitling it Perfectly Imperfect. When COVID-19 closed theatres, she turned the story into a novel, exploring her characters in a new light while keeping the same message at its heart.

She writes because she believes this story is familiar to all — and because she wants women to feel brave enough to truly understand themselves.

To learn more about Angela, visit www.AngelaWrote.com

You can connect with me on:

🌐 https://www.instagram.com/angelawrote